Coming Home Lost

Jennifer Button

Grosvenor House
Publishing Limited

This book is published by
Grosvenor House Publishing Ltd
Link House
140 The Broadway, Tolworth, Surrey, KT6 7HT.
www.grosvenorhousepublishing.co.uk

This book is a work of fiction. Any resemblance to
people or events, past or present, is purely coincidental.

A CIP record for this book
is available from the British Library

ISBN 978-1-83975-329-9

To my long suffering husband, Alan.

"Come you from over by there to over by here and stand you by me now. I don't want you coming home lost." Polly

Chapter 1

THE ROYAL COLLEGE OF SURGEONS
LINCOLN'S INN FIELDS
LONDON 2017

When the penny finally dropped, I struck my forehead with the heel of my hand and groaned. Stepping back briskly, the MC said, "I am sorry. Have I said something to upset you, Mrs Jenkins?" Mr Sullivan, who was usually so dapper, so commanding, so very in control, was anxious. I let him fill the embarrassing silence.

"I am sure your husband has a perfectly good reason for being late, but you must see my dilemma? We cannot possibly begin without him... you do understand, don't you? I can assure you, there is absolutely no need for concern." Receiving no response, he kept talking. "I realise how disconcerting this must be. Please believe me when I say I understand your frustration." I repeated my silence. "May I offer you anything, Mrs Jenkins? A drink maybe... or...?" Accurately assessing that his suggestion was not being well-received, Mr Sullivan took another cautionary step back.

It was a wise move, as I was seriously considering kicking him. Of course, I knew the cock-up was not entirely his fault. No. I laid the ultimate blame at the dinosaurs' door – whether Mr Sullivan numbered among them, I was not entirely sure.

"Damned, anachronistic, pompous, pea-brained pedants, too bloody busy patting themselves on the back to join the twenty-first century." The small space we were confined in, left no room for Mr Sullivan to retreat any further, so he simply lowered his head.

I was livid. I'd been kept waiting in this pokey anteroom – really, little more than a cupboard – for a good hour. It lurked behind the stage, behind the main dining hall, from where the sound of glasses clinking, and convivial chatter grew louder with every creeping second. Patience has never been among my strong points, and mine was fast approaching breaking point.

I felt a trickle of sweat travel from my hairline across my brow and into my eye. Hot, salty tears streamed down my cheeks. I yelled, "Bloody hell," and immediately regretted it. If I could hear the audience, they could probably hear me. Damn!

Ah well, so much for my cool facade, my carefully applied ivory-blush powder and my lash-thickening, coal-black mascara. My face was melting. And my hands – my most prized tools – were wet and clammy. What's more, they were shaking. I thrust them behind my back, clenching them in white-knuckled fury.

My reflection in a nearby mirror confirmed my worst fear. I resembled a margarita pizza, fresh from the oven, laden with extra purée. I braced myself for the explosion.

Tonight was important to me in more ways than one. It represented a lifetime's achievement, the icing on the cake of a long, successful, hard-earned career. But it was both a pinnacle and a beginning. This was a night to feel proud and an evening to celebrate. Yet here I was,

INTRODUCTION

A chance remark at my grandmother's funeral told me how little I knew about the remarkable woman who had raised me; the woman who had been mother, father, grandmother and mentor to me.

Sadly, I had left it too late to question her personally, so began to ask the people who had known her for most or all of her long life. Their answers were inconclusive, confusing, and at times conflicting. I had unearthed a maze, a jigsaw, with no clue as to what the complete picture should look like. Inevitably, some pieces had been lost, some damaged and some deliberately removed. Retrieving, sorting and piecing the remaining bits together became my obsession.

To tell more would spoil the story, so let me reveal the story as it revealed itself to me – piece by piece. I must, however, tell you this: in uncovering this story, I discovered how strong and resilient the human spirit is. I learned to recognise and trust my own strengths and to face and fight my weaknesses. I also discovered just how remarkable that woman I called Gran was.

alone, apart from a useless MC. I abandoned any remaining decorum and prepared to scream. That was when I heard Gran's voice...

"Hush, now, cariad. That's right, deep breaths, isn't it? Stand up, shoulders back. That's better. Remember this is your night, my girl. Dew, isn't this what you've been working for all those years? Now, you listen to your old gran, has she ever told you wrong? No! So, get you down off that high old horse and step out there where you belong. You show them what us Welsh women are made of! If you won't do it for yourself, do it for me. Better still, do it for all those other women who never had the chances you've had. Do it for them, cariad!"

Polly's voice, with all its familiar Welsh warmth and love, embraced me like a cool breeze from the mountain above our home town of Brynavon. A window had opened. All the pent-up steam and frustration floated away. The heat drained from my cheeks and neck, and my palms grew dry. My hands were as steady as rocks, and my heart regained its normal, regular beat.

I ran my fingers through my cropped, steel-grey hair, took another breath of mountain air, and drew myself up to my full five-foot-nine. I surveyed the calm, controlled woman who stared confidently back at me from the mirror. I was ready.

I blew a quick kiss to Gran, gave a defiant toss of my head, and with a swish of expensive black taffeta, I swept past the astonished MC, leaving him in my wake, and sailed from the anteroom onto the stage. I was unstoppable – a stately galleon, fully rigged, gun ports open, cannon primed, ready for battle.

Chapter 2

I stared out at the elite, the cream of the medical profession: my icons, my peers, my colleagues and my friends. They stared back expectantly. I cleared my throat, forced a smile, took a deep breath and launched myself.

"Ladies and gentlemen, fellow members of this most prestigious Royal College of Surgeons, firstly I must apologise for the inordinate delay. It appears we have been waiting for my husband to arrive. Well, I'm sorry to disappoint you, but Dr Matthew Jenkins is in New York this evening, so he cannot be here with us tonight. But I am here, and I too have been kept waiting. As far as I can ascertain, the delay is due to what I can only describe as a cock-up. Now most of you know me, but for those who don't, allow me to introduce myself. I am Mrs Phyllis Jenkins MBBS FRCS – your newly appointed president; your speaker for this evening."

After some gasps, a ripple of laughter then silence, I continued.

"To be appointed President of the Royal College of Surgeons is a rare honour. To be a woman and be appointed president is a unique honour.

"I spent many hours preparing a speech for this auspicious occasion. I intended to highlight the great strides we have made, and the enormous contribution both men and women make to this pioneering field of medicine. But tonight's 'cock-up' has led me to rethink what I want to say. There is a scourge threatening the very core of our profession. So, with your leave, I shall abandon my notes and speak from the heart.

"Many of you will have noticed that I was not alone when I walked onto this stage. You will have spotted a large, grey mammal lumbering on behind me. Now, you may be surprised to learn that despite its size, its pungent odour and its unavoidable presence, some of you cannot see it. Some claim it does not exist. Others can see it but refuse to acknowledge it, while a few stubborn old farts see it, but wilfully choose to ignore it. I refer, of course, to the elephant in the room – or to give it its proper name – gender prejudice."

There was laughter, loud voices of approval and some of disapproval, adding to the mounting applause. There were even a few stomping feet. I waited for the kafuffle to die down before continuing.

"It is a truth not universally acknowledged – *many surgeons are women!*" I emphasised the words... and the pauses. Again, I had to wait for the laughter to fade.

"While this evening's cock-up illustrates my point perfectly, I was witness to a far more disturbing example only yesterday. We had been in theatre for three hours, fighting to save the leg of a young gymnast, a vibrant thirteen-year-old girl. Sadly, we lost the battle and I was forced to amputate.

"As consultant surgeon, it was my job to break the dreadful news to her distraught parents, but, before I had even begun, her father brushed me aside and began questioning my F2. We were all still in scrubs, so we looked very much alike. My F2 was male, the anaesthetist was male. The theatre sister was also male. I was the only female. The father assumed I was the nurse. His confusion and subsequent embarrassment would have been avoided were such gender stereotypes not so deeply entrenched, or so infrequently challenged.

"Have any of you experienced a similar incident in… let's say the past year?" Hands shot up. I knew they would. "Okay, lower your hand if you are a woman." The hands disappeared. A buzz vibrated around the closely packed tables. I nodded, knowingly.

"The women among us will not be surprised. There is a sea of prejudice out there. It won't be expunged overnight. It will require effort. It will require time, and above all it will require education. We must all be proactive in this process. We must lead by example. It is only when we are passive or silent it spreads. We must be vociferous and active if we are to replace ignorance with knowledge.

"There is, however, a world of difference between ignorance and willed ignorance. Women surgeons operate – no pun intended – in a male-dominated world. Yes, we have made great inroads. We have come a long way. No doubt some of you are thinking, 'So why rock the boat? Let time sort things out. What harm does a little prejudice do?' Well, remember the elephant? Refuse to acknowledge its existence, and before too long you will be up to your necks in… I leave that to your imagination.

"Refusing to acknowledge that women have as much to offer as men – and I am talking across the entire spectrum of medicine – is tantamount to halving the potential of this essential branch of science. It is a profligate waste of human resources. Gender prejudice disrupts and disables team development. It is a travesty, developed a style of my own, and I am no longer a dedicated follower of fashion. Vanity is for the young. I no longer qualify as such, so I am free to bid farewell to fripperies. To prove my point, I kicked my ridiculous shoes under the bed.

Having freed myself from shoes, dress, underwear, pearls and earrings, I pulled my comfortable old dressing gown around me and let my swollen size-sevens slide into a pair of misshapen sheepskin slippers. Bliss! Feeling almost normal, I made for the kitchen where a bottle of very cold wine waited in the fridge. My ordeal was over. I had survived. 'Well done,' I said, congratulating myself, as there was no one else to do the honours.

I had hoped Matt would at least remember to ring, but the answer machine told me he had forgotten. I wasn't surprised. It would be 9pm in New York. He'd be checking in about now. Poor love. He hates night flights. I didn't envy him the next nine hours. Still, at least he'd be home in time for breakfast.

I had just taken my first swig of Sauvignon when the phone rang.

"Hi."

"Hi."

"Missed you."

"Missed you too."

"You haven't forgotten me then?"

"Not yet. Listen, I'll be home 9 or 10am your time – unless we get blown up somewhere over the Atlantic."

"That's not funny. I want you back safe and sound. I've planned a lazy day, and I want you home in one piece."

"What are you doing right now?"

"Downing a bottle of Sauvignon. Oh, and by the way, my speech was a great success..."

"Shit! Your speech! I meant to ask. Sorry. It went well then? Good. I knew it would. Oh! Damn, that's my flight, they're calling me... must go. Bye."

"Safe flight. See you soon. Bye... bye..."

I blew a kiss down the phone, although he'd already hung up.

I suddenly felt very lonely as I flopped onto the sofa. I was annoyed and hurt Matt hadn't been with me this evening. He's never been one for birthdays, anniversaries or celebrations in general, but tonight was an exception. I sighed. I should know better by now. Still, at least my practical, unsentimental husband would be home soon.

Not long after we got married, Matt gave up his post as a trauma doctor at London Middlesex, to work for Médecins Sans Frontières. Matt is a deeply caring yet emotionally contained man, but he needs to be mentally and physically stretched. MSF provides this by the bucketload. I have never come to terms with him being in the worst trouble spots in the world, but it was what he wanted. It's been the perfect job for him.

Unfortunately, Matt's job-change meant long periods away from home. His ability to focus purely on the job in hand meant he took these partings in his stride, while I have never been comfortable with them. I am not emotionally independent. I need to share things, to talk things through. I need support and encouragement in my moments of self-doubt. Matt never has such moments. He's the most self-assured person I've ever met. In fact, he's sickeningly self-contained.

Don't get me wrong, I am proud of what Matt has achieved, but it doesn't compensate for the way I feel when he's away. I can only describe a feeling of not a disgrace, an anachronism and an abomination. It is the height of rudeness, the epitome of ignorance and the last resort of cowardly dinosaurs who are terrified of having their power eroded. It is to our shame that it is still alive and well, even in this auspicious society."

The hall was silent. I closed my eyes, wondering had I gone too far when suddenly the esteemed guests erupted. There was cheering, stomping and clapping. Many were on their feet. I applauded them in turn, before appealing once again for quiet and resuming my speech.

"As you know, the Royal College of Surgeons was founded in 1800. Yet it took over a hundred years before women were allowed to sit the college exams. In 1910, Dossibai Patel became the first female member. Imagine what her life was like? Trying to carve a path through a herd of elephants, trumpeting disparagingly at every step she took. A year later, Eleanor Davies-Colley became the first female fellow. It has taken another hundred and six years, more than two hundred years for a woman to be elected president!

"I am honoured to be that woman, but I know I am not the first to be capable of doing the job. How many equally capable, probably far worthier women have been overlooked during that time, purely on grounds of gender.

"Gender prejudice is endemic throughout the medical world, from training colleges to its highest echelons, which, sad to say, includes this noble establishment. When such biased opinions are applied at board level, they become dangerous. Women do not threaten men's jobs, nor do we ask for favours. We do not want special treatment, we merely expect due respect, equality of opportunity, matching rewards, and similar recognition.

"In plain terms, we want justice. What branch of justice is it that decrees I am to be paid less than my male colleagues simply because I am a woman? So long as those in power cling to the myth that women are less capable due to some fictional, fundamental, genetic weakness, GP will never be eradicated. This is not to be tolerated in the NHS. And I assure you it will not be tolerated in this society while I preside over it.

"Can you see the elephant now? Can you smell him? Can you hear him trumpeting? He doesn't want to be here, but he can't go until we set him free. Women surgeons do exist, we are here to stay, what's more, we intend to make ourselves blindingly visible and deafeningly loud."

My voice had risen to a rallying cry. I felt a surge of adrenalin that took me back to the demos and marches of my student days. I was 18 years old and flying. Suddenly I realised I was shouting and dropped my voice to a whisper.

"Don't worry, you'll be fed soon. But first I must say a big thank you to Polly Evans, my grandmother, a brave, stubborn, working-class, Welsh woman. Her infinite patience and unstinted self-sacrifice is what put me here tonight. She longed to become a nurse. Time and events denied her that dream. But that only made her more determined to ensure that first my mother, who became a nursing sister, then I should go as far as we wanted in life.

"Polly raised us to believe it was our right to be given the same chances as any man. She worked tirelessly to place stepping-stones beneath my rapidly growing feet. These gave me the firmest of footings, enabling me to travel confidently to the very top of my chosen profession. Yet, she never once complained that she had been denied her own chosen pathway.

"We must never forget that throughout this world, women like Polly are still paving the way for the next generation. Their work is tedious, at times exhausting, often dangerous, and always undervalued. We have to offer them our support and help them continue their work. We owe it to the millions of unborn women – those wonderful women who will be the doctors, nurses, scientists, nuclear physicists, archbishops, deans, professors, artists and mothers of the future. They are the future. We owe it to women like Polly, who are our past. And we owe it to ourselves: the wonderful women of today. Thank you and goodnight."

Chapter 3

LANCASTER GATE
LONDON W2

It was nearly 2am when I closed my front door behind me. I was home. For the past 15 years, home has been the same well-appointed, well lived-in flat, in a posh part of London. I was exhausted, but I resisted the urge to sink to the floor and forced my swollen feet to carry me a few more steps into the bedroom.

My toes were crying out to be freed from the instruments of torture that had them in a pincer grip. It was as if every ounce of nervous energy, every drop of adrenaline, had sunk to my feet, rendering my indulgently expensive, stylishly fashionable high heels several sizes too small. Whose idea was it to 'go on' after dinner? It had seemed a good idea at the time: to combine celebrating with 'chilling out', but with hindsight, it had been neither wise nor cool.

At the sensible age of 63, I must admit I no longer have the urge to go clubbing. Not that getting older worries me – at times I find it a positive relief. I was about 50 when I stopped caring what people thought of me. I adopted a 'what you see is what you get' attitude that has since served me very nicely.

Don't get me wrong, I still like nice things, especially clothes and shoes. But, over the years, I like to think I've being whole. It's as though an integral part of me is missing. Don't get me wrong. I have an extremely successful career, and being a consummate professional, I never let this self-doubt manifest itself in my work. I am formidable in the theatre. Staff and colleagues hold me in the highest esteem. In fact, I have heard that some are quite terrified of me. It's in my personal life that I struggle with demons. I crave praise and approval, which Matt is incapable of comprehending.

So, two years ago, when Matt announced he was planning to retire, I was over the moon. He said he wanted to write, to deliver the odd lecture, and attend the occasional conference. No more travelling. No more fieldwork. No more periods apart. We could examine our relationship and mend any cracks that needed fixing.

Earlier that year, Matt had a TIA or mini stroke. It put the fear of God into me, and I know it alarmed him too. Of course, he dismissed it as a mere hiccup and went on to make a speedy and full recovery. But I have no doubt it was this scare that prompted thoughts of retirement. With the passing of time, he seems to have forgotten his fears and his plans. I sometimes think he still feels the need to prove he's the man he's always been. Anyway, lately, he has plunged headlong back into work.

*

An hour later, I was still sprawled on the sofa, ankles crossed, feet resting on the padded arm, indulging in the luxury of a long yawn. I got up to stretch my back and walked over to the window. It was still dark outside, or as dark as central London ever gets.

I resolved to wait up for him. I still love him, even though I could kill him at times. Oh, it's a different kind of love now, less frantic, more accepting – and definitely less passionate. My demons whisper, *You've both grown complacent. Matt only stays with you because you're the devil he knows, and he hates change.*

Marriage is not easy: many of our friends' unions have crashed on the rocks. If I'm honest, we too bear scars from the occasional buffeting. But we haven't floundered so far... In fact, those rocks have provided a solid foundation. They have served and saved our marriage well over the years. I am proud of that. I am proud of the fact that we're still together after 37 years. How sad to throw away all those years of work, all that loving and trusting, for the sake of a simple slip-up or a meaningless fling!

I have tried to imagine life without Matt. I cannot imagine waking up one day to find our marriage is over. To realise it had been seeping through hairline cracks that have been growing wider with time and expanded by neglect. What if our relationship has been trickling away in a slow, fatal, monotonous drip of tedium and resentment until every drop of love has been sluiced down the drain?

Deep down, I know it would take a mega-disaster to destroy what Matt and I have, but I sometimes find myself shivering at the mere thought.

Back on the sofa, I curled up like a foetus and dragged the throw over my head. Grief and guilt gripped my stomach. It was the same cramp, the same pain I had felt when I first heard Gran had died. That was in 1979.

Gran's death was my first personal encounter with loss, and it knocked the wind out of me. I had assumed she would always be there – she was eternal. She had taken me in the day I was born, the day I was orphaned. She had been mother, father, and best friend to me. She had been my rock, my blueprint, but most of all, my beloved gran. Life without Polly was unthinkable.

When my gran died, I thought I would crumble in a heap and never get up. Now, all these years later, I realise I have begun to transfer that burden of responsibility to Matt. For the first time, I realise what Gran had meant when she said, "Some lessons can only be learned by living them. Remember, one chapter has to end before a new one can begin."

Chapter 4

LONDON EVENING NEWS:
February 14th 1954
GERMAN BOMB KILLS TWO

Tragedy struck the London suburbs today. Squadron Leader David Marshall and his young wife Megan, a nursing sister in Croydon General, were killed when a German bomb exploded in their Surrey garden. The device demolished their new home and left their new-born baby without parents.

The couple had recently moved into the semi-detached house in Mulberry Road, South Croydon. The bomb, one of 2,620 that fell on Croydon during the last war, exploded when struck by the former squadron leader, who was digging a vegetable patch in his back garden.

The UXB had lain dormant since 1945. The ex-bomber pilot was killed outright. His wife, Megan, who came from Brynavon in South Wales, was rushed to hospital. Before she died, she was delivered of a baby girl. The baby, weighing only 5lb, is reportedly doing well and is expected to make a full recovery. The hospital staff have called the birth a miracle.

During the war, Squadron Leader David Marshall had been based first at Kenley, then at East Kirkby, Lincolnshire with the 57 Squadron. From here, he flew

Lancaster bombers, laden with 4,000 HC Blockbusters, deep into Germany on hazardous bombing missions. He will be remembered as a hero, while both he and his wife, Megan, will be listed as tragic casualties of war.

*

Whether my father's death was karma, poetic justice, ironic coincidence, or simply bad luck, is a matter of opinion. He was dead, his young wife was dead, and I was all alone in the world. Urgent action was needed.

Death was no stranger to Polly Evans. He had visited her many times during her life. He seldom gave any warning, often calling when least expected. On 14 February 1954, he came in the form of a telegram, informing Polly of the sudden death of her daughter and son-in-law. The unjustness of the situation was enough to try Polly's faith in all she held true.

But Polly Evans was a pragmatist. I was her granddaughter. I belonged in Brynavon with her. Polly would never have called herself a pragmatist – it was not a word she knew. However, she did know she was practical to a fault, and she was proud of it.

It can't have been easy for Polly. In 1954 she was 61 years old. She had been thinking about putting her feet up for the first time in her life. But she thrived on hard work. She had never played the martyr or the victim, and this was no time to start. Besides, the years ahead might have been lonely or unfulfilled, whereas they would now be filled with love, joy, and the satisfaction that comes from watching a child grow. Polly had been raising children since she was no more than a child herself. It was second nature to her. One more would not break her.

So, Polly rolled up her sleeves and got on with it, determining that her granddaughter's dreams would never be smashed, her ambition thwarted, or her chances curtailed.

This was a new post-war era. Women had the vote, they had education. They had opportunities that had been denied to Polly in her youth. She promised her granddaughter would get all the education and support she needed. There would be no limits placed on her ambition or prospects.

The Reverend Griffiths christened me Phyllis Aronwyn. There were no other Marshalls, so I took the name of Evans. Gran gave me the name Phyllis, but, with all its consonants, it was too much for me to get my tongue around, so I became Fliss – although, to this day, I am known in Brynavon as 'Polly Evans's little grandchild.'

Back in 1954, Polly had no idea to what heights I would aspire. I hope I have done all she could have wanted and more. Yet on the night of my triumph, I was alone with my thoughts. I felt exactly what I was, an ageing woman hovering on the brink of some unknown future, not sure if I was worthy or capable of the honour that had been bestowed on me.

Suddenly I could see the funny side of things. The assumption that the president had to be a man, the infuriating delay, my last-minute decision to ditch my speeches – it had Gran's fingerprints all over it. I threw back my head and laughed.

"It was you, wasn't it!" I shouted. "I should have known. Even when I was tiny, you knew exactly how to stop my tantrums, popping them like party balloons. You'd watch me wind myself up, pouting, puffing, stamping my little feet, my face turning blue with rage. Then you'd laugh.

"You were always there, watching, smiling, nodding your head knowingly, giving me that side-wise look that said, 'One day you'll go too far, my lady, and you'll meet yourself coming home lost.' The next second you'd be laughing, scooping me into your arms and holding me tight until we were both rolling round the floor, laughing fit to burst.

"Good God, Gran, I can feel you giving me that look right now. You'd give the devil a run round the bloody mountain and tell him not to come back until he was good and lost. You knew all along what you wanted me to say in my speech, didn't you? You knew every word I was going to say, didn't you?

"You promised me you will always be there if I need you, and you always have been. You calm me down when I'm high and lift me up when I'm low. You instil a quiet confidence in me so that I know I shall always find the way home in the end. Thank you. Thank you for everything, Gran."

Throughout this one-sided 'conversation', I had been looking up at the ceiling, as if my gran was hovering there, somewhere between heaven and earth. Having finished, I looked down. I felt totally at ease. Everything was as it should be. All I had to do was plump the cushions, fold the throw over the back of the Chesterfield, and ready myself to welcome my lovely husband home again.

I scooped up my glass and noticed it had left a slight ring on the coffee table. Grinning like a naughty schoolgirl, I wiped it away with the sleeve of my dressing gown. In the kitchen, I refilled my glass and carried on through to the bathroom, taking the rest of the bottle with me.

The full-length mirror behind the bathroom door showed me a woman of a certain age, stripped of all the trimmings, unkempt, alone but not lonely, perfectly at home in her loose-fitting skin. I raised my head, lifted my shoulders back, and pulled my tummy in, looking at the woman from the left then from the right. Finally, with a determined tug, I pulled the sash of my beautiful old dressing gown as tight as I could. I then took a large swig of wine and poked my tongue out at the crazy woman who was copying every move I made from the other side of the glass.

I bent nearer and watched as she leaned towards me. "I am going to run the deepest, hottest bath in history, and lie in it until my skin shrivels up and the morning papers plop on the mat. What's more, I don't give a shit if I wreck the national grid doing it."

I, Mrs Phyllis Jenkins, MBBS FRCS, the first woman president of the Royal College of Surgeons, gave the bath lotion a squeeze and watched a large pink tear hover and plop into the steaming water. Bubbles began to explode, multiplying until they formed a mound of sweet-smelling foam, turning my bathroom into a tropical paradise.

How different bath time was with my gran. We'd lift the tin bath from its nail on the kitchen door and place it in front of the kitchen fire. We filled as many kettles and pans that we could fit on the stove and wait, shivering until they boiled. Then we poured them into the tub with the same amount of cold water. The galvanised tin never warmed up, and the water never came higher than my ankles. You had to be quick, or the water was cold before the next one got in. What a palaver – no wonder we only had a bath once a week. God knows how Polly managed to wash nine children in the same water without the last dying from hypothermia.

Gran made me wash behind my ears and between my toes while she scrubbed my back. She scrubbed really hard. Sometimes I thought she'd draw blood. And no matter how tightly I closed my eyes, the soap got in. God, it stung more than the furry, green nettles that nipped my ankles as I ran home from school, through Ben Ward's fields.

So many memories, so vivid and fond, sadly that child had long gone. I was now of a certain age, or so they say. I was content. I felt safe wherever I was – so long as Matt was beside me. With him, I could face anything – anything life cared to throw my way. I lay back, let all the stress of the evening float from my tired body as I luxuriated in the deliciously hot scented water.

Chapter 5

FLIGHT BA114

The prospect of a long flight home with plastic food and a rubbish movie, squashed between total strangers talking non-stop and occupying twice as much space as they'd paid for, depressed Matt. He was steeling himself for the worst when a uniformed official sidled up to him and whispered, "It appears we have some spare capacity in first class. May I offer you an upgrade, Dr Jenkins?" He was delighted.

Minutes later, Matt was reclining in a comfortable first-class seat, with a leggy blonde pouring him a glass of chilled champagne. "Skol," he whispered, raising his glass. They, he and Fliss, had picked up the habit in Scandinavia, loved it and continued it to this day. By now, it was second nature. So, whether in absentia, or face to face, they would look at each other, raise their glasses, say skol, take a sip, skol again, then drink.

Matt smiled wryly. Fliss would be pleased he'd remembered, although she'd be frowning at his sexist appraisal of the stewardess.

At times, Matt felt they had been married forever and a day. He could no longer recall not being married. If asked how long, he'd say, "Too bloody long! Actually I really don't know. At a guess I'd say about 30 years. I know we've passed our silver wedding."

Matt's thoughts fizzed as aimlessly as the champagne in his glass. He'd never really liked the stuff, overrated and overpriced, but as this was courtesy of BA, he thought *Why not?* He felt quite proud of having been married for forty-odd years. Many, if not most, of their friends were on their second or third marriages. *We're doing pretty well, all things considered. Of course, that's down to Fliss,* he thought. Fliss was in charge of all things domestic. *She's what keeps me sane. She seems to be able to lift me when I feel I'm sinking, and God knows I've been going down rather too often of late.*

"Top you up, sir?" It was the leggy blonde.

"What? Oh, sorry, I was just saying 'skol' to my wife. Just something we picked up in Copenhagen. I don't make a habit of talking to myself."

"Don't apologise. I think it's rather nice. I wish my boyfriend was a bit more romantic."

Romantic! Matt thought. *Now that's something I don't get called every day.* The stewardess's rear sashayed down the aisle. He watched for longer than he should have before settling back to enjoy his wine.

He let his mind scroll back to the day he first met Fliss, or the day Fliss claims they first met. It was her grandmother's funeral – a cold, wet, Welsh day in April or was it March? 1978 or it might have been '79? It didn't matter as he couldn't remember much about the day, except of course it was the first time they'd met as adults. There was some incident with a hat, but that might have been at another do. One funeral was much the same as any other to Matt.

However, he had never forgotten his first sighting of Fliss, all grown up, and then some. *My God!* he'd thought. *She belongs on a catwalk in Paris, Rome or*

Milan – and those boots. Wow! The arrow hit hard and had remained embedded ever since.

Fliss's hair was long back then, reddish-gold, very thick and shiny as a mirror. She had tucked it up in a beret, a small, round, black beret, with a little stalk on the top. She'd pulled the hat to the side. It looked cute, but when she pulled it off and let her hair tumble over her shoulders, it fell like a cascade of molten copper. Matt's heart stopped, and he knew with absolute certainty that this was the woman he would marry.

It was the first time marriage had even crossed his mind. As a young doctor, Matthew Jenkins' vocabulary did not contain words like love, romance or commitment. He was dedicated to medicine and alcohol. There was no room in his life for women, marriage, mortgages or kids.

So why had he become so smitten with a certain Miss Evans? He knew nothing about her, other than the fact his grandfather had known her grandmother. But there was no doubt she was the most exquisite creature he had ever seen. What had triggered that instant recognition, how he had known they belonged together, was a mystery he never managed to solve.

Chapter 6

FLIGHT BA114

Chateaubriand with Béarnaise sauce, you don't get that in economy! Matt salivated at the sight of the thick red slices. His glass had been refilled, and he drank again, although this time he didn't actually raise his glass to Fliss. He was thinking of her, but he didn't want the stewardess to think he was under the proverbial. He was on the Merlot now.

Matt tried to recall more details about the funeral, but it was all a blur. Well, it was a long time ago. He remembered he had recognised most of the faces milling about, although he didn't recall their names. Names always eluded him. He certainly remembered Polly Evans, both her face and her name, because he'd had many wonderful lunches at her house when he was a child.

*

Mrs Evans was what you'd call a character – one of those big-bosomed, big-hearted women, kind yet indestructible, that Wales bred so well. Fliss had done a lot of growing since I'd last met her, but I knew who she was as soon as I saw her. She swears blind we'd never met before, but we had. We met as kids. We didn't like each other, but that's another matter. To this day, she won't admit it.

It's strange, but if I hadn't gone to that funeral, we might never have ended up together. I very nearly didn't go. I wasn't going to go. I only changed my mind because I got a pang of conscience at the last minute. I owed it to my grandfather, and it was a small thing to do after all he'd done for me.

*

As Matt tucked into his steak, he remembered the day he met Polly Evans and her horrible granddaughter – the day his grandfather took him to Mrs Evans's house for lunch.

*

One Sunday, Grandpa announced we were going out for lunch. The thought of swopping precious hours of exploring for an afternoon of sitting being polite seemed a pretty raw deal. It was the start of my first hols in Wales. I was not quite five and newly arrived in Brynavon. Grandpa was a new figure in my life, although I loved him instinctively, from the moment he welcomed me with a very grown-up handshake on the platform of Newport station.

I had no idea where we were going when we set off. Grandfather was an important man in Brynavon, being the local doctor. Mother had told me to be on my best behaviour at all times so as not to let the family down. I'd smarmed my hair flat with water (it was embarrassingly short and stuck up, given a chance), and I'd shined my shoes on my hanky. The good thing about going out was we'd be going by trap, and Grandpa had promised I could take the reins next time we used it. But the day was too hot to leave Betsy standing for any length of time. So we walked. God, it really was hot!

"Not far now, Matt." Grandpa wore a heavy grey suit and a stiff white collar. He must have been boiling. I was in shorts and an open-neck shirt, and I was boiling. His face was as red as the geraniums in the pot on his window ledge. We'd almost reached the top of a steep hill, and he was panting heavily. A minute later, he stopped. "Here we are," he gasped. "Give me a minute to tie my shoelace and I'll take you in."

We had stopped in front of a very small house. It was sandwiched between several identical houses, which ran along both sides of the narrow street. This one was on the right-hand side. It had a door and a window, with just one window upstairs. Grandpa doubled over; his hands pressed to his knees. He was breathing hard. I was about to point out that both his laces were perfectly tied when the door swung open and we were ushered inside.

"Hello, Emlyn. Come on in, come on in. Wipe your feet, there's a good boy, Matthew. So, you're Dr Jenkins's little grandson? Well, there's lovely! Come on through. I expect you men might like a glass of beer and a bottle of pop, is it?"

That was the first time I'd been called a man. I felt very grand as I scuttled behind this round woman in a wrap-around apron. All I could see was her large bottom swaying from side to side as it led me through a tiny parlour crammed full of furniture. A stone step dropped down to an even tinier kitchen, in which a black-leaded range boasted a roaring fire. The back door was propped open by a wooden rocking chair, but the room remained ridiculously hot.

The back door led out to a communal yard – little more than a scrubby piece of land with an enormous tea-tip. A cat's cradle of clotheslines made it hazardous for anyone over five foot, and a terrible stench hung around the long, low building that housed the communal lavs, which served the occupants of 10 or 12 houses. But to me, this door led on to the great outside – which was everything to a boy of almost five.

Mrs Evans was rotund, cuddly, as old as Grandpa, jolly and friendly. Yet, I was apprehensive. I had met women like her before. They had a habit of pouncing on you, of cuddling, of messing with your hair or worst of all, demanding kisses! As a precaution, I made sure that my grandpa was almost always between Mrs Evans and me.

The little house was polished and neat. If possible, it was even smaller on the inside than the outside. So, when Grandpa told me Mrs Evans had lived there all her life, and at one time there were 12 people under this very roof, my jaw dropped. My first question was, "Where?" Of course, I was too young to realise that people are not born full size. They start quite small – like the baby lying in a carrycot outside the open kitchen door.

I hadn't noticed the baby at first because I was too busy breathing in the wonderful smell of roast lamb, Welsh lamb with sprigs of wild thyme and rosemary. To this day, nothing makes my mouth water so freely. Mrs Evans must have read my mind on that first visit, because she chuckled and said, "I expect you're hungry, isn't it? Not long now. First, I want you to meet someone special." She stepped outside and picked up the baby, which she squashed against her enormous bosom, holding it as if it was the most valuable thing in the whole world.

'"This is Phyllis, my little granddaughter." Thinking she was going to hand the baby to me, I prepared to bolt. What a relief when she sat down on the rocker. "Come and say hello, Matthew. Isn't she beautiful? You two will be good friends one day – mind she's got a bit of growing up to do first, isn't it?" I remember feeling rather sick, although it didn't affect my appetite. I seem to recall scoffing second helpings of everything going.

After that, we were regular visitors at the small friendly house, never tiring of Mrs Evans's cooking. Her roast meats and fruit pies were to die for and all cooked on a simple open range. Baby Phyllis was always there, but she just slept or lay on the rug gurgling, so she didn't bother me. My school friends had warned me about girls. "They're wimps," they'd said, "and they're very clingy, so don't let them get too near." Their advice was to steer clear… "Especially if one of them is your sister or something. If you show any interest, you'll end up babysitting, and that's worse than a whacking from the headmaster."

By the time baby Phyllis was walking and talking, I was still following that advice to the letter I avoided little Phyllis like the plague. I remember she couldn't even say her name, so by the time she was four or five, she was known as Fliss. I had a very low opinion of girls in those days – and a phobia of girls called Fliss.

One hot summer's day – those summers were full of long, hot days – Grandpa and I arrived at number 26.

I suppose I must have been about 10. I know I hadn't started boarding, so I was still a kid – a kid with a voracious appetite. Mrs Evans sent Fliss and me out the back to play. Fliss had reached a really annoying age, about five, I think. We'd each been given a raw carrot to stave off our hunger, while Mrs Evans saw to the veg and gravy.

I was under strict instructions to "Play nicely now, Matthew." Along with a stern reminder that, "Fliss is only little, and she is a girl." God! As if I needed reminding.

We sat on the bottom wall, as far apart as possible, our nut-brown legs swinging as we munched our carrots like a couple of rabbits.

"When I grow up, I'm going to be a brilliant doctor, like my grandfather," I said. I'll admit I was bragging rather than attempting to make conversation. Even so, Fliss's quick-fire reply quite wrong-footed me

"Ha! I'm going to be a better doctor than you. I'm going to be the best doctor in the world."

"You can't, you're a girl. Girls can't become doctors. Anyway, my grandpa's the best, so there!"

Fliss stuck out her tongue and yelled, "Cachu hwch!" which was the only Welsh I knew, and I knew it meant pig shit, which was quite impressive. The next minute, she was gone, out of the yard and off down the valley road at a rate of knots. I didn't give chase. Well, she was just a stupid girl. Besides, I was pretty sure I couldn't catch her, and I'd have died of shame if I'd been out-run by a stupid girl – especially one five years younger than me.

When I got back to the kitchen, Grandpa asked where Fliss was. I told him most of what had happened, and he clipped my ear. He then gave me a telling off for not acting like a gentleman! If anyone had told me I would end up married to that horrid little brat, I'd have run up the mountain and let the mist take me.

*

"More wine, Dr Jenkins. Or would you prefer a brandy?"

"What? Oh, sorry, I was miles away! Yes, why not, thank you, I'll have a cognac. Thank you…" Matt paused, hoping for a name.

"It's Julie, Dr Jenkins. Will that be all for now, sir?"

"Yes, thank you, Julie. And please – call me Matt." He smiled. She smiled back. For one second, he wondered if she was coming on to him. She had been so attentive and charming throughout the night. Then reality hit. *Wake up, idiot. You're just another pompous, old fart, only flying 1st class because of an upgrade, and too pissed not to realise he's well past it.* With an expression halfway between a grimace and a grin, Matt resigned himself to the innocent pleasure of wondering if Julie was a natural blonde as he watched her wiggle back to the galley.

Chapter 7

LANCASTER GATE

The hot water was working its magic. I floated halfway between sleeping and waking, my mind wandering at will. Soon I found myself at my grandmother's funeral.

*

I remember that day as if it was yesterday. It was 1979. I was an angry 25-year-old – a skinny, overworked, underpaid junior doctor in a major London hospital. Chaka Khan's 'I'm Every Woman' was at number one. The Cambodian-Vietnamese war was raging. Ayatollah Khomeini had taken over Iran, while in America a 21-year-old woman had been on a rampage killing two people and wounding nine, including a police officer. When asked why, she said, "I hate Mondays." This was a Thursday, but I hated it already.

It had taken seven hours to get from Paddington to Brynavon, via Newport. I felt nauseous as I stepped from the train. I wondered if I would survive the day.

The little town was crying. Its slate roofs shone with the wet that bounced off them. Guttering overflowed as gallons of water splashed into already full downpipes. It gurgled and spluttered and spewed out onto pavements already running like mountain streams. It was not yet midday, yet the sky was dark as night. Thick cloud wrapped around the mountain like a sodden woollen blanket.

Water poured down the hills vainly searching for a resting place – a drain, a hole, a field – anything that would swallow it, or let it soak away. This was Welsh rain, colder and wetter than any other. I thought of making a dash across Market Square. I could shelter in the entrance to the Market Hall until it eased off. There might even be a taxi there... or there might not.

This was what my gran called 'proper rain'. The sort that makes you proper wet. I was too upset to smile at the memory. Instead, I cursed the umbrella I'd left behind on the train. I turned my collar up and rammed my hair under a beret, which thankfully I had brought in case they were all wearing hats. I then set off at a brisk march up the hill in the direction of the small, square, stone chapel.

A single bell tolled, summoning the mourners to chapel. I ran the last few steps and was ushered to a front pew. Every eye was on me as I knelt, head down, pretending to pray. To my horror, I saw a puddle pooling around my hassock.

There was a lot of coughing, some shuffling and sniffing, followed by a nervous silence. Eventually, the Reverend Griffith's rich bass voice boomed out from the pulpit. He was resplendent in black and white, standing against a shaft of light that turned his silver hair into a halo around his magnificent head. I don't recall his words; I just stared at the coffin and the growing puddle at my feet.

Eventually, they carried the coffin out with me following behind it. It was very small. I wished I too was inside it.

I stepped out of the dark into bright sunlight. Temporarily blinded, my foot hit the ground sooner than I was expecting, and as I pitched forward, I saw the entire contents of my bag spill over the path. All my personal possessions were on display – a pair of panties, a bra, a washbag, a comb, a train ticket, a purse, a lipstick, a couple of Tampax, a forest of crumpled tissues and, of course, the umbrella!

I crammed them back into my bag, which was suddenly too small for them. The umbrella was the last straw. I began to cry again. I was utterly alone. The rest of the congregation were already gathered around the grave – heads bent, scarves and coats flapping. The rain had stopped, the sun was out. A February wind blew down on us from the mountain, which was crowned with its halo of mist, having shaken off the sodden blanket. Once again it was watching over the little town.

I was calmer now – less self-conscious, brave enough to take a look around. The other mourners, all in bible-black, resembled a flock of starlings. I remembered there were two collective nouns for the awkward, shiny birds. One was a 'chattering', the other was a 'murmuration'. I began to chuckle. Both were so appropriate. It was the way they huddled together; their gleaming feathers proud against the grey-green stones. They were deep in private conversation. I imagined them taking flight at some awaited signal, rising as a dark mass, soaring and wheeling against the sky – their chattering voices building to a crescendo as they rose and fell on the wind.

Unfortunately, in my heightened state of emotion, I lost control. What had begun as a secretive chuckle became a rather obvious guffaw. 'Oh God, let me die now,' I whispered. He answered very promptly in a most unexpected way.

The Reverend Adollgar Griffiths, still a formidable figure at the age of 90, stood a good head and shoulders above his brethren. With the wind billowing in his white surplice, he was twice his already impressive size – a sole magpie among the starlings. My face burned with shame as his eyes bore into mine from beneath those legendary eyebrows.

The reverend's eyes softened. A hand was offered, and I took it. The next minute, his strong arm was wrapped round me as he led me to the graveside. He remained by my side until Gran's body was committed to the ground.

This spiritual man, Adollgar Griffiths, was no stranger to me. I had known him all my life. He had watched me growing up from babyhood. I, in turn, had stared in awe as his eyebrows burgeoned from greying bushes into snow-laden boughs. To my knowledge, they had not been trimmed in all their 90 years. As a child, I used to think a snowy owl had perched, spread its wings and fallen asleep on that proud brow.

In order to see his flock, the reverend was obliged to tilt his face towards heaven and let his gaze follow the beaky contour of his nose. This added to his already convincing appearance of absolute superiority. As he grew older, white fronds sprouted from his ears and nose, threatening to join with the snowy owl. I lived in hope of witnessing this inevitable meeting. In fact, I became so determined not to miss the magical moment, my gran was constantly reminding me not to stare.

When passive, Adollgar's face was impressive. But when he spoke, it came alive. His nostrils flared and the white plumes danced. It was phenomenal. And the Reverend Griffiths was a man who never merely spoke. His every word was an utterance; deliberate and articulate, formed, polished and placed into a perfect sentence, delivered as a ready-made quotation —befitting one who spoke directly to, and on behalf of, God.

Despite his great age, the reverend's hair was as thick and strong as ever. He wore it long, from habit rather than fashion, although it did make him look rather trendy. When the light was behind him, his great mane shone like a silver halo. He should have been an MGM star – he was perfectly fitted for the role of Moses, Abraham, or God Almighty himself.

In his heyday, the Reverend Griffiths could silence a congregation with the mere twitching of an eyebrow. Today, his deep, bass voice still carried more than a hint of fire and brimstone. It was well known that a single word from this illustrious man could make an innocent lamb confess. Yet despite his physical superiority, Adollgar never looked down on his fellow sinners. He never condemned anyone. His terrifying pulpit-presence belied a kind, forgiving nature. I know Polly Evans held this man in the highest regard and, although she might criticise the church, she never let a word be said against Adollgar.

I too held him in high esteem. He had been very kind to me when Gran died. It had been comforting to know that he had been with her when she passed. "Polly Evans was one of God's own. I am proud she called me friend and was proud to call her friend in return. She was an example to us all," he had said.

In fact, he came out of well-earned retirement to officiate at Polly's funeral. Remembering all this while standing by my grandmother's grave added to my sense of shame. I had been soundly admonished by a look, and quite rightly so. But what happened next was nothing short of a miracle. If it hadn't happened to me, I wouldn't have believed it.

Chapter 8

There was no mistaking my grandmother's voice.

'That'll learn you!' she said. I looked around but there was nobody there. No one else seemed to have heard anything. I thought I must have imagined it, but then I heard it again. It was as clear as if she was stood next to me. 'There's a time and a place for everything, young Fliss. So stop playing silly beggars! Us Welsh take dying very seriously, and there's nothing more serious than a Welsh funeral. Especially when it's mine!' Gran was chastising me.

I was so taken aback I hardly heard the Reverend Griffiths' loud, "Amen." I'm sure it rose on the wind to sail over the mountain, bound straight for the gates of heaven. I couldn't move. I was paralysed with delight and fear. I tried to concentrate. I'll admit I was in a vulnerable state, no doubt prone to illusions, maybe I was even a bit mad.

In an attempt to curb my wild imaginings, I began to count the faces I could put a name to. Was there anyone I didn't recognise? I was surprised to find only one, a young man of about 30. There was something familiar in his face, but I couldn't put a name to him. I began to run through the alphabet, hoping a letter would jog my memory. I had just reached the L's when a kerfuffle broke out.

A sudden gust of wind had snatched someone's cap and sent it spinning over the open grave like a Frisbee. The starlings watched open-beaked to see where it would land. What if it landed in the grave? Or worse still, on the coffin? A tall, gangly figure was jumping up and down in a vain effort to catch the flying hat. I began to giggle. It was quite involuntary, but far too loud. All eyes turned to me, their disapproval tangible. Once again, I heard Gran's voice.

'Pull yourself together, girl. Think of poor old Ifor. He'll be beside himself. He's one of God's gentle creatures, the last person on this earth to be disrespectful. Go you from here to over by him now and say something kind to the poor lost lamb.'

I hung my head in shame. Gran was right. The hat belonged to poor old Ifor. I had known him all my life. He had spent his life being ridiculed, and here I was, adding to his misery. I had behaved very badly. Gran was very fond of Ifor. Theirs was a special bond. I felt doubly ashamed.

Since anyone could remember, Ifor had been known as 'poor old Ifor'. Nicknames are given for many reasons; Ifor's may well have started as a term of endearment, nonetheless it was demeaning. It was also inaccurate as Ifor Williams was better off than many and was several years younger than most. He was just unfortunate to have been born with a severe speech impediment, which had condemned him to be cast in the role of town simpleton. He might well have been a genius, but he was never given a chance to prove it.

Polly was one of the few people who had taken the time to get to know Ifor. He was kind and honest, although he was unable to communicate fully. He had been born with a severely cleft palate at a time when nothing could be done to correct it. It is a fact that when someone is treated as an idiot, they learn to act accordingly. Gran was right to shame me for being so disrespectful.

Meanwhile, Ifor's renegade hat had landed on the far side of the grave, well beyond his reach. He looked utterly mortified. I went over to him and slipped my hand in his. He turned to me, his face lit up with a smile of recognition and overwhelming gratitude.

The next minute, his cap was being offered to him, brushed free of mud and almost back in shape. I looked up to meet a pair of soft brown eyes. One winked at me, and although I couldn't put a name to their owner, I knew his face. I watched as the stranger took Ifor's arm and gently led him back to the other mourners. He stayed beside him for the rest of the service. I couldn't say for certain if Gran had a hand in that, but I knew I had won back her approval.

The service was drawing to a close. Single flowers and handfuls of earth were tossed onto the coffin lid. I watched Ifor as he let a single daffodil drop from his hand, followed by a silently blown kiss. This final act in remembrance of a dear friend was beautifully conducted, unbelievably touching. I had a lot to learn about loss and much to learn about death.

It also struck me that I also had a lot to learn about the woman we were burying. I knew her as my gran, but who was she? I knew so little about her, her life, her loves and disappointments. To me, she was my gran, the centre of my life, as I was hers. Yet, she had in turn been a child, one of many siblings; a young woman with heartaches and romantic dreams; a woman of my age, with hopes and desires, and finally an old woman who had devoted her later life to raising her grandchild.

The Gran I knew was short, round, and grey-haired. I tried to imagine her as a young girl, buxom and rosy faced. Had she been thin when she was young? What colour was her hair before it turned silver? Why were there no photos of her, of her wedding day, her baby girl, of christenings, birthdays, weddings, anything that might shed some light on her past life?

My eyes were welling up again. This was my first taste of grief. I had never cried for my parents, as I had never known them. But as these tears fell, I felt real loss. It was surprisingly tangible. It tasted salty and bitter. It was liquid, it dripped down my nose, poured from my eyes and dribbled out of the corners of my mouth. I sniffed hard, but I was too late, the floodgates had opened.

Someone was offering me a handkerchief. I took it and blew hard. When I looked up, it was into those soft brown eyes. The young stranger signalled for me to keep the hanky. I smiled.

"Gran would have loved the gleaming brass and polished mahogany. 'There's posh,' she'd have said."

"There's boot-i-ful, she'd have said."

"Yes, she would have. How on earth did you know that?" I asked, confused, still unable to give him a name.

"I'm Matthew Jenkins," he said. "Dr Emlyn Jenkins was my grandfather."

Of course, he was. I could see it now. No wonder he looked so familiar. "Did you ever meet my gran?" I asked.

"Oh yes, often – when I was a child."

All was silence now, apart from the birdsong and the sound of the wind in the trees and tall grasses. All heads were bent in a moment of silent reflection. Last farewells were being said by mourners who had known Polly all her life or had at least known her all of theirs. Apart from myself and Matthew Jenkins, they belonged to a generation whose past was a foreign country to me – a place where loss and death were frequent visitors.

Death sat comfortably in the small cemetery. Two memorials erected to commemorate two Great Wars stood next to each other. The names of lost loved ones were etched here. The first, commemorating the Great War, was flagged by marble angels whose milky eyes stared blindly to heaven. The more recent monument had four stone soldiers leaning on rifles, one at each corner: young men, also empty eyed, eyes that looked towards the earth. Maybe they longed for a piece of their homeland where they could find eternal peace – instead of being lost in 'some foreign field'.

It struck me as ironic that many of those whose names were carved on these memorials had spent their lives tunnelling beneath this very earth. They were the men who had, for over a century, mined the coal that Brynavon was built on.

The task of keeping vigil had passed to those who still breathed. These mourners, these stalwarts, were the last generation to remember the flesh and vitality of the fallen. It was their lot to watch the etched names fade, worn away by the elements, by age, amnesia and time.

Today, we were remembering Polly Evans, the last name on their long list of departed friends. Brynavon was a tight little community. It bore its losses together. The town had lost a worthy citizen in Polly. The community had lost a loving friend. They knew they were the poorer for their loss.

This was a small cemetery, but it housed a great many graves. Most of the headstones were covered in lichen and moss, their epitaphs once fresh and clear now so worn that some were no longer readable. Many stones had toppled forward. Others had fallen back. All were worn out from their long, hard vigil. Some leant, propped against a neighbour, whether stranger, family, friend or foe no longer of concern. The few that remained upright marked the newly dead.

Death was still recruiting as we walked among them. One day he will call me, and I, like all the others, will holler back, "Not yet. I'm not ready yet." Yet, for all its morbidity, the old cemetery of Brynavon exuded a tranquillity that I found, and have always found, surprisingly comforting.

Eventually, the murmuration began to migrate towards the gate. Like the headstones, they each held onto or touched another – all but me. I was alone as I watched them go. I saw the tall figure of the Reverend Griffiths walking arm in arm with his wife. He stumbled. My heart missed a beat. But before I could move, his wife's arms had caught him and prevented his fall.

For a while, the couple stood bracing and embracing each other. The smile they shared, the love they transmitted, was palpable. Here were two separate lives, lived side by side, each lived always for the other. The look that passed between them needed no speech. It was a beautiful illustration of perfect communication.

Eventually, the old couple recovered and set off to catch up with the rest. I felt a lump rise in my throat. "What must it be like to trust someone that totally?"

I had spoken aloud, not thinking anyone was listening, when a voice said, "Never forget this sight. I doubt there'll be a generation like theirs again. They have endured more than their share of loss. They've been to more funerals than I've had..." I smiled at Matthew as he added with a broad grin, "I was going to say hot dinners, but to be honest, I've been travelling for bloody hours, I'm so hungry the thought of food might make me cry. I hope you've catered for good, hearty Welshman and women."

"Of course I have! I'm Polly Evans's granddaughter! Has anybody ever told you, you're the spitting image of your grandfather?"

"Umm, just a few. If you want to know anything about your gran, now's your chance. These people are a living record of her life. Anyway, that's the worst part done. It's literally all downhill from here." Matt was offering his arm.

What he had said was so true. The answers to all my questions were making their way down the hill to the Griffin Hotel. These were Polly's peers, her friends. They knew her better than anyone. I took Matt's arm and we set off together. I was amazed to find how natural it felt to lean on this young man.

Chapter 9

FLIGHT BA114

Matt opened his eyes. He wondered if he had been sleeping or merely daydreaming. It was the middle of the night, and he began to wonder if the correct term should be 'night-dreaming'. The futility of such a thought reminded him to take it a bit slower. He had already consumed a fair amount of alcohol, and the last thing he wanted was to arrive home drunk.

A quick glance at his fellow passengers told him he was the only one awake. He closed his eyes again, hoping for sleep to kill a few more hours. This night-flying was a tedious business, even in first class. Instead of sleep, he sank into that semi-conscious state of 'night-dreaming'. Work, Fliss, home, Wales – a cocktail of memories buzzed in his brain, like demented flies. Finally, one landed. It was his grandfather.

*

If it hadn't been for Grandpa, Emlyn Jenkins, I would never have become a doctor. I certainly wouldn't have met Fliss. It all started at that funeral. How weird, the funeral of someone I hardly knew has affected the whole of my life. How fickle life is. I very nearly didn't go. I don't believe in fate or destiny, but it does seem that I am linked in some mysterious way to that small Welsh mining town of Brynavon.

Grandfather had known Polly Evans since childhood. They had been friends all their lives. When Polly died, there was no one of my family left, well no one who had known her well enough to attend her funeral. But Adollgar Griffiths had written, probably out of politeness, to inform anyone concerned of the funeral arrangements. As I still lived in the family home, the letter came to me. I had meant to reply with a letter of condolence, but I forgot. I had absolutely no intention of attending the funeral, but as the day approached, I decided I owed it to my grandfather to put in an appearance.

For most of his adult life, my grandfather served as GP for Brynavon and the outlying district. I know he was held in high regard by the entire community. He must have been in his late fifties when I first met him. I was four. To me, he was an 'old man'. Yet strangely enough, although I changed over the years – getting taller, stronger, acquiring skills, and generally growing up – the old man hardly changed at all – until dementia took him. But that was much, much later.

When I close my eyes and think of Grandpa, it is his teeth I remember most. He took them out once – to show me the wonders of modern dentistry. I'd just lost my two front teeth and several others were getting wobbly. Nobody had thought to tell me that nature would replace them. The thought of going through life with no teeth was alarming. So, when I saw Grandpa's shiny, removable gnashers, I stopped worrying. Instead, I waited by the letterbox every day for two weeks, expecting my new set to arrive any day.

The first time I went to stay with Grandpa, I was just four years old and had all my teeth. Mother put me on the train at Paddington. I remember that first journey in great detail, and every subsequent voyage with a vividness and excitement that has not diminished with time. Now, faced with a long night passage back to England, I find my mind travelling back to those gloriously free years of boyhood.

The smell of Paddington Station still excites me. We'd got there early, so I could have a look at the locos and make a note of the names and numbers. I must have been a precocious brat. (I could read and write well before my fourth birthday.) The trains were huge. I had to climb aboard, the step was very high and there was a scary gap between the platform and the running board. Mother selected a window seat for me, but before I was allowed to sit down, she asked the woman opposite if she was going to Newport. Having established she was – and no doubt having mentally vetted the woman's suitability – my mother proceeded to fire instructions at her.

"Make sure that Matthew behaves himself, and that he remembers to take his bag with him when he gets off at Newport. He's being met by his grandfather, Dr Jenkins. Matthew knows he must wait on the platform until someone claims him."

Turning back to me, Mother said, "You've got your sandwich and your pocket money, yes? Matthew? Matthew?" Turning back from the window, I nodded. Mother continued, "Mind you keep it safe. Remember it's to last you six weeks. If you need the lavatory, ask to be excused, and mind you wash your hands afterwards, both sides mind, with soap. Now, I expect you to be a good boy for your grandfather. Write to me." Pressing her lips together, Mother made a sound like 'mwah'. I screwed my eyes tightly and counted to 10. When I opened them, she was gone.

Imagine doing that today! Social services would have a field day. Half the train would be calling Childline before Mother reached the barrier. I don't recall feeling scared – well, possibly just a tad the first time, but after a couple of holidays, I was a seasoned solo traveller.

I remember the first time I tried walking along the corridor while the train was moving. It was like being gloriously drunk – not that I had enjoyed that experience at this stage of my life. And going to the loo was something else. I wasn't very tall when I was four, so I could barely reach the bowl, and my aim wasn't great at the best of times, so peeing was a bit of a hit and miss business. In the end, I swallowed my pride and sat on the seat. It was safer and less messy. I've never told anyone that – not even Fliss. How sad is that!

I had to stagger the length of two cars to reach the nearest lavatory. The carriages were coupled together by huge steel hooks that pivoted – ingenious engineering. I'd make myself stand astride the join. I had to grit my teeth, forget how terrified I was, and concentrate on keeping my balance. If I fell, if the gap opened, if… I don't know exactly what I was scared of, which only compounded the fear. My aim was to stand there while I counted to a hundred. I'd count as quickly as I could. I knew it was just a silly, personal dare, but the adrenaline rush was fantastic.

One man rode the whole way in the corridor. He wore a duffle coat and smoked roll-ups. He showed me how to open the window. (Only the windows on the doors opened, all the others were fixed. The long sliding ones opened, but they were too high to reach and too small to get your head through.) The door-windows were held in place by stout leather belts with holes. You opened them by releasing the strap and lowering it to the next hole.

The windows weighed a ton. At first, I couldn't move them. Later, I found if I hung on the strap and bounced up and down, it would jump free. If I let go at this point, the whole thing crashed down and I'd end up on my backside, listening to my heart thumping in my ears.

*

Matt opened his eyes and found time had stood still. Through the small oval window, night was black and starless. Inside the cabin, passengers slept, strapped into their reclining seats. Everything was motionless. He had no sense of going anywhere, no feeling of speed. This wasn't travelling. They should be hurtling over cities and oceans, chasing rivers, skimming mountains and buffeting clouds. It was claustrophobic being shut in a tube – a stale, sterile world. There was no adventure in this. Matt closed his eyes and willed himself back to a proper journey.

*

I am standing tiptoe, leaning out of the window as far as I can and then some. I am as free as a bird, an eagle, soaring miles above the world. My whole body shakes. I have been gripped by a hurricane. It tears my face, pulls at my mouth so that my lips flap so wildly it hurts.

The wind grabs my hair. It drags its knife over my scalp, lifting it like a savage – despite the short back and sides and layer of Brylcreem my mother insisted on, hoping it would last the duration of the holidays.

The smell of soot rushes up my nose, into my ears, my mouth, down my throat. My cheeks are full, like round balloons ready to burst. My throat burns from the smoke, which makes me cough and splutter until I want to puke. Water courses from the slits where my eyes used to be. They get narrower and narrower with each bombardment of gritty, sooty air.

Suddenly I am being thrown to the left. This is it. We are banking to the right. I lean out even further, my fingers clinging to the doorframe. And then... there it is... the locomotive in all its glory, shrouded by steam, flying faster than the wind. Wow! Oh, yes! Watch it rising from the smoke, the whole kit and caboodle – the engine, the tender, the dining-car, the carriages, every section curving, winding, taking the bend like a wonderful mechanical snake which is carrying me to the four corners of the world. Wow! Double wow!

A whistle screams for the sheer hell of it. The pull of gravity, the power of the engine, the exhilaration of adventure sent tingles down my spine. The thrill... the sheer, exquisite thrill.

*

"We are travelling at a speed of 600mph at a height of 30,000 feet. The weather is..."

The pilot's voice droned on. It meant nothing to Matt. He was too busy hurtling through the sky on a steam-driven loco, the wheels gliding along endless tracks of cumulus cloud, hoping he would never come down to earth again. His memory still held the scent of smoke. His ears buzzed with the hiss of steam. He felt the thrust of giant pistons as they drove the metal wheels faster and faster. His body throbbed to the rhythm, and he found himself repeating the sound out loud —'da-di-di dah, da-di-di dah, da-di-di dah' —over the points, over the points, over the points.

Chapter 10

FLIGHT BA114

The plane banked, and the spell was broken. Matt opened his eyes. He was back, strapped into his first-class seat on flight BA114 from JFK to LHR. He adjusted his watch. It was 1am New York time – it would be the middle of the night at home. Fliss would be in bed, her arm tucked under her neck, and her legs drawn-up tight. He felt a pang of guilt at having forgotten her big night.

Still, she ought to know me by now, he told himself. *I'm useless at remembering things, but I hope her evening went well. She's worked bloody hard to get this far. Mind you, next year's going to be tough. President of the whole shebang! Bloody hell! Who'd have thought it? Rather her than me.*

I hope someone recorded her speech. She's a good speaker, I'll give her that. But then she's good at everything. Can't think why she married me? It's a funny old world. I hope she hasn't been drinking... too much booze makes her all nostalgic and maudlin.

Thank God she doesn't drink as much as me. I remember being pleasantly pissed that first night, after the wake. I really had the hots for her. I was sure she was going to ask me in. We'd walked slowly, arm in arm, hips bumping. I'd wanted to make love to her there and then, on the pavement, in a doorway, anywhere. But I didn't...

When we reached the doorstep, I kissed her. It was pretty damn good for a first kiss, not too passionate but promising. I was sure she'd ask me in. She didn't. She just said something about being tired, some lame excuse or other. Still, she had just buried her gran. It had been a stressful day. But one measly kiss was a bit of a let-down. I remember leaning forward to kiss her again, but she ducked aside and let herself in. At least she thanked me. I think she smiled. Then she shut the door on me. Oh my God! It's all coming back to me now... that long, agonising walk back to the hotel, nursing an enormous erection.

*

Matt's head sunk back against the headrest, and he allowed his thoughts to take him back to those earlier childhood summers in Wales, long before he was a doctor, long before he was married. Wonderful times when he was as free as a bird, as wild as a mountain pony, and as mucky as a slag heap.

*

Unlike Mother, Grandpa never checked my ablutions. A quick wipe with a flannel and I was free to go. In less than ten minutes, five if I ran flat out, I was out beyond any traffic, beyond grown-ups, beyond civilization. On my mountain, I could revert to the young savage that inhabits every young male.

I'll never forget the feeling of achievement that first time I reached the top of the mountain. The mountain!

I loved that place. It didn't have a name. It was simply called the mountain. Actually, it was more of a large hill, but to me it was every bit a mountain – mysterious, unconquered and deadly. Okay, there were no craggy, snowy peaks. In fact, there wasn't a peak of any sort, just a top. But there were sheep and ponies instead of Sherpas. And it took all day to reach the top and climb down again. Coming down was quicker but more hazardous. Everyone said that – which was true as I only ever came a cropper on the way down, never going up.

Mrs Mills had forbidden me to venture further than the Low Pond, which was about halfway up. But intrepid explorers like me didn't heed the warnings of elderly housekeepers. Later I learned that several people, including grown men, had died on that mountain, either from exposure or drowning in the pond. So, maybe she wasn't so silly after all.

The mist was the problem. That mist came from nowhere, as quick as a bird, making the temperature drop within seconds. Its victims got disorientated. They'd wander round in circles until they died of cold, but I wasn't frightened by a bit of mist. I was a savage. I was wild. I was indestructible. I was a boy.

I thought of that mountain as mine. That mountain. The grass was springy and short on the lower slopes, shorn by the sheep constantly munching it. Further up on the craggy slopes, wild-eyed, thick-coated ponies skittered shoeless over outcrops of grey stone and longer, wilder clumps of green. Those ponies were tame enough to nudge my arm if I had an apple or a slice of bread in my pocket. They were always hungry.

I learnt to avoid the boggy bits where grasses and reeds grew thick and tall – often taller than me – where the ground was soft and hungry. If you didn't know where to tread, it would suck you under and gobble you up. My left wellington boot was eaten by that bog. I used to tell the tale with pride. I never admitted I pissed my shorts as my boot disappeared. I remember staring as it got sucked under. I'll never forget the final, sickening, slurp. I never found it. Since then I've always bought my wellies a size larger than I need, even now – just in case.

I could spend all day exploring, yet never run out of new territories to discover. There were prairies teeming with bears, lions, buffalo and redskins, far more savage than even I was. There were caves and mines, cliffs and dells. There were jungles, swamps and impenetrable vegetation you had to hack your way through. I'd whoop and holler until my lungs hurt and my voice grew hoarse, and still nobody told me to be quiet. I'd pull my shirt off and let my skin turn as red as the natives I tracked. By the end of the summer, I was as brown as the bears I stalked and shot.

Freedom is a wonderful thing. It allows one to be reckless. I discovered my own limitations and learned to love living. Those summers stretched out in an endless succession of days. I never gave a thought to the weather: the sun was always shining, even when it rained.

I never met my grandmother, she died before I was born, but Grandpa had a housekeeper. She was a jolly lady called Mrs Mills. Mrs Mills saw to the shopping, the cooking, the washing, and to my grandpa, although he liked to think he was totally independent. After dinner she went to her own home, leaving us 'boys' to our own devices. Grandpa always treated me as an equal. He taught me to play chess and poker. He taught me almost everything I value today. The first time he called me boyo, I nearly burst with pride.

One morning, very early, when it was still as dark as night, Grandpa woke me, wrapped me in a coat and took me to the front door. I could hear singing, like nothing I had ever heard before. It was as if a choir of angels was marching along the street. Even now the sound of a Welsh male voice choir gives me goose pimples. I was witnessing the miners off to work, their steel-capped boots striking sparks from the cobbles as they climbed the hill to the deep, dark pit.

That first night in the pitch dark, I didn't know who they were or what they did, I just watched in awe, and they were truly awesome – like the heroes from my comic books, men of mystery, steel-clad night-warriors. Later, when I learned what they did, they were still every inch a hero to me. Yet, I never aspired to be a miner. My heart was already set on medicine. I was going to be a doctor – like my grandpa.

I was born when the second war ended. Britain had heaved a sigh of relief. Things weren't perfect, there was still a lot of poverty, but peace brought hope. Prosperity was just around the corner; it was a time of jam tomorrow. I never experienced war as hardship. For me, war meant heroes and villains, Germans and Brits, Tom and Gerry. London, with its bombsites, was one vast adventure playground.

If I was happy in London, I was ecstatic in Wales. Little did I realise it would end abruptly with my eleventh birthday when I was sent to a new school in north London. From then on, my holidays were spent working and studying, with just a couple of weeks to play. I was learning to be a grown-up.

Chapter 11

LANCASTER GATE

A hot bath was exactly what I needed. I let my head rest back on the rolled towel and relaxed. My toenails were still immaculate from yesterday's pedicure. The dark plumb colour was growing on me, although it had seemed rather extreme when I first chose it. I wiggled my toes admiringly. *Yes. It was a good choice.*

As my thoughts slipped back to that fateful funeral, I found myself wondering at what point Matt and I had realised we were in love. Had it been mutual? Had I been the first to fall? I slid down beneath the bubbles. When I resurfaced, I was in the lounge bar of the Griffin Hotel, Brynavon.

*

We were the last to arrive. The Griffin was the finest – the only – hotel in Brynavon. The lounge bar had been set aside for Polly's wake. In the centre sat a long table covered in a crisp, white linen cloth. It groaned beneath platters of sandwiches, cakes and freshly baked sausage rolls. A neat stack of plates and paper napkins waited beside a tray of schooners, each filled with dark, sweet sherry, or Amontillado for the more sophisticated.

I smiled at the waitress to show my approval. She smiled back. I had gone to school with her a lifetime ago.

The starlings had perched around, some sitting, some standing. Fingers tugged at unfamiliar collars and over-tight waistcoats. Toes tried to wiggle in seldom worn 'best' shoes, while hats sat awkwardly on the heads of women more used to headscarves. I counted 18 guests in all. Not one of whom looked at ease. Most had known each other forever, yet they were acting like total strangers. A pall of smoke hung over the room, suspended by silent expectation. What were they waiting for?

Across the room, I spotted Ethel Lewis – known to me as Little Aunty Ethel. She was no taller than Gran, but as I already had an Aunty Ethel – a grace aunt, long since dead, who was quite large, and from Abergavenny, with 10 cats and a succession of sacrificial canaries, all called 'Tweety' – Ethel Lewis was therefore the little aunt.

Little Aunty Ethel was a nervy, bouncy woman, always on the go, endlessly wittering or trilling some tuneless melody as she flitted from pole to perch. Her round-rimmed glasses were far too big for her and regularly slid down her miniscule, retroussé nose. It was only the upturned tip that prevented them falling off. Every so often she would give them a shove, which sent them shooting back up, which made her blink even more furiously than usual.

Uncle Jim wasn't with her. I guessed he was too unwell to attend. Jim suffered from emphysema, a reward many miners got for years working at the coal face. I knew he had been finding walking difficult for some years now. Hills were impossible.

Little Aunty Ethel sat squashed, like a sliver of ham between two thick slices of buttered bread called Mr and Mrs Pritchard. The Pritchards had once been dairy farmers and had owned the local dairy. For the past 50 years they had been cream-fed by their herd of coal-black Pembroke cows. With Ethel Lewis they filled a window seat designed to take six.

Both Mr and Mrs Pritchard had apple-round faces, with rosy-red, shiny cheeks. A picture of health, or so everyone said. I saw two cases of high blood pressure and potential diabetes. But they were happy, always laughing, yet oddly enough, right now, they too showed no hint of a smile.

The Widow Price sat opposite them, her face set in its habitual scowl. Opposite her was the familiar figure of Rosa May Davies. I'd always been in awe of Rosa May. She and her husband ran the haberdashers in the High Street, and they'd lived in a well-furnished flat above the shop. I thought Rosa May was very grand and rich when I was little. Her shop was an Aladdin's cave, crammed with amazing things, like skeins of brightly coloured wools and silks, and dainty mother of pearl or painted-china thimbles, like the one Gran bought me for my tenth birthday. Her flat was a palace, with painted china and a silver tea-service.

I smiled at Rosa May and gave a little wave, but she either didn't see me, or she didn't recognise me. I reminded myself that they were all getting on now, their eyesight was failing. Besides, I must have looked very different from the young girl who left Brynavon a good few years ago to go to study in London.

I was Dr Evans now, 25 years old, my sights set on making consultant by the time I was 35. There was very little of the gawky bookworm they would have known. When I was a child, Gran told me I had hollow legs. I could out-eat anyone yet remain as thin as a beanpole. I was still on the skinny side.

Rosa May Davies sat with the Widow Price. Despite their long friendship, they too sat in silence. Rose May had been Gran's closest friend. They had known each other all their lives. She must have been feeling her loss more than most today.

The grand old lady sat as straight-backed and serene as ever, just as I remembered her when I was a girl. She looked especially grand in her funereal finery – her powder-pale face half-hidden beneath a wide-brimmed hat, over which black floribunda roses rambled, their petals stiff with dust.

I hardly recognised Dai the Post out of uniform. He leant awkwardly against the bar, in a coat several sizes too small for him. Poor old Ifor loomed next to him – his gloved hands screwing his cap to a rope, clinging on to it as though fearful it might take flight again. The Reverend Adollgar Griffiths sat with his rotund wife, Aderyn. They faced each other at a table far too small for them, and so close to the fire that Mrs Griffith's fur coat was in danger of singeing.

The only sound in the room was the ticking of a large grandfather clock, the crackling of the fire. The starlings were silent. They were not even murmuring. They were waiting. Eventually I realised they were waiting for me. I began to panic, not knowing the right thing to do when my gallant stranger came to my rescue. He winked at me, patted my arm, and sprang into action in that practical way that I have grown to love.

It was as if a pause button was switched off. Sherry was being handed round. Everyone was alert, a full glass in their hands. Matt raised his glass – somehow, he had managed to avoid the sherry and get a pint of bitter. He tapped a teaspoon against the jug of beer, and the room fell silent.

"Ladies and gentlemen, let's raise a glass, the first of many, I'm sure, to Polly Evans. May the Lord bless her and keep her safely cwtched in his loving arms." He downed his pint in one. The mourners cheered and schooners were emptied; the hive was buzzing. Every corner echoed with chattering, laughing voices, old friends exchanging and sharing memories of my gran. Soon pints of beer, heavy and light, glasses of port and tumblers of whisky, rum and gin were passed over heads and behind backs.

*

Matt was the spitting image of his grandfather, Dr Emlyn Jenkins. Apart from the moustache and the accent, the resemblance between the two was uncanny. I found I was staring at Matt and was delighted when he stared straight back at me.

So, he was Dr Jenkin's grandson. How many times had I heard the name Emlyn? As a young doctor, Emlyn Jenkins had worked alongside his father, eventually inheriting the practice in Brynavon. He had been one of Gran's dearest friends since childhood, so I had known him not only as our family GP but also as a kind, supportive 'uncle'.

Polly adopted a certain look whenever she spoke of Emlyn. It held a mixture of pride and affection together with a shy, half-smile, making me suspect it was more than fondness she felt for him. It had never occurred to me that they might have been an item. Now I found myself wishing I had asked. It was an intriguing question. I looked over at Little Aunty Ethel. She would know if anyone did.

Little Aunty Ethel was still sandwiched between Mr and Mrs Pritchard, whose faces were redder than ever after several bumpers of port. They were obviously enjoying a good joke, both rocking with laughter. Their flesh wobbled like jelly with each chuckle, leaving Ethel's giggles floating an octave higher – like a sprinkling of caster sugar on a rich plum-duff.

Rosa May Davies, who by my reckoning had to be at least a hundred, was still sitting as upright as a school prefect. She was enjoying a cheroot and a pint of stout in the company of the Widow Price, who was every bit as old and still wore the same lace cap and frown she had sported at the turn of the last century. The two old women were putting the world to rights, as matriarchs of their age do, their eyes searching the room for the latest subject under scrutiny.

The air pulsed with the sound of friends at ease with each other. Smoke from the fire mixed with wisps and puffs from pipes, cigars, cigarettes and Rosa May's cheroots. Solemnity had given way to celebration. Everyone was content. And it was all thanks to Matt.

*

I turned the tap with my toe and released a gush of steaming water. It was bliss.

Chapter 12

FLIGHT BA 114

Random dots of light winked up from the rapidly approaching ground. Matt watched them with fascination as they began to organise themselves into recognisable patterns – houses, roads, an airport, a runway. Heathrow, he was almost home. He found his phone and dialled Fliss. Oddly, there was no answer.

"Fasten your seat belt please, Dr Jenkins." Matt smiled as Julie leaned across to help him with the buckle. She smelled delicious.

"What perfume is that, Julie?" he asked.

"Chanel no 5... Perks of the job. What does your wife use?"

"She likes Chanel too. Damn! I meant to get some. I don't suppose I can buy some now... I've left it too late, haven't I?"

"I think I can get some, but don't let on. We're not supposed to sell duty free now. Have you got your card? I can only get the actual perfume, is that alright?" Matt nodded. "Right, I'll be right back. Mum's the word, okay?"

Matt looked at his phone. It was still ringing out. He redialled and continued to listen while studying Julie as she moved down the aisle. She looked as fresh as a daisy, yet she'd been working all night. *How does she do it?* he thought. At that moment, Fliss picked up. Matt smiled, held the phone close to his ear and announced, "Hi. The eagle has landed..."

Chapter 13

LANCASTER GATE

I was trying to work out how I came to be buried up to my neck in snow when the white silence was shattered by a shrill, annoyingly-tuneless peal of electronic bells. They jingled inanely as they bounced off the tiles and crowded into my skull. For one startling moment, I thought my head would split in two.

Another chattering, clicking sound joined in, and I suddenly realised it was my teeth. I had fallen asleep in the bath, and the awful electronic din was my mobile phone. Resolved to change the offensive ringtone as soon as I was out and dry, I began to scan the bathroom looking for the culprit. I leaned over the bath and ran my hand over the tiles.

Luckily it was on the bathmat, just within reach. Unluckily my numb, wet fingers could not get a grip on the slippery plastic. The phone slithered and skidded across the floor, crashing to rest against the door. The damn thing was still ringing. In the end, I netted it with a towel and dragged it back within reach. As my finger hit the green light, there was a moment's peace before I heard Matt's voice announcing, "Hi, the eagle has landed."

*

An hour later, I was dried, dressed and ready to greet my errant husband, while the flat was warm with the seductive aroma of a full English breakfast. I hummed as I finished setting the table. Any minute now he'd be home, safe and sound.

Secretly, I hoped he would also be tired, contrite and malleable. In other words, I wanted him susceptible to my proposals regarding our future. I had a plan afoot. If we both left the front row of medicine, we could sell up and buy an idyllic cottage in the Brecon Hills. Somewhere we could spend our separate time writing and out together time reading, walking the dogs, and imbibing in the many fine local pubs.

I checked my watch then my lipstick. I had decided on a strategic change of plan. It was wiser to let Matt enjoy his breakfast in peace and not spring my plans on him until his stomach was full. With a full stomach he would be easier to manipulate. As I fussed over the final touches, my mind returned to the Griffin Hotel, and an innocent conversation which had exposed a secret my grandmother had taken to her grave.

*

I was really pleased with the way things were going. Everyone was relaxed. They chatted on, sharing stories and memories of Gran, and I knew she would have loved to know all her friends had come to say a final "ffarwelio" to her.

I noticed Rosa May Davies beckoning to Matt, she was signalling for him to come over and sit by her. Willingly, he crossed the room and squeezed in beside the old lady. She leant back, letting her sharp eyes focus better on the young man. From beneath the dusty roses on her hat, she threw a surprisingly coquettish smile and whispered, "Emlyn Bach, there's lovely! Stay you by me now and let me get a good look at you." She scanned his face for a while, smiled, and said, "Look at you, there's lovely you are. Dew, you don't look a day older than before!"

Rosa May lifted a bottle of stout and began to fill her glass. She didn't spill a drop. I was impressed as the black liquid settled beneath a crown of dense, white froth. She raised it to her lips, took a sip, smacked her lips in a surprisingly ladylike manner, and placed the glass on the beer mat in front of her. Then she delicately dabbed at her lips with a pristine lace hanky.

I watched Matt take his hanky, lean forward and remove the last speck of the froth with a gentle wipe. Next, he took her hand and kissed it. "Rosa May, you still look like a blushing eighteen-year-old."

Matt's familiarity, bordering on the flirtatious, surprised me. Did he really know this old woman that well? Seeing my raised eyebrow, he laughed. "She thinks I'm my grandfather. I take it as a compliment. Emlyn was a looker in his time, and from what I hear, he had quite a way with the ladies. For all I know, they could have been lovers once upon a time. Far be it from me to disappoint a lady."

"There's wicked you are." Rosa May was frowning as she continued to admonish Matt. "It was cruel what you did to Polly. Poor Polly! Broke her heart, you did. Mind, it cost you dear in the end. Fancy letting a prize like Polly Evans slip through your fingers! Not like you, Emlyn Jenkins, you being so smart and a doctor and all."

Matt laughed, and I noticed the slight gap between his front teeth and the lock of hair that fell over his eyes when he lowered his head. But I was curious to hear more. This was the first I'd heard of any romantic link between my grandmother and the doctor. Matt winked at me then turning to Rosa May, he said, "Ah Rosa May, Rosa May. I should have married you. Now that would've been a smart move."

Rosa May tapped the side of her nose. "Ah, but you didn't have a shop, Emlyn Jenkins, not like my Davy, I wasn't cut out to be the wife of a poor country doctor. No. It was Polly Evans as you should've wed. She'd have made a perfect wife for you, her being a nurse and all. Dew! Why, the whole of Brynavon knew as you two were made for each other. I tell you, boyo, you broke her heart you did."

So, Polly and Emlyn had been an item. That was news to me. And why had Gran never told me she'd been a nurse. I knew my mother, Megan, was a nursing sister back in the days. But Polly? When did she train? How much more didn't I know? For instance, who was my grandfather? No one ever mentioned him. Evans was a common enough name in Wales. It wasn't unusual for a woman to have the same maiden name as her married one. I'd assumed Gran had married someone with the same name as her father. Although, in all honesty, I'd never really given it much thought – until now. Come to think of it, there had been no photos, no certificates, nor any record of the past when I was growing up. I was beginning to realise I knew very little about my grandmother, Mrs Polly Evans – the girl or the woman.

*

I was barely a day old when I'd gone to live with Gran. I'd never known anything else. It was always just Gran and me. My father and mother died on the day I was born. But I didn't miss them as I'd never known them. All I knew was Gran, and she was enough for me. I certainly didn't feel the lack, or need, of a grandfather. Yet to realise I had no idea who he was felt disconcerting. It was also oddly exciting, and it certainly aroused my curiosity. Why hadn't I heard anything about him? Why had it been kept such a secret? Suddenly I wanted to know what he'd been like, what sort of man he was, and also, who he was.

Before I could ask these questions, the manager was calling, "Time, ladies and gentlemen, please." Guests were taking their leave. Goodbyes were being made; hands shaken. (There was no kissing – not in Brynavon. It was all very proper in those days.)

I remember Matt walked me home. We shared a brief goodnight kiss on the doorstep. I knew he wanted to come in, but I'd let him kiss me, so I didn't feel too guilty when I packed him off back to the hotel. He was quite drunk, and I wanted to be alone. I had things I needed to think over. God, was that really 40 years ago! We were different people then, or maybe we had not yet become the people we now are.

In 1979, all I wanted was to qualify as a paediatric surgeon. My ambition was to be a consultant surgeon by 40. Sooner would be better, but like most junior doctors, I had not realised quite what a long slog I was embarking on. And it was getting harder, not easier.

I'd already discovered how disadvantaged women are in the professional world. The fact that a woman's insight is often shrewder than a man's, their empathy is usually stronger, and their ability is on a par with, if not better than most, counts for zilch. Being a born fighter has been an advantage, but I still recall many hours and days of despair at ever achieving my goal.

Forty years on, I have accomplished most of what I set out to achieve. I know it has taken longer because I'm a woman, but now, at last, I am in a position to redress some of those injustices. I am a highly respected consultant surgeon. Tonight, I was paid the great honour of becoming President of the Royal Society no less. This is a position I had never knowingly aspired to. It delights and terrifies me. But it gives me the voice, the platform needed to effect change. I cannot back away from that. Life has placed this opportunity in my path, and it is my duty to make the most of it.

However, I also have a duty to my husband. His health is still a concern. What if he has another mini-stroke? He'll need me to look after him. Am I capable of being so selfless? As someone who never planned to marry, it feels alien to be holding such contra-feminist views. Knowing what I now know about Polly's life and the choices she had to make, I am beginning to understand the dilemmas she must have faced. When I was little and life was baffling me, she would say, 'Some things have to be lived through before they make any sense.' It didn't make much sense to me then, but now I understand exactly what she meant.

Anyway, I can't make any decisions now. I have to know what I am facing first and deal with it armed with the knowledge of experience. I shall plan to spend the next year devoted to my career and make any necessary changes as and when required. Hopefully, in that way, I shall be free to be there for Matt, should he need me.

If I've learned anything from life, it is this. Firstly: Absolute truth does not exist. Everything is dependent on something else. Life is conditional. It is fickle. And it can be cruel. In short, life is what we make of it, no more and no less. Secondly: Nothing is as it first appears. Never jump to conclusions or make assumptions. They are nearly always wrong, often damaging, and always way, way too simple.

*

As Matt's key turned in the lock, I felt a great surge of relief. "Mmm, that smells good." His voice, huskier and deeper than usual, echoed in the hall, which was instantly awash with bags, coats, shoes, and general clutter, mess and noise. The eagle had indeed landed. My world was whole again.

*

Matt wiped his plate with the last piece of toast. He pushed back his chair and rubbed his tummy. For a moment, I thought he was going to belch. Instead, he laughed. "Your face! God, I wish I'd been born an Arab... belching is remarkably satisfying."

"Only for the belcher," I remarked, wondering if this was the right time to broach the subject of retirement.

Matt was eyeing me suspiciously. "Are you softening me up for something? What happened to your 'no more fry-ups' policy? Don't tell me —you've bought a puppy?"

"Don't be ridiculous, darling. I've bought a house."

*

And that was how I broke the news to him. But all this is going too far into the future. Before all that, I need to go back to that funeral, to Brynavon in 1979, when I was just 25 and thought my world had come to an end.

Chapter 14

BRYNAVON 1979

The day after the funeral arrived with a beautiful spring morning. I was about to nip out to the shops when the phone rang. It was Matt. He apologised for having had too much to drink at the funeral and asked if I would meet him for lunch.

I had already arranged to visit Rosa May Davies for tea and asked if he'd like to join me. Rosa May lived in a retirement home in what used to be Brynavon House, where she was one of 60 residents. I was eager, if apprehensive, as I had several questions I needed to ask her. I'd bought biscuits, Welsh cakes, Yardley's lavender water, and six bottles of stout to take with us. I explained why I wanted to see her, and Matt agreed it would be best to let Rosa May chat away at her own pace.

Brynavon House was a large mansion, with iron gates and a long drive. The house was Georgian, with a grand portico and impressive steps, now scarred by an ugly, concrete ramp.

Matt and I were met at the door by the matron, Matron Manners, who led us to Rosa May's room – a small, bright room decorated in apricot and pink. The old lady sat in the only armchair by the only window. A stack of moulded chairs in bright orange plastic sat in the corner of the corridor, ready for visitors. Rosa May's face lit up as we entered, and before we'd sorted our chairs, she was chatting away.

"Hello, you two. Matron told me you were coming. Oh, I see you've brought some little treats, there's lovely. Now, I know you want to talk about your gran, my dear. Well, you'll have to bear with me, because my mind do come and go. Backwards and forwards it do go. Mind, I do prefer it when it do go back. I prefer the past, see. It can't surprise me anymore. I don't much like surprises. So, I prefer to go back to where I'm comfy.

"It's a funny old thing getting old, but when my mind do go it takes me back, so I don't know as I'm old. That's why I do prefer it, see? Better to be young and with it than old and past it, isn't it? They tell me I'm 92. Is it two or three? I don't know. What's a year here or there? Anyway, you should never ask a lady's age. That's right, isn't it?" With that, she winked at Matt.

Rosa May chatted freely, her powdered face full of life and enthusiasm. Whether she thought she was young, only she knew, but she certainly appeared youthful. Her voice was young, and her laugh was that of a young girl, flirtatious and beguiling. It was obvious that she had been enchanting in her day, beautiful too – attributes that still shone from her.

"Your name is Matthew, isn't it? I knew your grandfather. We were born the same year. 1887. Emlyn Jenkins was his name. Emlyn! He was a handsome lad, tall as a tree – a good head and shoulders above the other boys – long, straight legs see. Well-fed. No rickets in his family. I had to run like hell to keep up with him.

"He always carried himself as if he knew he was different – destined to be a doctor, see, like his father before him. Most of us were miner's kids. We knew we wouldn't have much time for learning. Boys went down the mines, girls helped at home, see. Or they found work in town if they were lucky. Mind we could all read and write and do our times-tables by the time we left school – except for the dunces.

"We were born the same year, Emlyn and me 1887, the year of the old queen's golden jubilee. My mother had a mind to call me Victoria, but my father swore he'd not have a child under his roof named after an English queen! He was that passionate about the English. Hated them, he did.

"I knew your grandfather, Matt. We were born the same year. He used to walk me to school, through Ben Ward's fields to the old stone schoolhouse. It's gone now, fell down after the war. I was mad in love with him then. Well, all us girls were. He was a one for the ladies even then was our Emlyn. He was clever, mind, but lovely with it. Not full of himself, like some I could name.

"And look at you, Fliss, there's lovely you are. Your gran was my best friend, even though she was three years younger than me. Funny name Fliss, isn't it? Well see, you couldn't say Phyllis when you were little. You could only say Fliss. 'What's your name?' they'd ask. 'Fliss,' you'd say, proud as Punch. Now, where was I? Oh yes, Emlyn and me were born the same year – 1887. Polly wasn't born 'til 1893, six years younger than me. But we were all in the same class at school, so we became friends straight off. Mind you, Polly never got much schooling once her brothers came along, with her mam being so poorly. Now let me see…"

Rosa May closed her eyes. I looked at Matt, thinking this was going to be a bit like pulling teeth. He smiled and raised an eyebrow. Rosa May opened her eyes and began again.

"...Owen. That was it. Owen was the eldest of the Evans boys, stocky – bright auburn hair and a temper to match. Thomas was quiet, deep as the Low Pond he was, while Rees was more like Owen. Alun was the clown, not very bright and always up to his ears in trouble. Fiercely loyal they were, mind. No one picked on the Evans brothers. Little Dafydd and Fred started the year I left. Inseparable they were – like peas in a pod – twins, see?

"Like I said, Polly was seldom at school, too busy with the little ones. Poor Polly, she was the cleverest of the lot of them. Wicked waste, but then she was only a girl, see? And girls didn't matter.

"It was chapel as brought us together. I used to set out the hymn books for the Reverend Pritchard and collect them in after. Had to count them too, I used to think, *Who'd want to steal a hymn book?* but old Reverend Pritchard didn't trust anyone. 'We are all sinners, Rosa May Thomas. Even I am a sinner in the eyes of the Lord.'

"Pompous old tup. Anyhow, one day young Polly offered to lend a hand, see? She was better at counting than me, so I said yes. Polly was always wise for her years. There was something special about her. She always knew what to do. It was more than plain common sense. She had this wisdom about her. She was born wise. Emlyn used to say as Polly Evans had more sense in her little finger than the rest of the town put together. And there's true.

"After chapel, we'd walk home arm in arm. Polly and me that is, not Emlyn. I lived on the bottom road.

The Evans's lived up Somerset Street. If you cut through their house, you'd save a good five minutes. Everyone did it see?

"Later, I began stepping out with a young man. My da was strict chapel, so I wasn't allowed to see my Davy without someone else was there. He didn't want any hanky-panky, see? So Polly used to play gooseberry.

"Davy and I did our courting down the valley. We'd walk as far as the Fairy Falls, give Polly a bit of taffy and tell her to wait 'til we'd pick her up on the way back. Oh dew! I remember getting carried away one day, and well, it was a good two hours before we got back. My blood turns cold even now when I think of poor Polly all alone. It was dark by the time we got back, see. Dew! We found her sitting by the falls, singing. Singing hymns, she was, happy as a mochyn mewn cachu!"

Rosa May cast a sideways peek at Matt while she took a sip of her Guinness, dabbed her lips and continued her story.

"Mind, Polly never told a soul, even when her da tanned her backside for stopping out so late. Luckily, Polly could keep a secret, see. Just as well when you think of what happened later with all that scandal. Tongues were wagging and fingers pointing, but Polly never let a word be said against her family – especially not against her baby sister. Well she was her favourite, look you."

This was the first I'd heard about a sister. I knew Gran had eight brothers, but I'd never heard of a sister. "I never knew Gran had a sister."

Rosa May lowered her eyes, so she didn't meet my gaze.

"Yes, there was a sister, although Polly didn't like to talk about her. She died when she was young. Her name was Phyllis. You were named after her."

Chapter 15

BRYNAVON

Although I was none the wiser as to my grandfather's identity, I had unearthed a very late great-aunt. But all this secrecy was highly suspicious. Had I stumbled upon a dark family secret?

Matt was shaking his head at me, urging me not to ask any more questions —not yet anyway. He obviously didn't want me to break the old lady's train of thought. I doubted I could keep quiet when there was so much to ask. I was about to protest at being told to keep quiet when Rosa May raised an already arched eyebrow and pointed her index finger in the direction of the Guinness.

Her fingers were thin, and her large black onyx ring had slipped so that the stone hung heavily to the side. I studied the finger. It was gnarled and bony with an enlarged, arthritic knuckle. So that was why she always wore gloves in public.

Memories came flooding back as I stared at that ring. I had often been allowed to try it on when I was a child. I felt a sudden urge to ask if I could try it now. Rosa May was nodding enthusiastically to Matt, who held out a bottle of Guinness. He popped the cap off, but before he could pour it, she reached out and demanded he hand it over.

"Give me that over by here, young man. It's very fussy I am about my stout."

The old lady winked at me and began to transfer the contents from bottle to glass. When the glass was full, she gave the bottle a deft twist of the wrist. Once again, a perfect layer of white foam lay on top of the black liquid. She took a healthy swig, closed her eyes and smacked her lips together. Having dabbed at her top lip, she then tucked her hanky up her sleeve and continued her story. "Dew, those two sisters were as different as chalk and cachu."

Matt's eyebrows shot up. Rosa May held his gaze. The twinkle in her eyes betrayed her delight at having shocked him again.

"Oh, so you do know some Welsh then, young Matthew." She threw me a sly wink and continued. "Like I said, they were very different. Polly was wise, Phyllis was silly; Polly was plain, Phyllis was pretty; Polly was a giver, Phyllis was a taker. But they were very close —— more like mother and daughter than sisters, see? Remember there was 12 years between them. Their mam was always poorly, weak as a kitten. It was Polly as saw to the housework, the shopping, the cooking and the washing. She was mother to the lot of them, father, mother, and babies, from the time she was seven until they'd all gone.

"Phyllis was her baby doll, even when another baby brother came along. Phyllis was the one that got pampered and spoiled. Apart from baby Dewi, her brothers were giants. Phyllis was petite and dainty. Polly loved that. The brothers were hefty lads, she fed them and kept them clean, but apart from that, they were men, and took care of themselves.

"Young Phyllis could charm the birds out from the trees. She could wrap boys round her little finger with a smile and a flutter of her long eyelashes. She had the look of an angel; Polly would brush that girl's hair a hundred times every night 'til it shone like burnished copper! Then she'd tie it up in rags, so it fell in tight ringlets. And there was always a pair of blue ribbons drying over the end of the bed ready to tie on fresh in the morning.

"That child was born graceful. She moved like a lady as soon as she could walk, and she spoke beautifully, like a proper lady. God knows where that came from. But, no, nothing was too good for that one. Like I said, Polly treated her like a little doll. Fussing over her, fussing, petting, grooming. Broke her heart when she left, it did."

"Why did she leave, if they were so close?" This time it was Matt who interrupted while I glowered at him.

Rosa May ignored his question, continuing her own train of thought. "You won't remember when this was the Llewellyn's place, I don't expect? Ha! Lord Bloody High and Mighty, Arthur Llewellyn. He'll be turning in his grave and serve him right. My God, he'd be tamping if he could see it now. Sixty batty old commoners living in his precious mansion! Ha! His father built this house, see? It had a farm and parkland, woods and hills, not to mention coal. I never went inside the gates in those days, mind. Now it's me is living here. There's posh! ... Where was I? I do get lost..."

Rosa May took a draught of stout, wiped her upper lip and straightened herself in her chair. "Oh yes, Brynavon House. The Llewellyns owned this house back then, see. Owned the mine, they did. Llewellyn, pah!" Rosa May spat the name out. She sat straight as a rod, her eyes smouldering with an anger that had not lessened in 9 decades. "That family owned the mine, half the town and most of the inhabitants." Rosa May sipped her Guinness thoughtfully, her eyes brimming with memories. Suddenly they misted over. Her voice dropped to a whisper, as though she couldn't bear to hear the rest of her story.

"1913 it was, June 27th, a Friday, 10 o'clock in the morning. At first, I thought it was the church sexton ringing the hour. Then I realised it was the colliery bell. Dew, that only meant one thing – an accident. I remember the crush as the whole village started off up the hill, running and scrambling to reach the pit head. Women with babes clutched in their shawls, children tumbling out of the school, the Reverend Pritchard puffing and panting up the steep hill, everyone heading for the mine. Davy and I had the haberdasher's shop in the High Street back then, but we ran with the others, leaving the door wide open, the takings still in the till, the cobbles ringing as we ran to catch up with the crowd charging up the hill.

"Emlyn was already there, in his shirt-sleeves, a helmet on his head. Polly stood with him. She was one of the first there, she was. I remember the two of them, heads together, arguing something fierce they was, you could see the steam rising between them. Suddenly Emlyn threw his hands in the air, shouted something to one of the men who took his tin-hat off and gave it to Polly. Well, she was in that cage before he could spit. It was her brothers as was trapped see, and her da. He was down there too.

"That was the first time Polly had been down the mine, first time for the young doctor too. It was always his father as went before, see? Mind you, Emlyn didn't hesitate, and well, no one could have stopped Polly – stubborn as a mule she was and fearless as a young ram.

"They were underground 11 hours, maybe 12. It was dark when they started bringing men out. Rhodri Evans was the last. And he had to be dragged out – wanted to stay with his boys, didn't he, wanted to die with them, see? But they were too far under. There was no way to get to them, they were buried too deep. They were never found. They're still down here, under the mountain.

"Poor Emlyn. Young Rhys Jones was pinned beneath a prop. Emlyn was no surgeon, but he had to take Rhys Jones's leg off to free him. Just above the knee he cut it. He told me later that Polly held the boy down, stroking his head, smiling and whispering to him while Emlyn sawed. He said Rhys never took his eyes off Polly. Saved his life they did. Mind, poor boy never worked again. Crippled he was. It was a wicked, evil day.

"Polly never talked about it. That's how she was. She never said a word. Not to me, not even to her da. It was too terrible for words, see. Even Emlyn was reluctant to talk, although he had to write a report. He accused Llewellyn of being neglectful. He told the authorities that the men were working in unsafe conditions. Well, that didn't do his practice much good. The old bastard Llewellyn had it in for him after like. I'll never forget Emlyn's face when he stepped out of that cage. He had the eyes of an old man.

"He'd no sooner stepped out when Rhodri leapt on him. Knocked seven bells out of him he did. He was ranting and raving, saying no proper doctor would have taken a slip of a girl down into that hell. Emlyn just stood there and let Rhodri beat him. It was the shock as did it, see. Mind, Rhodri said he was sorry after, which can't have been easy as he'd just left his four eldest boys down there. Seeing his daughter down there too just tipped him over the edge. It was the thought of Polly being buried with then. Turned him it did.

"There was something special between Polly and Emlyn even then. Made for each other, they were. It was like putting milk in tea or butter on bread. Each was good on its own, but together they were so much more. After the accident, they were even closer. They understood each other without speaking. A nod or a gesture was as good as a whole sermon full of words. Well, I don't know what you'd call it, but I'd call it love."

Chapter 16

BRYNAVON

Although still a junior doctor, I had witnessed a couple of amputations. These were carried out in sterile conditions, with state-of-the-art equipment and modern anaesthetics. Even so, given the best equipped theatre, with trained, skilled surgeons, and brilliant follow up care, they were deeply traumatic. I tried to imagine what it must have been like down there, inside that shaft. The dirt, the dust, the heat, the lack of equipment, and knowledge, the fear of being buried alive at any moment, made my blood run cold.

Why hadn't Gran told me these stories? Even when she knew I had set my heart on becoming a surgeon, she had said nothing. She had told me that my mother was a nursing sister yet said nothing of her own experience. I never realised Gran had done such things, or that she was so brave.

"I never knew Gran was a nurse," I said, still struggling to contemplate what effect that experience must have had on such a young woman.

"Oh, she wasn't a nurse... well, not a proper nurse, that is, not trained and certificated. Mind, it was not for the wanting. But see, you had to pay for your training back then. Polly had no money of her own. And even if she'd had the money, her life wasn't her own. She had the home to run. There was her mam to look after and the younger children to care for. There were still five at home."

For a moment, the old lady paused as she counted on her fingers. "Yes, that's right... there were the twins, and Morgan, Phyllis and little Dewi – he hadn't drowned by then – or had he? I do forget. Anyway, that's another story.

"Emlyn often took Polly with him on his visits. She was very capable, very caring. Then, after the pit disaster, he asked her to accompany him on all his emergency calls. Well, like I said, she was wise, sensible and not at all squeamish. She'd cope with anything would Polly."

Rosa May took another sip of stout. This was her third. She sighed, and I asked if she was tired.

"No, not in the least, besides, I want to tell you while I do remember. My mind do come and go so often now, I need to tell you before it do go again. I'm afraid one day it will go and not come back, see. What was it Polly used to say, 'Come you from over by there to over by here and stand you by me now, I don't want to take you home lost.' She was always saying that. Well, one day I'll come home well and truly lost, so let's make the most of it before then. Dew! I loved your grandmother. She was my best friend. Life was cruel to her. She deserved so much more. She was boot-i-full."

Rosa May pronounced the word with the exact same emphasis as Gran had. Letting the syllables rise and fall like the hills and valleys she loved so much. "Boot-i-ful." I repeated the word, and Rosa May smiled. I swallowed a tear. The old lady took out her hanky and offered it to me. Matt looked embarrassed. The three of us sat in silence. Suddenly we all smiled at once, and I knew Gran was with us. I could feel her, and I know Rosa May could too.

When the old lady spoke again, her voice was stronger, her eyes focussed and bright. "I remember now. Little Dewi drowned before all that business at the pit. He was the baby of the family. Rhodri's wife died giving birth to him. Some say as her heart burst with the strain, others that it was her lungs as gave out. I think she was just worn out. She was never strong enough to have one baby, let alone ten. It's like I said, Aronwyn was always weak as a kitten. It can't be right. Men have no idea. Believe you me, the day men are the ones to give birth will be the day the birth rate drops to nothing.

"Little Dewi didn't live much longer than his mam. Drowned, he did. Up the mountain, in the Low Pond it was. Treacherous that pond is. Fed by old shafts, see? Currents do pull and drag beneath the surface. You can't see them. The water looks as flat as glass, but it's always moving underneath see – pulling and dragging and cold as it is black. Like as not he'd swallow his tongue before he'd had time to drown – a blessing really.

"His little body was never found. He was lost to the mountain, just like his brothers. Mind you, fair dos, none of them died trying to save him. Although seeing as what happened, it might have been better if they'd all gone together.

"The first I heard, Polly, ran into my shop, weeping fit to burst. Young Morgan was with her, sopping wet, weeds stuck to his skin. He was screaming fit to burst. He kept saying, 'There was nothing to hold onto. I couldn't hold him. He was like a little eel, wriggling and churning the water up like a propeller. He was that slippery, there was nothing to get a grip of. Then he was gone, not even a bubble left to show where he'd been. It was as if he'd never been there. Vanished he had. Oh God, Polly, why did you cut his hair off? Why today of all days? Why, Poll, Why? I would have had something to get hold of. I might have saved him. Why, Polly, why?' The words went round and round, stuck, like an old phonograph record. 'Why, Polly, why?'

"Of course, they searched and searched. They were still searching when the mist came down and night fell. They never found him. It was his fourth birthday. It was Dewi as had asked Polly to cut his hair. He wanted it short, like the men, see? He wanted rid of his long baby curls. He wanted to be like his brothers, with men's trousers and shorn hair. He begged and pleaded, so Polly cut it. It was his birthday present. She never stopped blaming herself for his drowning. It was too much responsibility for a young girl. It wasn't fair.

"Rhodri Evans took it bad. He went to bed with hair like coal, and in the morning, it was silver as the moon. It was the shock, see. Some say as it went deeper than his hair, down into his brain they said. I don't know. I do know he was never the same after. Then, when the pit collapsed, he left the rest of his wits down the mine with his oldest boys.

"Polly never had a childhood. By the time Dewi died, she should have been thinking about courting, getting wed, starting a family of her own. But her hands were full now with her poor da. She had to watch him day and night for fear he'd harm himself. Dafydd and Fred, the twins, had to leave off their education and go down the pit, but that still left Morgan and Phyllis at school."

"So why did Phyllis leave?" I asked, hoping to get Rosa May back on track, although all this was fascinating news to me.

"I'm just coming to that. There's impatient you are. If I don't follow my thoughts, I'll get really lost and none of us will be able to find me, and you don't want that do you?"

I had been well and truly told. I hung my head by way of an apology and caught Rosa May winking at Matt. She was enjoying this.

"Mrs Llewellyn, her from the big house, had been asking after Phyllis. She had watched her going off to chapel every Sunday and asked who the pretty child was. The Llewellyns went to high church, see… chapel was too common for the likes of them. When she learned the girl spoke good English and could read, she asked if she would visit her and read to her for a trial like.

"Mr Llewellyn's wife was lonely in that big house with just two grown-up sons and a husband who only had time for his business. She wanted a daughter, but that wasn't going to happen.

"That's why young Phyllis was sent for. I don't remember when exactly, but I think it was just before the war started. It was definitely after the pit disaster because we had just had the new till put in the shop. That machine! Every time it snapped shut, I feared for my fingers! Something fierce it was. Mind you, once I'd got the hang of it, it was very useful.

"Anyway, Mrs Llewellyn wrote to Mr Evans, asking if Phyllis could go and work for her. Well, the poor man was hardly in a state to think, let alone make a decision. Polly was tamping mad when she read that letter. She blamed the Llewellyns for her brothers' deaths, see.

There was no way she wanted her baby girl to go and work for them.

"Besides, Polly was determined Phyllis would have the education she'd never had. She wanted her sister to go into nursing. Polly was wise enough to know you can't live your life through someone else, but that was what she wanted. Phyllis had other ideas though.

"They had a falling out. Phyllis liked the idea of going to the big house, see. She wanted to see how the rich lived. She ignored Polly and turned all her charms on her da. No doubt she cried and pleaded, grizzled and begged. Well, eventually Rhodri gave way, didn't he? He could never say no to Phyllis, and with his mind broken and his boys gone, he was putty in her hands. It hurt him though. It was like rubbing salt into his wounds to see his baby girl going over to the enemy.

"Even before the pit collapsed, there was no love lost between Rhodri and Llewellyn. But afterwards there was open hatred. Everyone knew it was bad management as caused those deaths, even before Emlyn's official report was out. But Phyllis was wilful. She didn't see things from her father's point of view. Mind, she was just a child, hungry for a bit of glamour and fun. So, off she went, up to the big house, to become Mrs Llewellyn's pet. A few days later she'd moved in."

Rosa May took a deep breath. Her eyes flashed with anger. Having been raised in South Wales, I was no stranger to the bitter history between the miners, the pit owners, and the government. It coursed through the blood of every Welshman. But this was the first time I felt it burn in mine.

I had never identified with the miners' struggle. I had witnessed Polly's rage, but it was her rage. I'd never stepped over the line that would enable me to feel the pain for myself. It was here now in this old woman's eyes. It was burnt into her generation, my gran's generation. It was to my shame that I hadn't listened harder to my gran's first-hand testimony. It is the same anger that fired Matt's desire to work with MSF, but I didn't know that back then.

Before World War One, most of the mines were owned by men like Llewellyn: upper-class English men who considered the Welsh to be an inferior race. 'Mine Barons' they were called – robber barons some called them. Arthur Llewellyn wasn't the worst as mine owners went, but he was bad enough. My great-grandfather Rhodri had lost four sons to the pit, he had been dismissed for being incapacitated, largely due to that loss, and now they'd taken his little angel. Polly had never told me any of this, I knew there had been a pit disaster, and her brothers had died. But she had never mentioned a sister. It was as though Polly had expunged her from her life.

Yet all this was still fresh in the mind of Polly's lifelong friend, Rosa May. And she was determined to tell me all before her mind 'did go again'.

"Young Phyllis thought she'd fallen into a pot of honey. Lady Llewellyn spent money on her, see. Shoes, frocks, bonnets, well, that's bound to turn a young girl's head, is it? Give the girl her dues; she did tip over her wages, which brought a little bit of money into the house. Polly had lost five wage packets with the pit collapsing and Rhodri being laid off and, even with fewer mouths to feed, every penny was welcome. She worked too, helping in my shop when I needed her, and Emlyn paid her when she helped him, but it wasn't much. Life was hard in the valleys in those days. Then came the war."

Rosa May's eyes were trying to focus on something too distant to take form, while her lips disappeared in a tight circle of wrinkles. Fliss was about to ask if she was alright when the old lady signalled for Matt to open another bottle of Guinness. Once refreshed, she sat up as straight as a ramrod and continued speaking.

"The government took over the mines just before the war. The men got better wages and conditions, and many of the Barons got the boot. It was too late for some, but others benefitted for a while. A price deal made sure the Barons who remained loyal to the government did alright. Sir Arthur (he was knighted by now) always made sure his bread was buttered on both sides. Later he was made Lord Brynavon, although that wasn't what we called him, but I'm too much of a lady to repeat what that was – even in Welsh!" She winked at Matt and gave a little laugh. I couldn't help thinking how beautifully she flirted at such a great age. What must she have been like in her youth?

"Right!" Rosa May let her eyes close and sighed. "They'll be ringing the dinner bell in a minute. Mind you, dinner's not up to much, but it's better than nothing, see? What was it Polly used to say? 'Very nice, much as there is of it and plenty of it, such as it is!'"

I laughed at the familiar phrase and apologised if we had overstayed our welcome.

"Not at all, but it's time for you to go. I don't tire easily, look you. Besides, I've loved every minute of it." She gave my arm a squeeze.

Matt lifted his corduroy jacket from the back of the chair. Knowing there was still a great deal I wanted to know, he asked, "Why don't we take you out to lunch tomorrow? We're dying to hear the end of your story, and I've heard the Griffin does a pretty mean Sunday roast?" Rosa May's eyes lit up.

"Oh, there's lovely! Mind, I shall have to talk very quiet. There's folk in this town as like nothing more than a juicy scandal, even if it is nigh on 70 years old!" The old lady tapped the side of her nose and winked at Matt.

Matt winked back. "Rosa May Davies, you are incorrigible. We'll pick you up at noon, okay?"

"I'll be ready. Go on, off with you now. I've got to powder my nose for dinner, isn't it."

Far from exhausting the nonagenarian, it was the two youngsters who were worn out. By the time we got back to Polly's house, we opted for a simple pasta supper and an early night – in our respective beds. I needed to wake up with a clear head. I wanted to be well refreshed and alert when I heard what the skeletons lurking in the cupboards of Brynavon had to say for themselves after all these years.

Chapter 17

BRYNAVON 1979

Bright and early the next morning I was up and raring to go. This was Sunday. I only had a week before I was due back at work. Also most of my key witnesses were either already dead or extremely old. I had to get a move on.

Last night I had sent Matt back to his hotel after a quick supper. I could tell he was reluctant to leave. We shared a goodnight kiss, and although we both wanted more, I turned away. I felt his lips brush my cheek and I knew he was hurt. But something didn't feel right. I told him I was going to see Little Aunty Ethel in the morning and asked if he wanted to come with me, hoping it would lessen his feeling of rejection. We were meeting Rosa May Davies for lunch, and I thought a whole day together would be nice. He made some joke about a cold shower, which I didn't quite get, but we parted friends.

*

By 9.15 we were standing on the back doorstep of Jim and Ethel Lewis's house, just across the yard from Gran's.

"Come in, come in." Ethel's chirpy voice ushered us through the back door. Matt and I were both a good head and shoulders taller than she was. "Come on in... let the dog see the rabbit. My, my, look at you two, there's lovely. Welcome, welcome. It's Dr Emlyn's grandson, isn't it? I saw you at the funeral – spit and image you are, it could be him stood by here now.

"Come, let me give you a kiss." Ethel threw her arms out, and I bent down for a kiss and a hug. "It was a beautiful send-off you gave Polly. She'd have loved it, Fliss. Did Polly ever tell you how you got that name? When you were little, you couldn't say Phyllis. Try as you would, it always came out Fliss. But Phyllis is your proper name. It was your gran's sister's name. Oh! There's sorry. I shouldn't have mentioned her." For a moment, Ethel was even more flustered than usual, but it passed quickly enough.

"Heavens, look at you now. There's grown up, you are. I'll have to stand on a chair to box your ears now, isn't it?! Mind, you were never any bother as a little one. Good as gold you were. Fancy! Little Phyllis a doctor! Your gran must be bursting with pride."

Nothing had changed in Ethel's house since the first time I had seen it. I had spent hours there as a child, playing with the old spring balance. Winding and rewinding the musical, wooden fruit bowl, making pretend phone calls on the wall-mounted telephone. It was all just the same, except the phone had been replaced by a modern one. But Ethel had not changed at all. She still twittered on non-stop.

"That was a lovely service. Adollgar always gives a lovely service. It was exactly what Polly would have wanted – all her friends around her, and the Reverend Griffiths leading his flock. There's fitting it was."

Ethel's little hands were constantly on the move, while her head's nodding kept time with her tongue's perpetual wagging. So, it was a shock when she suddenly stood stock still, with her hands clasped to her flat chest. "There's wicked I am. I haven't offered you a cup of tea, and you've been stood standing here all morning." With that she gave her glasses, which had slid down her nose, a hefty shove with her index finger, and sent them shooting up the bridge of her nose. The impact made her let out a tiny squeak. At first, I thought she'd done herself some damage, but then I remebered this was a regular occurrence.

"You used to love a cup of tea when you were little. Jim used to sit you on his lap and let you dunk his bread crusts in his tea. Do you remember? He likes his tea that sweet, you can stand a spoon in it. He still has a sweet tooth does my Jim."

Ethel's voice dropped to a whisper. "He'll be through in a minute. It takes him longer to do things these days." Then resuming her usual trill, she exclaimed. "We've missed you, Fliss. Mind I know it's busy you are, what with the doctoring and everything. My! Dr Phyllis Evans! There's posh.

"Polly showed everyone the photo of you when they made you a doctor, with your certificate and all. She was that proud. I was telling Jim what a lovely send-off you gave your gran. Lovely it was. Special. Well, she was special was Polly. We all knew that, didn't we?"

Ethel darted back and forth from kitchen to front room as she rabbited on. Eventually, she appeared with a tray of tea things and began to pour. The tea was steaming hot, strong and dark, made with loose leaves. 'Proper tea' as Gran would say.

"Fancy you two keeping in touch all these years. There's lovely. Still just friends, is it? Or are we sweethearts now?"

Matt looked at me and I felt my face redden. We hadn't met until the funeral. Although he later claimed we met when we were children. Ethel was obviously of the same opinion. Her little hands clapped with delight at my blushes, while she chirped on like an excited sparrow.

"Do you know you're the spitting image of your grandfather? I could swear it was him as was sat there. He was a good-looking man, mind, and I fancy he was a good bit taller than you. Come to think of it, his hair was darker, and he kept it short, combed beautiful, with a proper parting. Very smart was Emlyn Jenkins. Not that you're not smart. You look very nice. I do know as that's the style of today. Of course, Emlyn had a moustache, very fine it was, very stylish – rather trendy really." Her laugh rang out like wind-chimes in a breeze.

"Young Doctor Jenkins was considered quite a catch in his day. Rosa May Davies the shop claims as he walked out with her for a time. It's not true, of course. Rosa May always was one to exaggerate. Rosa May Davies the shop, that is. Rosa May Davies the post didn't have the imagination to story tell. Mind she was good at gossip was Rosa May Davies... The post that is, not the shop. And there were a good few others I could name – Bessy from the White Horse, Farmer Pritchard's eldest and that bottle blonde from over by Crickhowell. But everyone thought he'd marry Polly, eventually like. The two were made for each other, see.

"They do say that Polly asked the Reverend Griffiths to post the banns. They also say as he refused." She paused as if waiting for a question, so I obliged.

"Why would he object to the marriage? I thought everyone agreed it was a perfect match?" I asked.

"Ah! That's just it, see. Polly wasn't after marrying Emlyn. No. It was that other one... oh, I do forget his name." Ethel tapped the side of her head as if trying to jog her memory. Calling through to Jim, she shouted, "Are you there, Jim? I need to use your mind, my love." With that, Uncle Jim appeared in the doorway, a frail old man leaning heavily on a Zimmer frame.

It was barely a year since I'd last seen him, and he had deteriorated considerably in that time. The Uncle Jim I'd known when I was growing up was sturdy, strong and upright. He used to carry me around on his shoulders as if I was a lamb. I remember he had always had a wheezy chest and a cough, but it never stopped him from working – or being full of life. Over the years, his breathing had worsened, and he had developed a stoop, but his appearance today came as a shock.

His emaciated body was practically doubled over. He had lost all his hair, and his skin was the colour of dry slate. The web of fine blue lines – which I used to think he had drawn on for fun – were more pronounced than ever, and without hair, I could see they covered his entire head. These finely traced lines were the result of a thousand tiny cuts and scratches, which had filled with coal dust and healed over. They remained as permanent tattoos – the proud badges all miners wear.

It took Jim four breaths to complete one shuffling step. He covered the ground inch by painful inch, each snatched breath providing barely enough oxygen to keep a canary alive – another result of a life spent at the coal face.

Ethel fussed as she settled Jim in his chair by the window. "There you go. There's better, isn't it? I was just telling Fliss and Matthew about Polly wanting to marry that young what's name? You know who I mean. The simpleton... what did they call him?"

"Daf... ydd. Daf... ydd... Jon... es." The answer came in short gasps. Jim sat propped up by pillows. His eyes closed while he gathered enough breath to speak.

"Dafydd Jones! That's right. I remember now. What would I do without your head, Jim?" Jim nodded by way of a reply. I, however, was all ears, eager to hear more. Dafydd Jones was a new name to me, yet he must have played a significant part in Gran's life if she had planned to marry him. Had she really asked Adollgar to post the banns for their wedding? Had he really refused? If so, why? He must have felt strongly that it would have been a mistake. I know we all do crazy things when we are young... especially if we fall in love... but this really didn't feel like my gran.

It was a lot to take in. I'd only just learned Polly and Emlyn were once what we would call 'an item'. Suddenly there's another young man on the scene. Had Gran been a bit of a 'goer' when she was young? Somehow, I doubted it, but she did have a baby, and they aren't found under gooseberry bushes.

Ethel put her saucer down. (She mostly drank her tea from the saucer. Come to think of it, all the women I had known as a child had the same habit. It must be a Welsh thing.)

Ethel chewed her lip. "So, Polly never told you about Dafydd?" This was more a thought than a question.

"Well… why would she?" Ethel followed her answer with an explanation. "It was all past history by the time you came along, see. It was the same for me. Dew, even I wasn't born when all of that was going on. Mind, I don't know as anyone really knew Dafydd Jones – other than he was one of the Jones's boys from over Bryn Farm.

"Now don't get me wrong, I'm not one to spread gossip, not like some I could name, that Rosa May Davies for one, that's Rosa May Davies the post, not Rosa May Davies the shop. No. I'm only telling you what I was told, see? Young Dafydd didn't have the brains of a gnat, while Polly was as bright as a new penny.

"Apparently, he used to follow her around like a lost puppy – had done ever since they were kids. Mind, it's a big leap from puppy love to marriage vows. But then the banns never did get posted. They do say as that was the reverend's doing. He thought Polly was too good for the likes of that Jones boy. We'll never know, Reverend Griffiths would never share anything he'd been told in confidence. Still, he must have had a good reason to refuse Polly, and he was her minister after all.

"There's always tittle-tattle in a small town. 'Who's done what? Who's gone where? Who's kissed who?' I always say as gossip is like bread. It gets very stale in a day or two. I do forget who told me this in the first place. I don't think as it was Polly, I have would have remembered that, see. Mind, she always kept things very close did Polly – never told a secret, not even to me, and I was her best friend."

Ethel pushed her specs up so fiercely it made her sneeze, which sent them crashing back down again.

"Dearie, dearie me," she muttered, all of a fluster, her fidgety fingers shoving them back again. "Well, fancy you not knowing all this. Dear, dear. But look you, what do I know? Like I said, it was all over before I was born. I wasn't born 'til 1917, the same year as your mam. This all happened before that."

Ethel poured her tea into a saucer, blew on it, and slurped it down in one long slurp.

I was understating my confusion when I asked, "I thought you told me Polly had sworn she was never going to get married."

Ethel peered at me over the rim of her glasses. "She did," Ethel answered, dunking her ginger-nut biscuit in her tea. I noticed a hint of mischief in her voice.

"Well, can you explain why a confirmed spinster was so anxious to get married to someone like Dafydd Jones. It doesn't make sense."

"It does – if you're expecting." There was a soft plop as Ethel's biscuit dropped into her cup. "Drat it!" she exclaimed, fishing for it with her teaspoon.

Chapter 18

That was the first time anyone had actually mentioned Polly's pregnancy, and I found it strangely comforting. I'd always known she must have been expecting around this time because she had my mother, Megan, in February 1917. I have to confess; I was also excited. At last, the shadowy figure of my grandfather had substance. I could almost feel his presence. He was getting closer.

Meanwhile, Ethel retrieved her soggy biscuit, ate it and began to dunk another. And so we all sat in that small parlour, slurping, sipping, thinking and concocting. No one spoke. Eventually, Ethel answered one of my unspoken questions.

"Polly's baby came as a shock to everyone, even Polly. She hadn't realised she was expecting until the baby popped out. You'd think Emlyn would have known, though, him being her doctor and all. Thankfully, Polly's da died before the baby was born, or the shock would have finished him off even sooner, poor man – him being so upright and chapel and all."

Matt chuckled at Ethel's lack of reverence. It gave me quite a start. To be honest, I'd forgotten he was in the room. He'd not said a word throughout the discussion. Ethel carried on quite oblivious that she might have displayed a certain lack of sensitivity.

"Polly said her da died of a broken heart. Broken bit by bit, it was, until there wasn't enough left to keep him alive. First, he lost his wife giving birth to little Dewi. Then little Dewi got drowned up on the mountain. (They never found his little body, you know, although they do say as the boys searched that pond every day for weeks.) Mr Evans's hair turned white when he heard the news. Fancy that! Pure white – overnight! Then, as if that wasn't bad enough, the pit fell in."

Ethel buried her face in her apron and began to rock gently back and forth. Eventually, she straightened up, rearranged her pinafore and patted her hair, which was held in a tight bun by a handful of pins and a stout hairnet. "His four eldest sons were taken in that disaster. All strapping, handsome lads – buried alive they were." Ethel sighed. She looked at Jim.

Jim had closed his eyes as if he couldn't bear to remember such horror. "Then the war came. That took the twins and young Morgan. They never came back, killed at the Somme they were. Still, at least they went together. Poor Mr Evans! Eight sons gone, yet not a single body for him to bury. His poor old heart couldn't take much more, see? When his little girl ran off with that Llewellyn boy, it finally broke."

Once again Gran's sister Phyllis was in the picture. Rosa May had told me about her moving into Brynavon House but her running off with one of the Llewellyn sons was news to me. Was that the scandal she had talked about? If so, we would hopefully hear more over lunch.

I was puzzled as to why Gran had never mentioned her sister to me. Why on earth not? What had her sister done to deserve being written out of history? What sin warranted being disowned by someone as loving and forgiving as Polly? It must have been something quite dreadful.

There were so many unanswered questions – and more waiting to be asked. I was, however, pretty sure by now that my grandmother had never married. I assumed she kept her maiden name and simply called herself Mrs instead of Miss. She had obviously had a child, a baby girl called Megan, born February 1917. Although, so far, the identity of the child's father remained a mystery.

There were two candidates, the innocuous Dafydd Jones, or the erudite, young doctor, Emlyn Jenkins. My money was on the latter. I confess I was biased, although in my defence he was the more likely of the two. Emlyn and Polly had a history. They were definitely in love at some point. They were both free. But – and it was a big but – why hadn't he made an honest woman out of her by marrying her?

I was struggled to digest all this when Ethel began chatting again.

"Polly's baby was born on February 19th, 1917. She called her Megan. Megan and me became best friends, so I never forget her birthday, see. We were born the same year. Sixty-two she'd be – same age as me."

This was quite a surprise. I had always thought Ethel was older than Gran. She certainly looked older. I'd also never realised that she and my mother had been close, but then, as with Gran, I knew very little about my mother. Gran often talked about her. She told me how lovely she was, how clever and what a good nurse she had become. But I was never that curious. Gran had obviously done a good job in raising me because I can honestly say I have never actually missed having parents.

I looked at Little Aunty Ethel, this bouncy, nervy little woman, and tried to imagine her as my mother's best friend – two little girls, hand in hand walking to school. Lying on the same grassy banks I had lazed on – making daisy chains, picking wild berries, and blowing dandelion clocks. My eyes met Ethel's, and I guessed she was thinking similar thoughts.

"I've always known you were Gran's friend and neighbour, but I never realised you were my mother's friend before that."

"Oh yes. Polly, or Mrs Evans as I called her, always said as Megan and I were joined at the hip. And we were."

"What do you remember about my mother?"

"Megan? Well, she was as plump as I was thin. I have to say I was a bit jealous of anyone with a bit of flesh on their bones. Not that it came between us. Oh no! We were always close. Megan had curly, pretty hair. Brown it was, always tied up in braids. She was comical, mind. Always in trouble at school, was Megan – mimicking the teacher, or telling stories. She often got sent out of class for telling stories."

"What sort of stories? Lies?" I asked.

"Oh, no. Funny stories, like when she told us how she'd seen Tommy Morgan's willy!"

I raised my eyebrows and Ethel giggled.

"I take it you haven't heard that one? I'm surprised Polly never told you. It was all over the town at the time. Some said as it was a miracle.

"We were about six or seven. August it was, hot as hell. We'd planned to go down by the river to cool off, but Megan's mam told her she was needed to help make a batch of bread, and Megan always did what she was told by her mam. So, she rolled her sleeves up and began to sprinkle the flour over the table.

"Her mam was knocking back the second lump of dough while the first proved in the tin. Both she and her mam were sweating fit to burst it was that hot in the kitchen. The door was shut to prevent unwanted draughts, see, but all of a sudden it crashed open, and they both jumped out of their skins.

"The whole door was filled by a giant figure of a man. He was so large his body blocked out all the sun. He had forearms as big as the lower branches of the old oak on the top road. He was holding a bundle of washing, all steaming and wet – cradling it as if it was a new-born.

"Eventually they recognised Morgan Morgan, the new pit manager from two doors down. Mr Morgan was still in his working clothes, black as the coal he cut. His washing – blue and white striped it was – dripped down his trousers, making dark puddles round his enormous, steel-tipped boots.

"Before Megan realised what was happening, Mrs Evans had spread a clean towel on the floor, taken the bundle from Mr Morgan and laid it on top. That was when Megan realised it wasn't washing. It was little Tommy Morgan, dressed in his pyjamas.

"Megan said Tommy's eyes were wider than any she'd ever seen. His lay rigid like a stick, his eyes rolling and stretching even wider. His lips were pulled back as if he was trying to scream. But nothing came out. Not even a moan.

"His da stood frozen solid in the doorway. His whole body was shaking, and he was jabbering like a madman. Tears ran down, leaving white streaks on his sooty face. It was the first time Megan had seen a grown man cry.

And Morgan Morgan had grown more than most men do in a whole lifetime.

"Megan said her mam went right up to Mr Morgan and slapped him hard around his face. Twice she hit him, hard enough to make him reel each time. Suddenly, he dropped to his knees and whined like a baby. 'God forgive me,' he cried, 'I was filling my pipe – filling my bloody pipe! Gwenny was doing the washing, see. Tommy was charging about, larking around as usual. As he pushed past, he nudged my elbow, spilled my baccy over the floor see. So, I reached out and cuffed him. I didn't hit him hard like, but he lost his balance and sat down backwards, more from shock than anything.

"'I watched him go, ever so slow like, he just sat back. I'd just helped Gwen lift the copper off the fire. The boy landed right in the middle of it. I swear to God it was all over before I could spit.

"'Tell me he'll be alright, Polly? I know you can save him. You can save him, can't you, Polly? If anyone can, it's you, Polly Evans. It'll finish my Gwenny if we lose another. She's already lost six, isn't it?'

"Megan said her mam didn't turn a hair. She stayed very calm as she told Mr Morgan to pull himself together. 'There'll be time for all that later, Morgan Morgan. Now, hurry and fetch Doctor Jenkins; then go home and look after your poor wife.' When he didn't move, she slapped him again and shouted, 'Now!'

"Megan said she was staring open-mouthed. Her mam had just slapped a grown man three times and shouted at him. Then she realised her mam was shouting at her. 'Don't stand there gawping, child. Take that dough and divide it into three. Knead and roll the first bit into a twelve-inch square, about an inch thick, give it to me, and start on the next bit.'

"This was an order, not a request, so Megan did as she was told. Poor Megan. The last thing she wanted to do was make bread, but her mam gave her such a look, she knew this was no time to argue.

"While she had been talking, Polly had cut Tommy's pyjamas off him. Megan told me, 'He looked like one of the skinned rabbits hanging in Mr Barnet's window.' Well, I was nearly sick just hearing her description. That's when she mentioned the willy. Megan had never seen a willy before. She said it was all red and shrivelled, like a boiled sausage. She wanted to throw up, but she remembered her mam's order and began to work on the dough.

"Meanwhile, Polly had stripped and examined Thomas. Megan handed her the first sheet of dough and watched her mam lift the boy by his ankles and slide it beneath him, wrapping it around his private parts like a nappy.

"'Right, Megan,' Mrs Evans said, 'keep kneading and rolling until I tell you to stop. I need you to keep those nappies coming as quickly as you can. You can do it. You're a clever girl, you are. You can do it.' Megan said her mam's encouragement made her feel she could tackle anything. She suddenly felt very grown up, very strong and important.

"Polly was like that, see? She brought out the best in people. So, Megan kept kneading and rolling, working the same three pieces of dough over and over, not daring to stop until she was told to. Mind, she did tell me later that she thought it was a pretty daft idea – and a waste of good bread.

"The two of them carried on like this for what seemed an age, Megan kneading and rolling, her mam wrapping fresh nappies round Thomas's scalded bottom. All the while, Polly bent over Tommy, stroking his head and telling him how much his mam and da loved him, and how his da was out at this very minute, buying him a puppy.

"Later, when we were alone, and things had settled down, Megan whispered, 'While Tommy Morgan was lying on the floor dying, you know what I kept thinking?'

"'What?' I asked.

"Megan looked up to heaven then back to me. 'I thought, *I'm not going to eat this bread. I'm not going to eat it. I'd rather starve than eat this bread. I know where it's been.* Was that very wicked of me? Do you think God will be angry with me?' I said of course he wouldn't... but what did I know? Who knows what God is thinking?

"After Dr Jenkins had taken Tommy Morgan to the hospital, still wrapped in Mrs Evans's weekly bread supply, Polly told Megan she deserved a medal. Megan said she had never felt so good. Mind she felt even better when her mam told her to throw the remaining dough into the pig-bin. She never did find out what God thought, though."

Ethel took a long breath. She topped up Jim's cup, tucked the rug around his legs and let out a long, heartfelt sigh. "Now I come to think of it, I never heard Polly tell that story. Still, that's not so surprising, what with Polly being Poll. I mean she wouldn't, would she?

She wasn't one to seek praise or glory. It just wasn't in her.

"No. Come to think of it, it was Emlyn who boasted of Polly's quick thinking and foresight. He said, 'It is a wonder the boy didn't die from shock and a miracle his manhood was still intact. Do you know? By the time he got to the hospital, he hadn't a mark on him. It was a stroke of genius to use the property of yeast like that. I'd never have thought of it. Polly Evans is a remarkable woman, a natural nurse and a powerful healer.'

"Later, when he asked Polly how on earth she'd thought of it, she simply said, 'I just used my common sense. I often think doctors could do with a little more common sense. It's a powerful thing, Emlyn Jenkins.'

"When people began to call Polly a miracle-worker, she just smiled and said, 'If you want to understand how the Good Lord works, just ask yourselves, who it was that made sure Megan and I were making dough exactly when it would be most needed?'"

Chapter 19

BRYNAVON 1979

Ethel's story, or rather Megan's story, told me more about the mother than the daughter. I found it quite staggering that in all our years together, Polly had never told me about her nursing exploits with Emlyn. Oh, I knew she had helped out, mopping brows, feeding broth, rolling bandages, that sort of basic stuff. But she had apparently been working as an actual nurse. I was only just beginning to learn that there was far more to Polly Evans than I had ever dreamed.

I knew Ethel was eager to tell me more – but I was beginning to realise I was unlikely to get the direct answers I wanted from this source. Lovely though she was, she always took a while to get to the point and often didn't quite make it. Nevertheless, her haphazard wanderings were informative and amusing. No wonder Gran had been so very fond of her. Clearly, she was enjoying relating her stories to a new listener or rather two new listeners. Matt was still with us, even if he remained very quiet.

"Of course, I always called Polly 'Mrs Evans' in those days." Ethel was polishing her glasses on her apron as she spoke. Her hands were never still, and neither was her tongue. "It wasn't until Megan matriculated and went off to become a nurse that Polly and I got close. There was a big difference in our ages, see. Mind, that didn't matter so much as we got older. Funny that. You'd think it would work the other way."

Here Ethel paused to breathe, replace her specs, reflect on her own wisdom and take a sip of tea. I seized the opportunity to cut in.

"Did Polly always call herself Mrs Evans? I know Evans was her maiden name. It was my name too. But as she didn't marry, she was actually Miss Evans. I'm right, aren't I? Polly never did get married." I needed to confirm what I had already surmised – my mother was born and conceived out of wedlock.

"No. Polly never married. I don't know when she began to be called Mrs. I only ever knew her as Mrs. But you are right, I suppose. By rights she was Miss Evans. Well I never. I've never thought of that before. But then I'm Mrs Lewis, so it only seemed right to call her Mrs, more polite, more fitting, like."

"So, we come back to the sticky question. Who was Megan's father?" There. I had asked it.

Ethel looked at Jim, then back to me. "Well now, that's a fair question. Mind you, I have to say as I don't rightly know."

"But you must have an opinion, Aunty. My money's on Emlyn. He was the only man she truly loved. Do you think Emlyn Jenkins was my grandfather?"

Ethel sighed. Then she shrugged. "Well, like I said, I'm not one to gossip, but, as they're all dead and gone, I don't suppose as it will do any harm." She shuffled forwards in her chair. Instinctively, I leaned in towards her.

Ethel dropped her voice and whispered, "Like I said before, Polly never knew she was expecting until the baby arrived. You see, girls knew very little about such things back then, although Polly knew more than most, her working as a nurse and all. But we didn't talk about private things in those days. They do say the whole thing happened so fast, there wasn't much time to point fingers.

"Of course, there was some talk. Some said as Emlyn was the father. No one mentioned Dafydd. There was some talk as it was Polly's father, what with him being a full-blooded man and losing his wife and all... some even said it was a miracle birth. Adollgar Griffiths soon put pay to that, mind.

"As I said, I'm not one to gossip. All I know is that Polly had always wanted a child of her own, and she never wanted a husband. She believed women got a raw deal out of marriage. So, maybe she tricked Emlyn into bedding her, got with child, then refused to marry him.

"Emlyn was very proud – almost as proud as Polly. But men can be too proud for their own good. If Polly was carrying someone else's baby... and I only say if... well... happen his pride wouldn't let him marry her. Or maybe Polly was too honest to trap him into marrying her, so she told him he wasn't the father. Maybe she denied it was his to protect his reputation, him being a doctor and all. Maybe they'd never done the deed. Maybe she was too honest for her own good. Oh, I don't know, I really don't know.

"But see, Emlyn wasn't the type to go and get a girl pregnant and leave her. He would have offered to do the honourable thing. All I know for sure is what I've told you. So, it's sorry I am, but, like it or not, your guess is as good as mine.

"Like I said, I'm just a silly old woman, what do I know? I'll tell you what I do know. Polly and Emlyn were close until the day he died. They never fell out. Even after Emlyn married little Lucy Morton, the two of them stayed close, working together and all that. Why Polly was Godmother to their boy. Oh, but that was your da, wasn't it Matthew? Well, there's lovely, isn't it?" Ethel poked Matt in the ribs. "Anyhow, that's all behind us, like the cow's tail."

We sat for a while, lulled by the gentle slurping of tea, the chinking of china, and the occasional crunching of biscuits. Questions hung in the air, unasked and unanswered. I was no nearer the truth than before. So, I decided to ask a question that had been nagging at me for some time.

"Do you think Polly got pregnant on purpose? Goodness knows it's hard enough for single mothers nowadays. I dread to think what it must have been like back in 1916. It would have been a huge decision to make. It would take a very brave or determined woman to put herself through all that stress intentionally."

Ethel smiled. "Well now, the Polly Evans I knew was always determined. I never knew her do anything as wasn't planned. She'd spent her whole life bringing up children. She knew exactly how difficult it was. But look you now, they'd all been her mother's babies.

"As I said, Polly always wanted a child of her own. She never wanted a husband. And you can have one without the other. Maybe that's why she picked young Dafydd Jones. He'd have been no trouble, being simple-minded. Biddable, see? Emlyn was as stubborn as Polly. He'd have insisted on marriage and a proper family. Polly was fiercely independent, as well as stubborn.

"You must never forget that Polly Evans was Rhodri Evans's daughter. Everyone in Brynavon looked up to that man. His boys had all died heroes. There weren't many in the town who hadn't called on Polly for help of one kind or another. So there was always a lot of respect for Polly.

"Polly spent her own childhood raising other people's children. This little one was the first one that was truly hers. She worshipped that baby from the moment she was born. Poor Megan died far too young, the Lord bless her soul. But she left you for Polly to love. You arrived like a blessing from the Lord himself. You were a part of Polly see? Her granddaughter. Polly was that proud of you and your mam. Fancy! Her a nurse, and now you a doctor! There's lovely, isn't it?" Ethel wiped away a tear and sighed.

The story was beginning to make sense to me. I was beginning to see a whole new side to my grandmother. I had known her generation was tough, but she really must have been an exceptional woman, way ahead of most at the time. I wanted to know her better. If only I'd listened harder or asked more questions when she was still alive. Had I left it all too late?

I realised that although willing and interesting, Ethel probably wasn't the best person to ask. The age gap between Polly and Ethel meant that most of what she'd told me was hearsay. I decided to ask Rosa May what she knew about the enigmatic Dafydd Jones.

Matt must have been thinking along the same lines as me, because at that moment he said, "So what happened to this Dafydd chap? Did they stay friends? Is he still alive?" This was exactly what I should have asked. Matt was displaying his usual, cool, matter-of-fact manner, but even he was surprised by the answer.

"Got knocked down by a horse, didn't he?" Ethel paused to help Jim to a biscuit. "It was the same day Polly asked Adollgar to post the banns for their wedding. Killed outright, he was. Tragic that, him being so young and simple."

It was indeed tragic, but the way it had been told made it almost comical. Matt was trying to suppress a smile. I looked away. I'd been caught by his infectious laugh before, and I didn't want to appear disrespectful.

I doubt Ethel made her next remark to lighten the mood, but it made us all laugh when she exclaimed, "Gracious! There's lucky. If Dafydd Jones was your grandfather, let's praise the Lord you got Polly's brains, not his!"

Chapter 20

BRYNAVON 1979

It was 12 noon precisely when Matt and I arrived at Brynavon House. Matron met us at the door. I thought she spoke rather dismissively as she led us through to Rosa May's room.

"You won't get much out of her today. She's away with the fairies," Matron said as she marched into the room without knocking. We followed.

Rosa May sat in an armchair facing the window, which overlooked a brand-new housing estate. The ever-present mountain peered over identical rows of box-like houses, their brickwork clashing with the landscape. A tray of tea things sat on the small table beside Rosa May's chair.

"We have good days and not such good days, don't we, Mrs Davies?" Matron looked at us as she spoke. Rosa May said nothing, but the look on her face told me she didn't appreciate being talked down to. As if to show her disapproval, she lifted the lid of the teapot and whipped the suspended leaves into a whirlpool, like horses on a not-so-merry-go-round.

"Thank you, Matron. Shut the door when you leave." Rosa May continued stirring as she snapped her order.

Matron raised her eyebrows to me. "Ring the bell if she gets too difficult." With that, she left. Rosa May continued to stir.

"I was wondering when you two would show your faces. Waiting I've been – a whole afternoon gone never to return. There's me on tenterhooks and here you are, marching in, bold as cheap brass. Well, what have you got to say for yourselves? Polly's gone; she couldn't wait any longer. Tamping mad she is. Just wait 'til she gets her hands on you, young lady. Serve you right if she tans your hide to within an inch of your life." Her long, thin finger pointed directly at me. I felt about 10 years old. "She says she daren't tell her father what you've done for fear the shock will kill him. Well? What have you to say? I'm waiting..."

Matt walked calmly over to Rosa May and put his arm around her. Knocking his arm away, she har-rumphed loudly. He signalled for me to keep back while he spoke softly and reassuringly to the irate woman.

"You haven't forgotten we're taking you out for lunch, have you, Rosa May? It's exactly 12. Are you ready to go? Shall I get your coat and hat?"

Rosa May stared at him. "What makes you think I'd go anywhere with you? I'll not be seen out with that... that trollop." Her bony finger pointed once more. I think I may have cowered.

"Who do you think she is, Rosa?" His voice was gentle yet firm.

"Don't play games with me, young man. You get that hussy away from me. I'm surprised at you being seen with the likes of her!" She looked at Matt, her eyes demanding an explanation.

"And who am I, Rosa?" he asked so gently, it was really quite touching. "Do you know my name, sweetheart?"

"Don't you play games with me, Emlyn Jenkins. You may be a doctor and all that, but I'm nobody's fool. And don't call me sweetheart or Rose. My name is Rosa May, Mrs Rosa May Davies. Besides, it's Polly as you should be talking to." With that, she looked at me, and if looks could kill, I'd have dropped dead on the spot.

"That's right. I'm Emlyn, your friend. Remember when we used to walk to school together? You used to say my legs were so long you had to run to keep up with me? Remember?"

"Through Ben Ward's fields!" Rosa May whispered the words, her face relaxing, her eyes suddenly lit up bright as a schoolgirl's.

"So, what has this young woman done to make you so angry?"

The old lady straightened up. Her eyes locked on mine as she spat the words out. "She knows, well enough. I suggest you ask her." Again, the finger pointed at me. I had no idea who she thought I was or what I was supposed to have done, but I felt guilt weighing like a millstone round my neck. Welsh honour is power-ful stuff.

Matt didn't flinch. "I'd rather hear it from you, Rosa. Why don't you tell me? We can ask her later whether it's true or not when we let her give her side of the story. There are two sides to every story, isn't that what your friend Polly used to say?"

I was amazed at Matt remembering that. I was always saying it myself. I smiled at him, but he ignored me. God, he was good at this role-playing.

At the mention of Polly, Rosa May began to talk more freely, as if it was just two old friends alone in the room.

"Polly never wanted her sister to go and work at that damned house. Everyone knows as there's bad feeling between her da and Sir Arthur. Rhodri hates the man – hates everything he stands for. We hoped things would improve, now the government's taken over the mines. But they've left Llewellyn in charge, and he still rules the roost. The men still have to doff their caps, still play servant to their master.

"Does she give a damn about any of that?" The finger pointed again, this time the look followed. "No. You want a cushy life, selfish you are, for all your angel looks. I know as you can twist your da round your little finger, all eyes and smiles and ringlets, isn't it.

"That Mrs Llewellyn spoils you rotten, makes you think you're a proper lady along with all those airs and graces. Well, imagine how that makes Polly feel? 'Madam does this, Madam does that. Where's your napkin? You shouldn't serve food from the saucepan. Never go out without a bonnet and gloves, it's so common!'... Dew! Poor Polly, after all she'd done for you, you ungrateful creature."

At this point, Matt interrupted. "That hardly warrants loving sisters falling out. Those two were always so close."

"Oh, that was just the start. It's her behaviour with Master Edward that caused this ruckus. First the flirting and eyelash fluttering, I've seen it myself, immodest and shameful. Well, gentry won't stand for that sort of behaviour, not coming from a miner's daughter. But then you shamelessly run off with their youngest son. Yes. It's you I'm talking about, Phyllis Evans."

This time, I know I cowered. Guilt was eating into me like a virus. Ah, but Rosa May wasn't finished with me yet. "Off up to London they run, bold as brass. Not a letter, not a word to anyone. Like I say – selfish through and through." She cast a look of utter disdain at me.

So that was it. Rosa May thought I was Polly's sister, Phyllis, and I was toxic.

"They said they sacked you for being light-fingered." The finger still pointed at me, as the vitriol poured out. "Pah! No! They didn't want the real truth getting out. It was too much of a scandal! Their son carrying on with a common tart! That would never do, what with Sir Arthur being a Sir and his wife a Lady and all."

I cringed now, knowing she was speaking directly to me. "So, what brings you skulking back to Brynavon, you hussy? Your posh young lover abandoned you, has he? I suppose you expect your sister to take you back, all forgiven, like. Well, look you, Phyllis Evans, I don't think even Polly will forgive you after what you've done to your poor da."

"What has she done to Mr Evans?" Matt asked.

"Killed him, hasn't she. It was just like Polly predicted. He dropped down dead from shame, the moment he heard what she had done. It split his poor old heart in two – killed him dead, sure as eggs is hens' fruit."

"My God, I didn't do that, did I?" This was the first time I'd spoken, and by now, I was not sure who I was supposed to be, my great-aunt or her great-niece. It was obvious from her reply that Rosa May still thought I was the aunt, and so did I, given my reply.

"Oh, don't play the innocent with me, young Phyllis. Polly wrote to you and told you your father was dead.

She told me so, and Polly never lies. But you never even bothered to reply. Too busy leading the high life with your rich young gentleman."

It isn't easy to be wrongly accused. It is even harder to accept the accusation without retaliating. I wanted to shout, 'I'm not Phyllis. I'm Polly's granddaughter. None of this is my fault.' But there would be no point. Rosa May was in a time-warp and we had no means of entry.

Whether it was Matt's prior experience, having coped with his grandfather's dementia, or his natural skills as a carer I don't know. But he knew exactly what to do. Putting his arm around Rosa May, he gave her a hug.

"Let's find your hat and coat. I'm taking you to the Griffin for lunch. I've got a friend who wants to meet you. It's Polly's granddaughter, Fliss. You like her, don't you? Remember Fliss? You'll know her when you see her. She's meeting us at the hotel. She's a lovely girl, very like Polly. We can have a glass of stout and talk about the good old days. How does that sound?"

Matt signalled for me to leave. I mouthed my thanks and indicated that I'd see him in the hotel. He winked, and I left, relieved not to be cast as the evil sister anymore. I had no idea if his ploy would work, but it was worth a try.

*

Half an hour later, the three of us were sitting in the dining room at the Griffin, raising a glass of red wine to Polly Evans and Emlyn Jenkins, Matt, Fliss and Rosa May Davies the shop. Matt was right; a short walk and a breath of fresh air had revived Rosa. She was quite her old self again. The past was over, and she was contentedly talking us through Polly's funeral for the umpteenth time. For the rest of the day, my investigation was put aside, but only for the time being.

Chapter 21

The next day, Matt had to leave for London. Work was calling. He had been offered a job at the Middlesex and needed to find a flat nearby. He also had to organise the sale of his mother's house. I saw him to the station. I was sorry to see him go. I had grown very close to him in the past few days. I had also begun to rely on his help with my enquiries. His calm common sense kept my feet on the ground and stopped me shooting off impulsively. I knew I was going to miss him, but I understood why he had to go.

Determined to carry on, I arranged to meet up with the Reverend Adollgar Griffiths. Ethel had suggested that I speak to him, and it was a good idea. His position gave him unique access to certain facts that could potentially shed light on the shadier aspects of the story that was emerging. I agreed to meet him in the Three Feathers, a rambling old pub at the head of the valley, which he told me was conveniently on his daily walk.

*

I arrived early and ordered a white wine before settling at a table in a bay that looked out over the valley. From here I could see a view that held magical memories for me, yet for some inexplicable reason, butterflies flittered around my tummy. I felt I was on the brink of something as I waited in the smoky air of that low-beamed pub.

The reverend was wearing a brown polo-neck sweater, beige cardigan and a pair of corduroy trousers. A large black and white collie followed him close to heel, the only one wearing a dog collar. This was the first time I had seen the minister in 'civvies' and he was every bit as imposing as he was in uniform. He spotted and waved, sending his dog over to join me. Bryn ambled across, slipped under the table and lay down, his head on his paws. His eyes never left his master. Even the dog was in awe of this man.

Adollgar was striking. As a nonagenarian he was remarkable. His stature, his thick mane of hair, and those incredible eyebrows meant there was no way of ignoring him, even without his 'uniform'. The other drinkers – three old men sitting by the fire, and four more playing cribbage at a large central table – acknowledged him by name as he entered. He signalled to the landlord to refill everyone's jugs, shared a joke and a laugh with the landlord and then came over to join me, bearing a glass of wine and a jug of dark ale. His popularity was palpable and was not simply as a result of his generosity.

"Well now, young Phyllis. I hope you were satisfied with Polly's send-off. I think you could say Brynavon did her proud." His voice filled the bar, dark and warm like the beer. There was a slight hesitation as he sat down, as if he was making sure the chair was directly beneath him. I recalled watching him stumble at the cemetery.

I think he guessed what I was thinking because he smiled. Then, dropping his voice almost to a whisper, he said, "Ah yes, decrepitude catches up with us all in the end. Just when we have convinced ourselves that we are among the immortals, the Good Lord sends us a reminder to the contrary – in my case a touch of arthritis in the left knee." With that he raised his hands to the heavens and shouted, "Thank you, thank you, my God, for rebuking me in my pride and reminding me of my mortality!"

His hearty laugh boomed round the bar. Then his voice dropped again, this time he whispered, "I have asked the Lord for a dispensation allowing me to talk to him from my rocking chair to save my poor old knees, but I haven't had a reply as yet. I think he may also be getting somewhat hard of hearing these days!" He winked at me, or at least something moved beneath the left snowy eyebrow.

We shared some small talk about Brynavon, my job, recent births, deaths and marriages, until inevitably the subject of Polly came up. "She was a rare woman was Polly Evans. I don't know how much you know about your grandmother's youth, but I'll bet I could astound you if I were of a mind to. I'll get another round in first. Who knows, it might loosen this old tongue." His finger made a circular motion and the landlord began to refill all the glasses. As a man, the locals raised their jugs with a loud, "Iechyd da, Reverend."

I raised my glass and repeated the toast, "Iechyd da! Cheers, Reverend Griffiths!" We bumped glasses and I began, careful to pick up where we had left off.

"You knew Polly all her life, didn't you, Reverend Griffiths? I wish I'd known her better. I was too busy being a kid. She gave me a wonderful childhood. I was as free as a bird, much loved and made to feel safe.

That's what I am going to miss – it's what I already miss – the feeling that my gran was always there for me."

"Your grandmother had the rare ability to make everyone feel safe. She was a natural earth mother as well as a healer. She had a remarkable faith, did Polly. And I know she died regretting that she failed to pass it on to you. You don't share her belief, do you, my dear?"

Adollgar's left eyebrow rose while the right eye winked. After see-sawing for a moment, the great white bird settled on the bridge of the beak-like nose. Those eyebrows fascinated me now, almost as much as they had when I was a child, but I had been asked a question. "Well, I don't go to church, or follow any set religion, although I do believe in spirit if that makes sense. I often feel Polly is with me, I mean I can feel her here." I pointed to my heart. "Do you think that's wishful thinking?" This old man was easy to confide in. He exuded compassion. I wanted to tell him that I had heard Polly speak to me at the funeral – I mean I'd actually heard her voice, but I was afraid he'd think I was blaspheming, or worse.

"Ah, well now, shall I let you into a little secret, my dear? Most set religions, as you call them, are a load of mumbo jumbo. Religion should not be 'set' in any way, certainly not in concrete. It should be a living, growing organism. God has spoken in many ways, to many prophets in many different lands, at many different times and in many different tongues. Yet his message is always the same. It carries and is carried in one word: love. Love the Lord thy God. Love one another. Love is all that matters. God is love. His love never dies. Polly's love for you comes from that same great source. How can it die? She's with her maker now, so she too is that love and that love will be with you whenever you need it."

At this point, he threw back his great white mane and roared. "Ha! Knowing that woman as I do, she will be popping up even when you don't need her. She never could help sticking her nose in, could Polly. She'll be chatting to you next. Telling you what's what. Now, young Phyllis, don't be afraid. Welcome her, talk back to her. I often chat to her. Her wisdom is a comfort to me still. We argue the toss more often than not. Polly likes nothing more than to play devil's advocate. Dew! She's always challenging me, poking her sharp, little pitchfork, forcing me to face those doubts I am too weak to challenge, or too proud to acknowledge. Polly taught me more about faith than any Bishop.

"She used to say, 'God put us here for a reason. It's not for us to question why. Mind you, when I meet Him face to face, it'll be the first damned thing I shall ask!' And I'll bet it was.

"So, young lady, what is it you want to know about your grandmother? If I can fill in some of the gaps for you, I will. But to be honest, and I will be honest, I shall not bear false witness, or tell you what I think you want or ought to hear, so if I think it is against your interest, or it is something Polly would not want you to know, I will hold my peace. Is that understood? I am so vain that I must remind myself each and every day that I am just a man. But I am a man who has been charged with God's work. I cannot undo what he has prescribed."

His words puzzled me at first, but since he told me his version of Polly's story, they have begun to make sense. Adollgar Griffiths may only have been a man, but by God, he was a man to be reckoned with. I found myself forming a deep affection, a profound respect for the man. He was a man of total integrity, and you can't say that about many men.

Chapter 22

The reverend raised his head, fixed his gaze upwards, and began to tell me his fascinating tale.

*

"To begin at the beginning, I began my ministry as a cocky twenty-one-year-old. I thought I had all the answers and a direct line to God. And by God, I was raring to go. I was, excuse the expression, like a young ram set loose for tupping. It was sheer chance that I was chosen as minister for the chapel in Brynavon. This was where I was born, see, where I was raised, and when the post became vacant, I was there ready to fill it.

"The Reverend Giles Pritchard had been the preacher here since the dawn of time. He was a God-fearing, powerful man, a difficult act to follow. Yet, being blessed (or cursed) with the arrogance of youth, stepping into his shoes didn't daunt me. I had come to save the world – and Brynavon was as good a place to start as anywhere. Or so I, blinded by that same arrogance, assumed.

"With hindsight, becoming minister in my home town was always going to be an uphill task. Everyone knows everyone, and everyone's business, in a small town. Its people are good folk, but what they don't know they invent. The congregation, the elders, the

Pharisees and the sanctimonious old women, all knew the young Adollgar, and they, God bless them, had forgotten nothing. I can hear them now:

'I do remember as it was him as stole the teacher's bicycle!'

'Oh yes! They never found it, but Adollgar came home black and blue, caked in mud and shamefaced. Ych a fi! Little muchun!'

'He was a little muchun right enough. I can see him now, backside always hanging out of his britches. Why, those britches had more patches than one of Blodwyn's quilts.'

'They do say as God works in mysterious ways, but Adollgar Griffiths, as our minister? Dew! The Reverend Pritchard will be turning in his grave, he will.'

'Well may God forgive me, but if it wasn't so wicked, I'd turn from chapel to church! The Reverend Adollgar Griffiths – there's funny. Funny peculiar, mind... not funny ha ha!'

"The inhabitants of Brynavon are blessed with exceeding long memories. It took a good few years for me to find my feet, and a few more to plant them on terra firma. That was where young Polly came in. She was a good friend to me. Even as a child, she possessed a rare kind of wisdom. Solid as St Peter she was. Not as I'm saying Polly Evans was a saint. Oh no, our Polly was much more fun than that.

"Polly was sweet sixteen when I took up my ministry. And like I said, she was as wise as the hills even then. By contrast, I was as green as the grass clinging to the sides of the valley. I had an over-filled heart and an empty head. I was going to do so much. I was going to save the world. I was too young and idealistic to realise that all one can ever do is one's best. It was Polly who taught me that lesson. Invaluable it was, yet painful and humbling.

"The year was 1909, my first month as minister. We were in for a long bitter winter, and the snow had come early. I'd been told of a family over by the other side of the mountain, in one of the hovels the pit euphemistically called 'miners' houses'. The children, 11 in all, had caught the measles. The father had been laid off from the pit as he'd broken his arm in a fall on his way home from night shift. As he wasn't at work when it happened, he wasn't entitled to a penny's help. The mother was at her wits' end, not knowing where the next morsel of food was going to come from.

"Up I rode, like Sir Galahad, leaping from my horse with a bible in my hand and a head full of good intentions – the Good Lord must have been weeping, although as Polly told me, years later, He was more likely to have been laughing his halo off!

"Anyway, going back to that awful night, I recall Dr Emlyn was already there when I rode up. He'd come in his pony and trap, with his great leather bag full of medicine and bandages and was already taking temperatures and examining the little ones.

"Then Polly arrived, trudging through snow up to her knees. Strapped on her back was a basket as big as she was. This was stacked with freshly baked bread, tarts, basins of dripping, and a jar of jam. She'd brought assorted baby clothes and a thick woollen blanket. And she'd carried it all on foot, right round the base of the mountain, in a blizzard.

"Well, she put me and the good doctor to shame, she did. Within minutes, she had rekindled the fire, boiled a kettle, brewed a pot of tea and was cutting bread into chunks piled high with dripping for the little ones to suck on. That was Polly Evans, see. Practical, down to earth, filled with the love of God and made fearless by His strength. She was always ready to get stuck in, sleeves rolled up, determined that nothing was going to stop her doing what she believed to be the right thing.

"I remember her laying into Emlyn, tearing him off a strip for not calling for her and bringing her with him. He said he didn't want her to catch anything or take the measles back home with her. Fair dos, there were five children under eight in her care back home. It was quite a risk. Measles was a killer in those days, a killer and a crippler. Well, I thought she was going to explode when Emlyn reprimanded her for putting the children's lives in jeopardy.

"'You pompous old tup!' she exclaimed. I thought she was going to hit him with the bread knife. 'I don't need your permission, or anyone else's, to do God's work.' At that point, her eyes had the fire of righteousness burning in them. I'll swear to God, I trembled as she looked right into my soul. Oh dew! She looked magnificent with her blood rising to her lovely face. I think I fell in love with her right there and then.

"I can hear her now, challenging the young doctor, 'Do you take me for a fool, Emlyn Jenkins? There's a copper full of water boiling waiting back home. They've got blankets ready to rig up on the clothesline to form a screen. They're going to put the bathtub out the back, so all I've got to do is strip off, have a scrub down with carbolic, put on fresh clothes, dump the contaminated stuff into the tub, so they can place it back on the fire to boil. No one will catch anything from me!'

"What a woman! I remember her auburn hair catching the light from the fire as she tossed it back where it had fallen loose. Her voice was soft as she continued to put the poor doctor in his place. 'I will never bring fever or sickness to any child in my care, or to my neighbours' homes. I may not be a proper nurse, I might not have a certificate, but I do know a thing or two about infection, Doctor Jenkins.'

"Well, that told him! Oh, my God, Polly was tamping that night. I'd like to have been a fly on the trap when the doctor drove her home. That woman had a magnificent temper on her. She rarely lost it mind, ah but look you, when she did it was best to run for cover. Anyway, all those little ones survived. Polly traipsed over there every day for two weeks and, true to her word, she brought nothing back with her, but a kind heart and an empty basket.

"I loved Polly. I even asked her to marry me once. Oh dew! I've never told anyone that, before now. She turned me down, of course, which was embarrassing. When I asked her why she didn't want me, she said she was never going to marry. She was going to become a proper nurse, and in those days, hospitals discouraged their nurses from marrying. Pity, she would have made a fantastic wife, although I have no regrets, as I then met my angel, Aderyn, God bless her. But I tell you now, so help me God, I was a handsome young buck in those days. I had plenty of girls to choose from. But it was Polly Evans as broke my heart.

"And then there was Emlyn." The minister shook his head slowly and took a long draught from his jug of ale. "Polly adored Emlyn Jenkins. Oh, she'd rebuke him, give him a good ticking off when she thought he deserved it, but deep down she had a great deal of respect and love for that man. And it was mutual. Like everyone else, I thought they would marry. I remember praying that they wouldn't because I dreaded having to marry her to another man.

"Then I met my beloved Aderyn. The Good Lord has seen fit to grant us nigh on 70 years together. We weren't blessed with children of our own, but the Lord knows what he's doing, see. A minister's children can have a hard time of it. The flock takes a lot of shepherding, and a minister's wife is kept busy enough looking after God's lost sheep. As I say, this old heart harbours no regrets – and I know Aderyn feels exactly the same. We have gone through life holding hands, and I trust we will be hand in hand when the Blessed Lord sees fit to call us home."

With that, Adollgar downed the rest of his beer and slammed his jug down on the table. "Well now, young lady, before we get onto the scandal and gossip, I suggest we walk back to my house. Two pints is all I'm allowed these days. Aderyn will be waiting with my bread and cheese already on the table. Come and eat with us. It's only humble fare, but good Welsh cheese takes some beating. Besides, I've got something to show you, which might just interest you."

Chapter 23

The three of us walked back to the minister's house just outside the town's centre, where his adorable wife served a simple but delicious meal. When we'd finished, we sat comfortably by the fire drinking tea, and I waited for Adollgar to take up his story.

*

"Right, young lady, if I recall correctly, I told you I have something to show you, but first I need to tell you about the scandal involving Polly's younger sister, Phyllis. How much do you already know?"

I shrugged. "Rosa May started to tell me, but she was confused. She thought I was Polly's sister. She was quite nasty to me. I gather there was no love lost between her and Phyllis. I didn't even know Polly had a sister until the day of the funeral. So, anything you can tell me will help."

"I see. Well, it's not a pretty story. I have lived longer than most, but even I am shocked by the amount of hatred people can amass against one another, or how a lie can become familiar enough to become fact. Rumours, if repeated often enough, become truths and scandal can arise from the most innocent of happenings if the wrong people own the telling of the tale. Rumours and scandal! Like I said, the sanctimonious women of the chapel, and other Pharisees that attend my church, had a field day over poor Phyllis's disgrace. To this day, I'm not sure as I ever fully got to the bottom of it. But, well, let me begin at the beginning once more.

"The first I knew of anything untoward was when Polly came hammering on my door, asking me to help her. I expect you knew that there was 12 years difference between Polly and her sister. Your great grandmother, Aronwyn, was a sickly woman. So, the children were left in Polly's care. This wasn't ideal, her being no more than a child herself, but it wasn't unusual in those days. Needs must, and many children had to grow up long before they had lived as a child themselves. Polly was one such child. She raised her sister Phyllis from the day she was born.

"Many is the argument I've had with Rhodri Evans. I remember him punching me once when I dared to suggest he stopped having marital relations with his wife. Like Jacob, Rhodri was a potent man. But Jacob was allowed several wives, so there were more to bear the load, so to speak. Suffice it to say, my advice was not well received, and a new baby, young Phyllis, duly arrived. Apart from Polly, all Rhodri's other children had been boys. Now along comes the prettiest little thing you ever saw.

"Polly was ecstatic. I don't remember ever seeing her more happy. In her eyes, Phyllis was her baby, hers to nurse, to dress, to pamper and to spoil. Oh, she adored her boys, and they worshipped her, but her sister was her special joy. And that child did radiate light. It was as though all the love that was poured into her transformed itself into sunshine and shone out of her, mesmerising everyone that met her.

"Things weren't easy though. Dewi was born a year later, and the Lord saw fit to take poor Aronwyn in his stead. Now young Polly had two babies to care for. The older boys were already down the mine, and anyway, the division between women's work and men's work was clearly defined in those days. Anything to do with babies fell to the women.

"Phyllis always was headstrong. Some said she was selfish, and that Polly had spoiled her. Maybe she had, but understandably so. The child had been taught to put herself first and that she did. Polly knew this, of course, but she was determined her sister should have the life she had wanted yet been denied.

"All was fine until Mrs Llewellyn asked Phyllis to go work for her. Polly came to me, concerned about letting Phyllis go and stay at the Llewellyn's house. Oh, I knew the Llewellyns, Sir Arthur and Lady Anne. I'm sure you know he was the mine owner – a bigwig in the town. They were English, rich, and privileged. They were churchgoers, so they considered themselves superior to those who attended my chapel.

"Lady Ann had never had a daughter, and she wanted a young, female companion. Well, Phyllis was an obvious choice. The girl was pretty, well behaved, spirited, and amusing. She was also overawed by the opulence at Brynavon House. I won't repeat the words that Polly used when she first came to ask my advice. She was incandescent with rage, afraid Lady Llewellyn would turn a spoiled child into a monster, someone who would never be satisfied with her own humble home again.

"Polly said no in no uncertain manner, but her sister was a wilful little girl. She hated school and was only too eager to challenge her sister's authority. Apparently, she screamed at Polly, 'You're not my mother. You can't tell me what to do.' Those words cut deep. Polly didn't mind being called a spoilsport, told that she was jealous, that she wanted the job for herself – comments like that rolled off her like water off a duck's proverbial. But those words were cruel. I told Polly that Phyllis was just pushing to see how far she could push, playing the little madam to rile her sister. Mind, Polly already knew that. With the wonderful gift of hindsight, I now think she could foresee something ominous looming.

"The General Strike, the war, the boys joining up and her father's deteriorating health, weighed heavily on Polly. The thought of losing her baby sister, even for a few years, was too much to contemplate. Polly really didn't know which way to turn. In the end, Rhodri undermined Polly's authority and made the decision himself, despite all Polly's protests: Phyllis was to go and live at Brynavon House.

"Polly told me she began to lose her sister that first day she left. Afterwards, whenever Phyllis deigned to come home to Somerset Street, she affected the airs and graces of a lady. Polly hated it. She never hated her sister, mind. She loved her more than life itself. She knew God teaches us to love the sinner but hate the sin – not that any sin had been committed at that point – if indeed it ever was – but their relationship changed there and then. They were individuals now, not just siblings.

"Phyllis stayed at the House, enjoying her new life and privilege. Polly often came to me to unburden her heart. She truly believed she had lost her sister. Then one day in June a letter was delivered by hand addressed to Rhodri Evans. It was a letter from Lady Ann Llewellyn. Vitriolic it was, accusing Phyllis of theft.

"Polly gave me the letter. She said she didn't want it in the house. I still have it. Here, I'll fetch it for you."

Bryn's ears pricked up as the reverend started up. "Alright, boyo, sit you back down." The old dog settled back, but his eyes followed his master's every move. Reverend Griffiths levered himself from his chair, his arthritis obviously giving him considerable pain. Before he took a step, he paused, waiting until he was steady enough to stand upright and walk. Again, I was reminded of his stumble in the churchyard.

He crossed over to a large bureau which filled the corner of the comfortable parlour. Selecting a key from his watch-chain, he unlocked a small side drawer and produced a pale blue envelope, still pristine despite all the years that had passed. The letter it contained was handwritten in blue ink on pale blue vellum.

Chapter 24

Dear Mr Evans,

It has come to my notice that taking your daughter into my house has been a terrible mistake. I have been harbouring a viper. Not only has she behaved inappropriately toward some of the gentlemen of the house, including my sons, but she has also been stealing from my household. Several items of value have disappeared over the period of her employment – trinkets, jewellery and such like – my eldest son's gold cufflinks and shirt studs among them. He also informs me that numerous sums of money have been disappearing from his dressing-room over the course of the last year.

I am a God-fearing woman, Mr Evans – church, not chapel – and I expect my staff to be honest and obey the Lord's commandments, as I do. It would appear, however, that your daughter has not been raised to follow Christian ethics. It horrifies me to think I have allowed her to sit beside me in my pew every Sunday, morning and evening, only to discover she has no moral compass, no comprehension of right and wrong, with no idea of repentance nor any sense of shame.

I have no intention of contacting the police at this juncture. However, I no longer wish to associate myself with your daughter, or any other member of your family. I am, therefore, severing all connections from this instance.

Your daughter is no longer welcome in this house. Furthermore, I consider it my duty to ensure she does not find employment in Brynavon or any of the surrounding towns. I urge you to publicly disown her, with the hope of redeeming your own good name, and in order to teach her the lesson she deserves.

Yours faithfully,

Lady Anne Llewellyn.

I let the letter drop to my lap. So this was the source of the rumours. Adollgar retrieved the fallen letter. "Vengeful, that is!" he declared. "Believe you me, there was never any evidence against young Phyllis. No witnesses came forward, no members of staff confirmed Lady Llewellyn's claims. But dismissed young Phyllis was, stamped with the stigma of unseemly behaviour, branded with disloyalty, deceitfulness, and theft.

"Polly was tamping when she saw that letter. She marched off up to Brynavon House demanding proof of her sister's so-called crimes. If there was no proof, she demanded a complete and public apology. Of course, they didn't even let her in, let alone speak to her. Eventually, she went to the police, but they said they could not, or would not do anything. The Llewellyns were too powerful, see.

"Fair dos, though, Polly stuck by her sister. She swore her sister was innocent. I knew there was more to this letter than the words on the page. Something evil was going on. Polly's eyes took on a haunted look. I tried to question her, but she closed up like a book. I decided, maybe wrongly, to wait for her to come to me if, or when, she needed to.

"I never saw Phyllis again, and neither to my knowledge did Polly. Nor was she ever seen again in Brynavon. She had run away with Llewellyn's youngest. Gossip had it they had eloped, but only the Good Lord knows the truth. Polly was despondent.

"God bless them both. Let us hope that the wretched, young woman was not abandoned by her young man. Let us trust that she is safe. Polly never got over her loss, and the shock was enough to kill poor Rhodri. But that was all a long time ago, my dear."

At this point, the reverend paused as if he had entered some silent place that he did not want to share. Bryn sat up, alerted to the sudden change in his master's mood. The old man bent forward and stroked his companion's ears, first the black, then the white. Reassured that all was well, the dog settled at his master's feet, head on paws, watching. Eventually, the old man resumed his tale.

"Those were difficult times, my dear. The valleys had it hard for decades, centuries even. Strange as it may sound, when the war started, things began to look up for the miners. But it was false hope.

"I remember the strike of 1915. The men were fighting for half-decent wages and reform of the disgraceful conditions they worked under. It was like the Hebrew slaves challenging Pharaoh —without a Moses to lead them. The 'Robber Barons' had never been richer. Coal had never been in more demand, see. Remember we were at war now. Our young men began going off to fight, where the conditions were no worse, and wages were higher.

"Then the government decided as they'd be better employed at home. Coal fuelled the Royal Navy see, and it was Welsh coal as kept the foundries going to make the armaments and ammunition. Most of the boys who'd already signed up had been sent off to the Western Front. Well, there was no one as could dig tunnels like Welsh miners. My God, those poor boys, digging like moles they were, miles under the enemy lines – often within inches of the Hun. Dreadful work, hard and dangerous, but their wages were better than at home, and some even said the odds of survival, although grim, were pretty even.

"Then the government declared mining a reserved occupation, but it came too late for Polly's three remaining brothers. The twins, Dafydd and Fred, and young Morgan – who lied about his age so as to go with his brothers – had already signed up, see? They'd joined the 38th Welsh division earlier in the year of 1916 that was. I recall the three of them, like peas in a pod, marching off arm in arm, singing at the tops of their voices. Three good, strong tenors – the choir's rendition of Cwm Rhondda was never the same after... after...

"God forgive me, but I sometimes think He wasn't on our side in that war. So many young men died. And for what? As Polly would say, 'God only knows, and he isn't telling.'

"They were that close those three boys. Barely a year separated the twins from Morgan. The telegram came about two months before Phyllis ran off. Polly never really recovered, and the shock put another nail in her father's coffin. He'd already lost the will to live, poor man. He'd outlived eight sons, then his precious little girl ran off shrouded in shame. Some say that it was the shame that killed him. I think he just had enough. Poor Polly was left all alone to pick up what pieces remained.

Maybe Rhodri thought it would set her free to have a life of her own. Who knows? God rest his soul."

The old man wiped his eyes and murmured something about needing to get his eyes tested. I wondered whether to ask him if he ever learned what happened to Phyllis but decided it could wait. Surely, he would have told me if he'd known.

When Adollgar got up, only his eyes betrayed the pain he was in. Whether the source was his arthritis or the stress of recalling such long-buried memories, who could say? He'd said enough though, he was tired out. So, I suggested we call it a day.

"I was just going to suggest that myself," he said, patting Bryn, who was now sitting alert and upright by his master's side. "The next bit is complicated and still painful to me. I shall find it hard to tell. It was hard enough at the time, and contrary to what people may claim, some things do not heal with the passage of time. Sometimes the wounds fester and the pain worsens. There is stuff I have only ever talked about with Polly, and with God. Not even my dear wife knows what I shall soon relay to you. But, being Polly's granddaughter, you have a right to know. I feel she would want you to know, but I should like to pray on it. If there are details I am not meant to tell you, my God will let me know."

Bryn rested his head against my legs, and I gave his ears a vigorous rub. He growled affectionately. I bent down and kissed his head. I remember he smelled of toast. "Good night, Mrs Griffiths," I called through to the kitchen. "Thank you for your hospitality. I hope I haven't worn your husband out." Then turning to Adollgar, I put my arms around him, and he held me close for a moment. "Nos da," I said, kissing his cheek.

"Duw bendithia, Phyllis bach," he whispered as he placed a kiss on my forehead and blessed me. And, despite his ominous warning of worse to come, my butterflies had vanished, and I felt very peaceful and content. I would sleep well that night, I was sure of that.

Chapter 25

The next day I felt rested. My butterflies had also been recharged as once again they whirred around my stomach at Mach 1. As arranged, the reverend and I met in the Three Feathers and, although it was still February, there was a definite touch of spring in the air. The sky was clear with a sun the colour of cowslips. When Bryn saw me, he wagged his tail vigorously, his black lip lifting in a crooked smile of recognition.

"You're honoured, young woman. That old dog doesn't do that for many. Maybe you have the smell of Polly about you. He was fond of Polly was Bryn." After we had shared a drink together, the reverend suggested we made the most of the sunshine by taking a walk.

"I thought we might walk over by the mountain, only as far as the Low Pond, mind. I have to get back for the chiropodist at one. This nice young woman comes over from Merthyr once a month – special rates for pensioners on the last Thursday of the month see. I used to think as it was a bit self-indulgent getting my feet done, but by God, they feel as good as new when she's finished with them."

We walked on in silence for a while, the sun ahead of us, shining on our faces. It was warm enough for me to remove my Barbour and tie it round my waist by the sleeves. The reverend was dressed as before, looking comfortable and restored. I decided to let him open the conversation as he had obviously finished yesterday's chat at a natural stopping point where, I assumed, he would begin.

We had descended by a well-worn path, and now the lower mountain slopes rose ahead of us. Keeping a steady pace, we maintained our silence until the Low Pond came into sight. Suddenly, the minister stopped and let his eyes travel up as if searching through the hovering mist to find the top of the mountain. He must have seen this view so many times I wondered if he ever tired of it, but the look of wonder and joy in his upturned face told me it was still a thing of awe to him. I closed my eyes to soak up the sun and heard his powerful voice reaching up to blend with the wind.

"I shall lift up mine eyes unto the hills, from whence cometh my help? My help cometh from the Lord, who made heaven and earth."

The old minister fell silent again, his eyes still lifted to the horizon. I can't explain why it felt so special – it was just an old man and his dog, standing beside me on a breezy hill in Wales, but it did. I have never believed in God. I have never believed in angels, seraphim or divine power. But in that moment, I felt as if I was held in a prayer. I have thought about that moment many, many times over the course of my life. I have never told anyone else about it, not even Matt. But I can honestly say I have never experienced anything that comes even marginally close as a spiritual experience. I shall never forget it.

I would have been quite content to stand there soaking up the early spring sun forever. The mountain breeze was the only indication of how far we had walked, or how high we had climbed. I have no idea how long we had been standing there in silence, but I remember when that rich, dark voice spoke again, it gave me a start.

*

"This might have been the very spot where David first sang those words of praise. Psalm 121. Blessed indeed. I have been coming here all my life. Once to dump a stolen bicycle, but many more times to stand close to God in his beloved hills of Wales, from whence cometh my help." Adollgar took in a deep breath of mountain air, sighed and began to share his memories with me. As the story unfolded, I could hardly believe my ears.

Chapter 26

"It was 1916, about two months after young Phyllis had run off. I remember it was a gloriously hot, dry summer's day. I stood in the cool of the chapel, although truth to tell, I was feeling hot and bothered. I'd better explain.

"One of the choristers had been caught with his fingers in the collection box. I had been advised by – shall we say advisors – to dismiss him and I had refused. He was a poor little runt, father out on strike, no money coming in – an all too familiar tale. The box had been left open with seven shillings and ten pence ha'penny sitting there for anyone to help themselves to. Well, he did, bless him. I told him off, saying what he'd done was wrong in the eyes of God. I told him he had broken the eighth commandment.

"The boy looked at me. Red raw his eyes were, a great big sty on the left one. Bold as brass he challenged me. 'My da told me not to come home without a loaf of bread. He said as God always provided for the poor, and we was poorer than most. I was going to ask you, Reverend, honest I was, then I saw the box sitting there open and all. It's a sign, I thought. So, I took three and eleven pence. That left three and eleven pence ha'penny for Jesus, that's more than half, isn't it? So, I reckon as I only broke a bit of the eighth, but I kept the fifth.

"'My da said as when you get down towards the bottom of the list, they don't matter so much. Sorry, but I had to honour my da, the fifth being higher than the eighth, see? We got bread and dripping for us tea, and I got a ha'penny off my da.' His grubby hand opened to reveal the coin. 'Here, you can put it back in the box if you think God would like that. Only we've eaten the rest. What would God say, Reverend? Can I keep my ha'penny?'

"I couldn't fault the boy's logic or his arithmetic. 'Out of the mouths of babes' etc. etc. But the wise women of the church were listening. They didn't quite see it my way – they seldom do. Sometimes I think the Lord Jesus could sit himself down beside them come Sunday, and they'd tell him to shift himself as the front pews are reserved."

"I was still seething, burning with anger from their lack of compassion when Polly came charging in like a bat out of hell. She ran full pelt down the aisle, stopped just short of the altar, dropping to her knees in front of the cross. Like the picture of the Rock of Ages, she was, one arm reaching for the cross, the other clasped to her bosom.

"The words tumbled from her mouth too quickly for me to decipher until I caught the word 'banns'. Polly was asking me to post banns for a wedding... her wedding.

"Now, it's my experience there is only one condition that makes a young woman so desperate to get wed, and that didn't fit with Polly Evans. At least not the Polly Evans I knew.

"I remember using my pulpit voice, so she'd know I was speaking as her minister. 'Calm down, my child. If you have something to tell me, I will not stand in judgement over you,' I said.

"She fixed me in the eyes and declared, 'I don't want a discussion. I just want you to post the banns for my wedding. It takes three weeks, doesn't it? I have my reasons for being in a hurry, but I do not intend to go into all that just now.'

"To my great shame, I laughed. 'I'm sure you don't, Polly. But marriage is a serious commitment,' I said. 'There are questions that must be answered. One, how long have you been courting? Two, is he a God-fearing man? Three, does he attend chapel? Four, what is his name?'

"Polly took a deep breath and told me, in a very matter-of-fact tone, that she was engaged to a young man from over by Crickhowell. It was someone she'd known since school. She said she didn't know if he went to chapel, although he would if she told him to. He was a bit younger than her, but not by much and his name was Dafydd Jones. This was most unlike Polly. She was in her mid-twenties, a grown woman, rational, calm and level-headed. I suggested we might pray together then have a serious talk.

"I took her into the vestry where we sat by the little kerosene stove and talked well into the night. My wife, I'd been married for, oh goodness, about five years by now, anyway Aderyn came looking for me. She'd brought sandwiches because I'd missed my tea. I think she'd guessed I was with a parishioner and might be talking most of the night. As always, she left us alone. Midnight soul-searching is a frequent occurrence in my ministry, but Aderyn saw that tonight was different.

This time it was a dear friend in need, one whose soul was in obvious torment.

"I remember my mind racing nineteen to the dozen. My first instinct was that Polly was with child, and she never denied it. But who in heavens was the father? Certainly not Dafydd Jones! I knew him, of course, although he wasn't one of mine, nor was he a churchgoer. He was a nice enough young man, but not known for his brains, or his prowess with the ladies. Rather slow as I recall. Good with horses, inept with people. Not at all the sort Polly would choose – totally unsuited. I'm afraid I was thinking he was not good enough for her, which was uncharitable of me.

"Something was very wrong. I could feel it in my bones. I am ashamed to confess that my money was on Emlyn Jenkins. We all knew how much he loved Polly. But I knew him to be a moral man, a man of integrity and honour, a good doctor, not the sort that would take advantage of a God-fearing young woman.

"This is hard for me to admit. Very hard! I handled it all so badly. Oh dew! I betrayed my calling. I have begged God to forgive my recklessness— my zealous way of jumping to conclusions, my self-righteous pomposity and my lack of charity. Later, much later, Polly said she had forgiven me, but for me this marked the lowest point of my ministry, the lowest point of my life. It comes back to me now still heavily weighted with shame, laden with the guilt of my un-compassion. God forgive me.

"You must judge me as you see fit – as I know He does. My actions caused me to doubt my calling, to make me want to resign and withdraw from public service of which I felt so unworthy. I had judged and would be judged accordingly. The Lord my God is a forgiving God, yet I can never bring myself to forgive that conceited young man that was me. I was not fit to be called reverend. Now I must ask you, the next generation, to forgive me for the hurt I have caused and the rift it put between Emlyn and Polly... and me.

"Our conversation was uneasy, Polly was holding back, afraid to confide in me. I decided to confront her with my doubts and trust that our friendship would be strong enough to cope with the results. I realise, with hindsight, I was heavy-handed. I recall saying something along the lines of, 'Don't you lie to me now, Polly. I shall know if you do, and, even if I don't, our Lord Jesus Christ will. I like to think we are friends, Polly. If something is troubling you, I implore you to share it with me. We can sort it out together. I am here for you. You know that, my dear.' How patronising, how unhelpful I must have sounded. I know that now.

"Polly knew it then. Her face was set, that strong jaw of hers clenched tight. 'Reverend,' she said, 'I too value our friendship, but you are also my minister. I am simply asking you to read the banns in chapel next Sunday and for the two following Sundays so that I can get married to the man of my choice. Is that too much to ask?'

"I felt I could not agree to such a request unless she admitted she was with child and confided in me the identity of the father. I felt convinced that, whoever he was, it was better to force the truth out of her, and try to talk her out of an unsuitable relationship, than allow this bright, intelligent young woman to live her life with a man who was so beneath her in intellect and wit.

"I demanded that she told me. 'Tell me who the father of your child is. I cannot help you unless you are honest with me. Secrets cannot be kept from God, Polly. You need to confess everything to Him. I want to help you, but you have to meet me halfway.' I can hear my voice now. The arrogance!

"Polly raised her hands, and I swear to God I thought she was going to strike me. Instead, she clutched at her temples and tore at her hair. 'If I am 'with child', as you so aptly put it, it is nobody's business but mine. I will not tell you any more than that. Now, will you let me marry Dafydd Jones or not?'

"My God, I still recall exactly what I said and will regret it to my dying day. As God is my witness, I looked that innocent young woman in the eyes and said, 'I can't, Polly. It would be a sin. You are a member of my flock. I cannot let you make such a terrible mistake.'

"Polly left me standing in the chapel. I can still see her silhouette as she walked into the pale dawn light. Her head was high and her shoulders back, yet she carried the weight of the world upon them. It was my job to ease that burden. I had failed, but being an impetuous, self-righteous ass, I took things into my own hands and, God help me, I decided to challenge Emlyn."

Chapter 27

"Emlyn was dead-heading roses in his small garden. The gate had not swung shut before I accosted him. I told him I knew Polly was with child, and I knew he was the father. I demanded to know what he intended to do about it. His words haunt me now as if he spoke them yesterday.

"He was outraged. 'Good God, man, have you taken leave of your senses?' He spat the words at me. 'Polly isn't pregnant. I'm her bloody doctor, man, I'd know if she was expecting. And before you go any further, I have never done anything that I ought to be ashamed of as far as Polly is concerned. What right does that bloody dog collar give you that you come barging in here accusing me of... of... Well, what exactly is it you're accusing me of? What am I supposed to have done? What has Polly told you?'

"We continued bandying words back and forth, not getting anywhere, for what seemed like an age. I told him the whole town knew he was in love with Polly, and it was obvious she was fond of him. There were bound to be rumours, speculation... Gossip, you see? The devil's work... and here was I spreading it myself. Had I been listening to a dark voice? Could it be that I was jealous? Did I still hold a candle for Polly Evans?

"I tell you, as God is my witness, I have never faced such inner doubts, before or since. I had insulted Polly. I had accused a loyal friend and a decent man of acting immorally, and I had been unfaithful in thought to my beloved wife, Aderyn.

"Emlyn's temper was up; the man was visibly shaking. I could feel his need to hit out, to release the pent-up rage he was holding back out of common decency. Part of me wanted this. A good scrap could defuse things. A few punches might be what I needed to bring me to my senses. Then all of a sudden, he sat down, there in the rose bed. He sat down cross-legged and held his hands up in defence. He had turned the other cheek. Well, I can tell you it worked. Shame flooded over me and, before I realised what I was doing, I had sat down beside him.

"When we had both cooled down, he offered me his hand. I took it, and we grasped each other by the elbows before falling into an embrace. Eventually we pulled apart, and he rose to his feet. 'Well, are you coming in for a glass of beer, man. Or do I have to fetch it out here?' He was standing over me, rolling his sleeves down and fastening the cuffs as he spoke. 'We don't want the whole town gossiping now do we, Reverend.'

"He was as concerned as me when he heard what had happened between Polly and me, the request for banns to be read, the alarming urgency of the request and the unlikely choice of groom. Emlyn was less willing to believe that Polly had got herself into trouble than I was. In fact, he was adamant that it was so out of character that he flatly refused to believe it. He then went on to confide in me, something I have no doubt he would never have divulged if the circumstances had not been so bizarre.

"We were on our third beer, chasing them down with large whiskeys, when Emlyn suddenly said, 'Did you know Polly turned me down? It was only last year. We'd been attending a difficult birth in the top road, and she asked me to call to see her father when we got back, as he was unwell. He'd never really recovered from losing his lads down the mine. Polly was exhausted, but so stalwart. I think that was what I most loved about her – her solid, unshakable courage.

"'She was right about Rhodri. I was pretty sure he'd had a slight stroke. He would recover with rest and care, which Polly was the best person to deliver. Having settled the poor man, Polly and I sat in the kitchen. She was being her usual, stalwart self, and I remember telling her it was alright to cry. I'll never forget the fire in her eyes that night. I am ashamed to say I took her in my arms, kissed her and asked her to marry me.'

"'You kissed Polly Evans! God, there's brave, boyo!'

"'Foolhardy, more like! She pushed me away and told me to leave. She wasn't asking. It was an order. "Get out of here, Emlyn Jenkins. How dare you presume that I either need your permission to cry or am in need of a husband to survive? You will never ask me again, is that clear?" She was like a tigress. God! What a woman!'

"'What a woman, indeed!' I repeated, wondering if I too should confess to having also been rejected. I remember thinking it might soften the blow to discover he wasn't the only one Polly had turned down. I decided to hold my tongue and save my own embarrassment. Instead I asked, 'Did she give you a reason? Did she say she was in love with someone else?'

"'No,' Emlyn answered emphatically. 'But she wrote me a letter. It's personal. I don't think she would want me to share it with you, Adollgar. I can tell you that she was adamant she would never marry. For the first time in her life, she could smell independence. Marriage would erode that. It would snatch it away before she had time to taste it.'

"'So, will you?'

"'Will I what?' asked Emlyn reaching for the whisky bottle.

"'Well, ask her to marry you again, of course?' I said, feeling exasperated and strangely jealous."

"'Well, I won't say never – it's a long time is never. But I shall hold back for now as I've started seeing Lucy Morton. But that's another story. Listen to us, two bloody fools arguing the toss over a bloody woman who doesn't want to get wed at all. There's mad we are.'

"'It must be the whisky,' I said, trying to stand but falling back into my chair. 'God, Aderyn will kill me if I fall home drunk.'

"'Don't worry. I'll fall home with you. The fresh air will do me good. You are a good man, Adollgar. No hard feelings, eh?'

"'My God, Emlyn, it's me as should be apologising, my friend. Let's draw a line in the sand and start again. It's lucky the Good Lord loves sinners. Let's hope my wife is as forgiving as Him.'

"With that, we made our way back to the little house next to the chapel, where Emlyn waited until the door was opened and he could apologise to Aderyn for plying me with alcohol. I'm not sure that helped, as we were both as drunk as skunks, see? But our friendship was unshakable from that night. I didn't mention Dafydd Jones... it didn't seem right as Polly had told me in the confines of the church. But all the same, God does indeed work in mysterious ways."

Chapter 28

A few days later, Matthew came back to Wales. He was jubilant when I met him off the train, but he wouldn't tell me why, which was infuriating. As we climbed up the hill to Polly's, I told him what I had learned from Reverend Griffiths, including the fact that Phyllis had died young, although I didn't know any details. But, instead of congratulations, I received a dismissive laugh, "Ah. But wait till you see what I've found," he said, rather smugly I thought.

He was like a child with a secret. My instinct was to smack him, but when we got into the parlour, he opened his holdall and produced a bottle of champagne.

"Wow! What have I done to deserve this?" I asked. Matt lifted me up and swirled me round.

"This—" he began tearing the foil off the bottle "— is for me... because I'm so clever..." He released the metal guard and the cork shot across the room. Placing the bottle on the table, he reached behind him and took a box from his bag. "But this is for you."

'This' was an old chocolate box held together by string. Painted roses, violets and ribbons, faded and worn were still recognisable, although the corners of the box were battered and there had been various attempts to patch the cardboard with brown sticky tape. It must have been quite something in its time. I stared from the box to Matt. His eyes were bright with excitement.

"What is it?" I asked expectantly.

He shrugged. "Read the label. That's Emlyn's handwriting. I don't know what's inside. I thought you'd like to be the one to open it."

The label was the sort the post office issued years ago – Manilla card with a reinforced hole for the string. This had been knotted onto a thicker, stronger string that wound round the box, holding it together. The label read, MISS POLLY EVANS – PRIVATE AND PERSONAL. GIVEN TO EMLYN JENKINS 1918, FOR SAFE KEEPING

"You darling, darling man," I exclaimed, throwing my arms around Matt's neck.

With a sardonic snigger, Matt said, "It's Emlyn we should be thanking. To think he kept this tatty old box safe for 60 years. Hang on a mo, I'll go grab some glasses. We might want to remember this moment."

But I couldn't wait. I began untying the string. "Hurry up," I called through to Matt, "…and bring some scissors with you. They're in the drawer, by the sink."

Matt came back with two tumblers. "I couldn't find the crystal," he jibed. "But here." He produced a stout pair of scissors and I set to cutting through the impossible knots. Without the string, the box fell apart, as eager as I was to share its contents.

"Right – first things first," Matt said, putting a full tumbler in my hand and raising his own. The heavy glass gave a dull thud as we chinked them together, making us laugh as we guzzled the bubbles.

"Here's to Polly and Emlyn and whatever we are about to discover." Just then a horrible thought struck me. "You don't think Polly will mind us rummaging through her private stuff, do you?"

"Why did she keep it safe if she didn't want anyone to see it? She could have burned it or binned it. No, this was obviously precious to her, but I'm sure she'd want you to have it, whatever it is."

'It' comprised several bundles of letters, lovingly tied with thin black ribbon. Some looked as if they had never been opened before, others were dog-eared from constant reading and re-reading. It was an Aladdin's cave.

"Where on earth do we start?" I said, pouncing on the top bundle.

"Well, why not start with the one in your hand. But I suggest we do this systematically after that. There'll be postmarks giving place and date of posting, it won't be that hard. We can arrange them chronologically."

I couldn't help but think, how tediously boring, but I was impressed by Matt's clarity of thought. He was right, of course. We needed to work systematically. This lovely young man was going to be a huge asset in my quest. I was comfortable with him. He had this solid sense of reality that made me feel safe.

Then a thought struck me that sent a cold shiver down my spine. It was still highly likely that we were related by blood, sharing the same grandfather. Falling in love would be reckless. I decided to dismiss any such thoughts as ludicrous. I was getting carried away to the realms of fantasy. I forced my mind to return to the letters, nevertheless that cold chill didn't leave me.

It felt uncomfortable reading someone's private letters. I reminded myself that Polly wanted me to read them, yet I couldn't help asking, if that was the case, why hadn't she told me when I was of an age to understand? What had she been hiding all these years?

My need to know sat uncomfortably beside the fear of discovering something sinister. What if she had done something so awful, I would hate myself for revealing it? What if I ended up hating my gran? I stared at the paper in my hand.

"What's up?" Matt asked.

"I feel rather guilty, like a peeping Tom. Do you think Gran's watching me? Is she angry because I'm waking sleeping dogs?"

Matt shook his head, a wry smile on his face. "Listen, from what I know about Polly Evans if this isn't what she wants there'll be a hurricane, or these letters will self-combust. And, like I said, why keep them all these years if she didn't want someone to read them? And who better than you, the person she loved most in the whole world?"

Chapter 29

I opened the first telegram. It was dated August 8th, 1918.

IT IS WITH REGRET THAT I HAVE TO INFORM YOU OF THE DEATH OF MISS PHYLLIS EVANS AUGUST 8TH 1918. SHE DIED IN THE LINE OF DUTY WHILST VOLUNTEERING WITH THE FIRST AID NURSING YEOMANRY IN AMIENS FRANCE.

Matt whistled. "My God! Turns out that our young 'hussy' was a bloody hero, a frontline nurse no less, dying for King and country. I think Amiens was the last battle of WW1. Wow, that's tough luck. Now we have another piece of the jigsaw... we can contact the war museum. They'll have records."

I was still digesting the thought of Phyllis, a young girl from the valleys, in France, in that dreadful war. It did not fit the mental image I had been forming of a spoiled brat, selfish and frivolous. Maybe I'd jumped to the wrong conclusions.

Meanwhile, Matt had opened the second telegram. This was also from the War Office. It brought the news of Polly's brothers, the twins, Dafydd and Fred and their younger brother Morgan. All three had been killed in action, in the woods of Memetz.

I have lost count of how many times I have seen such telegrams being presented in films or TV dramas. The scenes, always poignant, often tragic, had never begun to compare with the wrench my heart suffered on reading that small bit of paper. The abruptness of such monumental news being conveyed by the briefest of messages was cruel. I had to fight back my tears as I replaced the telegrams in the box, vowing that tomorrow I would find a new, stronger home for Polly's treasures.

By midnight we, or rather Matt, had sorted all the letters into chronological order. I wanted to carry on through the night, but Matt insisted it would be wiser to wait until the morning. We agreed to compromise by limiting ourselves to the first and smallest of the three bundles.

These were all on similar stationery, personalised, watermarked, rather posh, and strangely familiar. All were written in the same hand, which we soon discovered to be our hero, Phyllis. I was glad we had been allowed to review our opinion of my great-aunt before we read her earlier letters, as I found myself approaching them with a softer heart and a fondness for the young girl. After some strong black coffee, we examined the first letter.

"There's posh!" I said, mimicking Polly, as I opened a blue vellum envelope. It contained two letters, written on consecutive days. A shiver ran through me – I was in direct contact with my great-aunt Phyllis and my grandmother when a young woman. And the notepaper was that of Lady Llewellyn. I was holding a piece of history, which would give me a glimpse of a woman I didn't know existed a week ago and might reveal a side of another who I had thought I knew so well.

Brynavon house

Brynavon   *May 8th 1914*

Dearest, darling Poll,

I know I'm a bit daft writing this as I shall see you on Sunday afternoon, but Lady Llewellyn said as I could use her notepaper and I just had to let you see how lovely it is.

Oh, Poll, you have no idea how grand everything is. They use the best china and silver at every meal, I mean real silver knives and forks. Mostly I eat with Lady Anne, sometimes in the summer house, sometimes in her sitting room. Imagine that. She has a sitting room of her own! She is teaching me how to use the correct cutlery and flatware. (Knives and forks) She says my manners are very common. She is a very grand lady and I have a lot to learn.

This afternoon, we are going shopping in Abergavenny. She wants to buy me some nice clothes, befitting to my position. Imagine, me with a position! I am so excited. She is terribly kind, very generous and so elegant. I hope to be exactly like her when I grow up. Give my love to Da and the boys.

Lots and lots of love,

Phyll

PS I'll bring this letter with me when I come on Sunday.

The second letter was posted in Brynavon.

May 9th 1914

My dear sister,

I hope you are well. I slept my first night at Brynavon House last night. I have my own room, my very own *bed and a wardrobe for my very own clothes. Imagine all that space, just for me. It is so nice not having to share everything. Although of course, I do miss you. But I expect you are pleased too, as you have so much more space for yourself now that I have gone and, well, now you are just there with Da the twins and Morgan. How is poor Da? I hope he is well. I was hoping to come and visit on Sunday, after church, but Lady Llewellyn wants me to go to Tredegar with her. She has been invited to The Gough's for luncheon. I don't like to disappoint her as her youngest son, Mr Edward, left to join his regiment yesterday and she is inconsolable.*

Hope you are well.
Your loving sister,
Phyllis

Further letters followed at weekly intervals, then they dwindled to one a month. They got shorter, briefer, of the 'I am well, hope you are too' style, except when they contained descriptions of the many fine possessions the Llewellyn family owned. Rosa May was right. It did seem as if Polly was losing her little sister.

Phyllis loved to brag about the number of servants in the house, how Lady Anne never did any washing up, laundry or cooking and how she was learning how to dress her mistress's hair and lay out her clothes. Polly learned how many chairs there were in the big house, how many mirrors, how many horses in the stables, how heavy the cutlery was and how light the china.

The war was seldom mentioned, but it was noticeable Phyllis was growing up – and apart. She was adopting sophisticated tastes. The Polly I knew would not have approved. Like me, she must have read the signs of dissatisfaction – the odd remark or phrase indicating that her little sister was reviewing her status, starting to look down on her origins. It would have irked Polly to have to take a back seat and watch her darling girl turn into a stuck-up little snob.

Then there was a gap of several months without any correspondence until we came to the very last letter in the pile. Gone was the posh paper, the fountain pen and the blue ink. This was scrawled in pencil, on a piece of lined paper torn from an exercise book. The handwriting was unmistakeably Phyllis's, but it was uneven and shaky, no doubt written in haste and under considerable stress. Most intriguingly, it had been posted in London, in Chelsea to be precise, and two years after the first.

29 Tite Street, Chelsea. London   *May 30th 1916*
My dearest Polly.

How can I begin to thank you? We are now in London. Letters will reach me at the above address, care of Mrs Elsie Conway.

Captain Edward has rented a room for me, in Mrs Conway's house. She is a kind lady who looks out for me. I help her around the house with the housework. Don't laugh, I know I'm no good at domestic chores, but I am doing my best. Captain Edward has gone back to France now. I miss him. He has been very kind. He rents a studio at the top of the house. I go up there sometimes and sit looking at his paintings. They are very beautiful. Sometimes, before he went back to the war, I would let him draw me. He is awfully talented. I think he will be famous when this war is over.

His family have disowned him because he came away with me. Fortunately, he has a private allowance which he says it is enough to keep the wolf from the door (His words) as I shall never be able to repay him.

My heart breaks when I think of Da. I hated not being able to come to his funeral. Did you lay a flower for me?

Please don't blame me for his death. I don't think I'd want to live if you thought it was my fault that he died.

I know I can never come back to Brynavon, which breaks my heart. Please forgive me for all the pain and shame I have caused. I love you and miss you so much. Write to me. Let me know you believe in me. I am s o desperately unhappy – and I love you more than my own life. Think kindly of your little sister. Please let me know you still love me, if I know that I can face anything.

Your loving sister,
Phyll

There was something wrong about these letters. An element was missing. The selfish girl depicted in these letters did not marry with the war heroine of later years. What had happened to change her. I began to wonder if Phyllis was the sort of person who always got centre stage. She was doing it now, her part, however intriguing, was side-tracking the search for my grandfather.

I looked at the unopened pile of letters, then at Matt. He was yawning. "I vote we call it a day. This lot will still be here in the morning, and we'll be much fresher." With that, he leaned over and kissed me on the lips. "Can I stay here tonight? It's bloody cold out there."

The kiss was quite innocent, but it completely unnerved me. My heart began racing, and my thoughts became a jumble.

"No. You must go to the hotel," I said, adding the word 'Sorry' and feeling like shit.

Matt hovered in the doorway. I could barely look at him. "Would it be so awful if I stayed the night? I'll kip in the back room, or down here. You do know I like you, don't you? I thought you liked me. Actually, I'm in love with you, Fliss, and I intend to marry you."

Chapter 30

Matt stayed the night. We made love. We rowed. We made up. Made love again and spent most of the day in bed, talking, making love and drinking wine. Matt stayed the next night too. The letters were shelved for now. Then suddenly Matt announced, "I'm going back to London. I'll catch the 10.50 from Newport and I want you to come with me." He was perched on the edge of the bed, obviously expecting a reply.

I was stunned. When, with all this going on, had Matt decided to go home?

"I thought we were going to read the rest of Polly's letters," I said, "Then we are going to Brynavon House to see if Rosa May is well enough to answer some more questions. I've also got to go to the solicitors this afternoon. I'd hoped you'd tag along."

Matt had his head in his hands. He began to shake it slowly from side to side. "No. It's best if I go back."

I began to panic. "Okay. You go. No problem. Do what you want, but I'm staying." I tried to act blasé, but I was angry, and it showed.

"Whoa! Don't be like that, Fliss. Listen, I only popped down to bring you Polly's box. I'm in the middle of moving, and I've got a mountain of work to catch up with if I'm going to make consultant next year. Besides, I don't think this 'research' is doing you any favours. You need to take a break. You're becoming obsessed. Honestly, it's all getting a bit unhealthy."

How could he say such a thing? I thought he was as eager to continue the search as I was. Was he really saying, "Who cares who your grandfather was? What's the big deal? I'm not really planning on getting married or having kids, or anything. That was just a ruse to get you into bed."

I turned so he couldn't see my face as I clambered over him to get out of bed and get dressed. I was livid.

"Why don't you go now? If you hurry, you might catch the earlier train. I have to see the solicitor this afternoon and I want to have another chat with Rosa May Davies. I'm still on leave, so I'll stay. You go. It'll give me time to think."

I gave a loud grunt as I forced my head through the neck of my polo-neck sweater. As I emerged into the light, I heard myself say, "It's best if you do go. I need space. I'm feeling pressurised. All this talk of love and marriage, it's stupid. My life is in too much of a mess for all this. I don't know who I am or where I'm going. And it's not just you. It's everything. I'm confused."

Matt's silence encouraged me to carry on with my tirade.

"I'm not cut out to be a surgeon. I'll certainly never make consultant. Besides, I'm not sure it's what I want. I'm thinking of moving back to Wales, maybe going into general practice, probably staying on in this house. I haven't decided yet."

Matt's eyebrows had shot up. "Where's all this coming from? You're in no state to make decisions like that, Fliss. Stop this now and come back to London with me."

"How dare you presume to know what's right for me?" I was shouting now, determined he would not interrupt me until I had said all that was in my mind. "You have no idea what I want. I'm up to here with studying." My fingers jabbed at my temples, while I blinked furiously to stop myself from crying. I was determined not to cry. "My mind has stopped functioning. It's saturated. My memory's stuffed to bursting point. I've been trying to remember the names of 31 pairs of spinal nerves for two months now, but there simply isn't room in my tiny brain for any more facts."

Matt was standing by the door. I could feel him listening. Was he smiling? His cool rationality was infuriating. My voice dropped to a whisper.

"I've had seven years of med school, two years of being mentored and I'm still only a 'junior doctor'. It's insulting. I work twenty-hour shifts, often nine days in a row. I've swallowed sexist remarks, been groped and suffered putdowns. I've made life and death decisions about patients, yet I am deemed incapable of deciding which specialty I want to follow.

"I am beginning to wonder if all the hard work and sacrifice has been worth it. Once I had everything worked out in precise, achievable detail. Suddenly everything depends on this next round of exams. I can't face them. My future is up in the air. And now you ask me to think about marriage. Ha!"

Matt had sat back on the bed. He stared at the counterpane while I prattled on. I pulled my jeans up and wriggled until the zip would close.

"What if I'm not good enough, Matt? People do fail, you know. What if I'm one of them? The thought of failure terrifies me. It would be so much simpler to chuck it all in – to throw my books away, fly off to the other side of the world and fry on some deserted beach while my guts pickle in cheap plonk. Why am I putting myself through all this? What's it for? What if you're right and our only glimpse of eternity is to end up suspended in formalin in a jar on a laboratory shelf?"

When I finally looked at Matt, he was grinning. I wanted to smack him. "Listen," he said in his calm, rational voice. "Every junior doctor on the planet has felt like that. It's a hard slog to become a doctor. I can remember giving that exact same speech, many times, and not so long ago. Now, look at me." He held my shoulders and physically turned me to face him. "Is it worth it? Of course it is. It's in your blood, Fliss. You're bound to make consultant. So it's going to take another five or six years, or even ten. So what? You're already a bloody good surgeon. You have the makings of a great surgeon. Okay, so let's say you do quit? What then, eh?"

His voice had the cool, calm quality of someone who never wastes energy. I sighed. He was right, I knew that. But I had no energy left. I had no plan B. I'd never dreamed of being anything other than a surgeon. I never questioned my ability to become the best paediatric surgeon in the world, until now. Before this, I'd had Gran there, encouraging me, prompting me. She never once questioned my ability or doubted my strength to achieve whatever crazy goals or dreams I decided to chase.

"But, Matt, what if these are Polly's dreams, not mine? What if I have taken on her dreams and lost my own? God, I'm so confused. I feel I am teetering on the edge of a precipice, terrified of what lies ahead."

"Crap! You've just got a hefty dose of self-doubt. It's not surprising. Polly was your prop. She's gone. Now you have to stand alone. Don't you see this is what she spent her life preparing you for?"

Matt wrapped his arms around me. I tried, physically and mentally, to push him away, but he was gripping my arms, literally holding me at arms' length. I wanted to scream, but instead I crumpled up in a heap, too tired even to cry.

"Look at you. You're exhausted. You have to take a break. You haven't even grieved for Polly yet; you've been too busy pursuing your damned crusade. The truth isn't going to vanish, so what's the hurry? Believe me, you'll be burned out if you carry on like this. I don't know why you're so obsessed about this grandfather thing. Your grandfather, my grandfather – who gives a shit? I don't care if it turns out that *I'm* your bloody grandfather. I'm still going to marry you."

I laughed, but it was a very lame laugh. Matt was right. It seemed he was often right. He had a logical, analytical brain. I needed to learn to argue the facts without letting my emotions get in the way.

I gave a long, worn-out sigh. "We can't get married, Matt. We're probably related."

"Who says so? There is nothing in UK law that says first cousins can't marry. It's only mindless cretins, morons who have seen *Deliverance* too many times, who worry about such nonsense. Consanguinity isn't an issue in first cousins. The likelihood of any problems is less than... oh I don't know off the top of my head, but they're negligible. Anyway, I intend to spend my life with you, grandfather or not – full stop. End of discussion."

*

In the end, it was agreed that Matt should return to London, leaving me in Wales to tidy up the legalities of Polly's death. I promised to deal only with the necessities and return to London the following week. I also assured him I wouldn't make any drastic decisions regarding my career, at least not until we'd had time to discuss it more thoroughly. We vowed to call each other every day, and by the time I waved him off on the first leg of his journey, I was feeling much calmer.

Matt was becoming a fixture in my life, although I still knew very little about him. His approach to life was refreshingly direct, his moral code very black and white. He believed that if he didn't hurt anyone, they would have no reason to hurt him. I doubt *The Water Babies* had ever featured on his reading list, but he was a dead ringer for Mrs Do-as-you-would-be-done-by. Of course, I didn't tell him that, not then.

Later I learned that Matt's parents were staunch atheists, who determined their only son would grow up free from religious indoctrination. They made sure that his education was purely secular. Apparently, it worked, because I remember him telling me, shortly after we met, that he didn't know the words to the Lord's Prayer.

Although Matt had subsequently read up on the major faiths, he had never felt inclined to adopt one. He had become immune to all things spiritual. I found this uniquely refreshing, although there were times when his ability to dismiss spiritual matters so readily, so abso-lutely, sat uncomfortably with my conformist heart. And at this time of my life, being riddled with personal doubts, I had no intention of challenging his ideas. Besides, I had nothing to offer in their stead.

I was, however, determined to follow my own instinct in one respect: I would not drop my investigation. I would not give up until I found the truth. So far as I was concerned, my quest was only just starting.

Chapter 31

BRYNAVON

I left the solicitors office at 3pm, having been told that Polly had bequeathed her house and its contents to me. I had also inherited the sum of five thousand pounds, which in 1979 was no small amount. How on earth she saved so much from her meagre pension was beyond me. Mr Blackmore, senior partner of the practice Blackmore and Clegg, was overly charming. He had given me tea and biscuits and an envelope which, as he said, contained, "The deeds of 26 Somerset Street and a few other bits and bobs, nothing for you to worry your pretty little head about, Miss Evans."

"Actually, it's Dr Evans," I replied, coolly. "And I'm a big girl now." His face was bright red when he closed the door behind me.

*

On the way home, I called in at Brynavon House. A whole week had passed since Matt and I had taken Rosa May out to lunch, and I was anxious to check that she was alright. I also wanted to ask a few more questions. Matron Madders opened the door to greet me.

"I'm glad you're here, Miss Evans. I'm afraid Mrs Davies has taken a turn for the worse. I was going to contact you if there was no improvement by tomorrow, you being her next of kin."

This was news to me. I knew Rosa May had no children, but surely there were lots of people closer than me?

"I'm sorry, but I'm not related to Mrs Davies. I'm certainly not her next of kin.

"Oh, but you are Polly Evans's granddaughter, aren't you? Miss Phyllis Evans?" I nodded. "Yes, well, Mrs Davies told us you are the closest she's ever had to a granddaughter of her own. Apparently, she was exceptionally close to your grandmother. That's right, isn't it, Miss Evans?"

"It's Dr Evans actually," I said, taken aback. I was well aware that being named next of kin would inevitably incur responsibilities and was not sure if I welcomed them. It would appear that, like it or not, the ties that bound me to this small Welsh community were tighter than I had thought. The idea brought a sense of belonging that was not unwelcome. This was my home. And although just a few weeks ago, Rosa May Davies had been little more than a sweet old lady with whom I had a childhood connection – someone I associated with the past – she was beginning to feel like family.

Rosa May Davies the shop had gained her title when Rosa May Brown married Michael Davies, who ran the post office. Rosa May was already married to David Davies who owned a haberdasher's shop up the High Street. To save time, the two women were referred to as Rosa May Davies the post and Rosa May Davies the shop, a fact which the latter disapproved of profoundly. This particular Rosa May had been Gran's close friend since childhood and had featured regularly in my own early years.

The sight of her sitting straight-backed, taking tea in Gran's front room, or socialising at the minister's house after chapel, always corseted, booted and bonneted, was very familiar to me. Even behind her shop counter, she was as elegant as the fine silk she sold by the yard, although I'm sure the hard-wearing cotton-duck sold better.

I used to watch with fascination as she tossed a bolt of cloth with perfect precision; the fabric rising in the air, floating before falling along the counter to be measured out. I loved to watch the enormous, heavy silver blades, sharp as swords, slip through the cloth as easily as slicing butter. Rosa May would slide the two lengths apart with her bejewelled fingers and, with four deft moves, fold the customer's portion into a perfect square to be packed in brown paper and tied with bright white string.

Rosa May's fingers were long and thin. Each displayed a ring. I remember those rings so clearly. My favourite was a large, oval stone the colour of summer sky. I later learned it was an Indian sapphire. It sparkled when her finger moved. Another favourite was more mysterious, being larger, almost black and set in an elaborate silver shank. It was either very heavy or too large for her finger, as it always slid to one side. She used to fiddle with it, using her thumb to push it back so that it sat correctly

But of all her jewels, my favourite was the locket, which hung on a long black ribbon, tied at the back of her neck in a small, neat bow. It was shiny, black as coal and always cold to the touch. On the front was a large carved cross. If I was very good, which meant if I had been quiet and not fidgety, she would open it and let me see inside. Here intertwined locks of white-blonde baby hair curled around each other as they nestled on a bed of black satin. I was allowed to look, but not touch. I never saw Mrs Davies without that locket. I imagined she went to bed in her jewels. I know I would never have taken them off – if they were mine.

Mrs Davies also had a large collection of hats. These I was permitted to try on. Rosa May was older than Gran – older than anyone else I had ever met. The age gap between us stretched across a chasm of time. I always thought she had been born old. She was at least as old as Queen Victoria and every bit as historic. Children don't see adults as people who had once been young and who still have a future ahead of them. Such is the splendid ignorance of youth.

Matron Madders led me into Rosa May's room. It was unusually dark and the air smelled stale. The old woman lay propped up in bed. Matron had not been exaggerating, there had been a marked deterioration. Her skin, un-powdered or rouged, was yellow and dry as parchment. Sparse strands of white hair straggled across her pillow. Her eyes were shut, and her chest rose and fell with each breath, which came in hard, shallow gasps. Matron signalled that she would leave us alone. I waited for the door to close before moving towards the bed.

Once I was sure Matron had gone, I drew back the curtains. Outside the mountain stood tall, its crown obscured by the mist which hovered round the top like Rosa May's wispy hair. Pale blue strands scratched through the cloud, leaving bright streaks against the grey. It was breathtakingly beautiful.

I opened the window and a rush of cool, invigorating air floated in, diluting the depressing smell of age and sickness, which began to fade into the mountain mist. Rosa May stirred. I bent down and pulled the covers up in case she felt chilly. She coughed lightly, opened her eyes and smiled at me. For a moment, I wondered who she was looking at. Was it Polly? Or maybe it was young Phyllis? Had she gone to a place beyond her memory? I hoped she would know it was me. But I was resigned to play whichever part she wanted.

"Let me look at you, Fliss." The strength in her voice was surprising and encouraging. "You are the spitting image of young Phyllis; do you know that? But then I expect it's everyone as tells you that. It would break poor Polly's heart to look at you, her sister being gone so long. You are so like her. You have her hazel eyes and the auburn hair. Her hair curled just like yours, although she wore it much longer. It was the style then. I had hair I could sit on. Black as coal, mine was."

The old lady was trying to sit up. I eased her forward, resting her upper body against my chest, while I plumped her pillows. Then I pulled her further up the bed and rested her against the mound of pillows. Even that tiny amount of exertion seemed to exhaust her, and she closed her eyes for a moment to recover.

"I was talking to Polly when you came in," she said.

"I'm sorry. I didn't mean to…" Instinctively she opened her eyes and signalled that it wasn't a problem. Then she beckoned me nearer. I drew my chair closer and bent my ear to her mouth.

"I do know as Polly's dead. I'm not gaga. But she does come and sit by me, see. Sometimes she talks to me, quiet and comforting like she always did. Mind I do come and go. Still, I seem to be here now, so that's good, isn't it? You are Fliss, and I'm Rosa May Davies." She paused before saying, quite defiantly, "I am dying, Fliss. That's right, isn't it?"

"No, no, Rosa May. You're not going to die for a long time yet."

The old woman raised her eyebrow and lifted her hand from beneath the covers. She held it there, signalling to me to shut up. I wondered if I should call for help, but again she read my mind and wagged her finger as if to say, "Don't you dare."

"Polly told me you were coming. She's always been a good friend to me, has Polly. I can't wait for us to be together again, running through Ben Ward's fields. It's a long old time since I hitched up my skirts and ran with the wind. Mind, Polly always beat me. She was that fast. Always in a hurry, was Polly Evans. I expect she still is, God bless her. I don't think eternity will be long enough for her. By the time I get there, I'm hoping it'll be scrubbed clean as an angel's wing. She'll find me a job, otherwise, and it's a nice long rest I'm after wanting, isn't it?"

Rosa May's body slumped over as her chuckle turned into a coughing fit. I held a glass of water to her lips and she sipped at it, looking directly into my eyes all the while. When she pushed the glass away, she winked and whispered, "You haven't got a drop of stout, have you?"

Suddenly the mood changed. Her voice took on a serious tone. "Now I haven't got long, so listen up. I'm leaving a tidy sum when I go. What with the shop and the house, it all mounts up. Did you know I had a shop? Haberdashery? Yes, of course you knew. Rosa May

Davies the shop they called me, on account of there being a Rosa May Davies in the post office, see? Dreadful woman she was! Anyway, we won't mention her. I'm leaving everything to you. I know you're a doctor, but Polly tells me you're going to be a surgeon, a children's specialist. Oh dew! She did tell me, but I do forget – I find long words do get tangled up inside my head then come out wrong, especially medical ones."

I patted her hand. "They can be a bit of a mouthful. I'm training to be a paediatric orthopaedic surgeon."

"That's right, that's exactly what she said. Did you know my babies were born linked together? They died together and are buried together. Nowadays, what with the National Health Service and doctors like you, they might have lived a little longer."

This was the first time I realised that Rosa May had given birth to conjoined twins. Suddenly the locket and the entwined curls made sense.

"I remember you used to let me look at your beautiful locket. That was the twin's hair, wasn't it?"

By way of answering, the old lady pointed to the drawer in her bedside locker. Inside I found a cotton hanky, embroidered with mauve and purple pansies. I lifted it out gently and placed it in her hand. She raised it to her lips to kiss it. It contained the jet mourning locket.

"This will be yours when I'm gone. I'll only need it for a little longer. Then I'll be able to kiss their beautiful faces and stroke their golden curls, and I shan't be needing this dead, old hair. They were perfect, my little ones. Not twisted or unnatural – two perfect little boys, sharing one hip. We christened them Simon and Peter, as they were one and the same. Look at me, getting all sentimental, isn't it? And I'm making you as sad as me, oh dew! We should be celebrating we should. I'll be with them soon, God willing."

I placed her treasure back in the drawer for her. What was it Matt had said? Her generation was on familiar terms with death? He was so right. I found myself almost envying Rosa May her faith, just as I had envied Polly hers. I resolved to call on Adollgar in the morning and ask him to help me find some peace for myself. I knew I would not tell Matt. Was it in case he laughed at me? I know I wanted his approval.

I bent forward and kissed Rosa May's cheek. It was dry, and I caught a familiar, sickly odour. I remembered how silky soft it had felt just a few days ago, under its dusting of musky powder. At that moment, I did envy her. I was jealous of that utter certainty that death is a beginning, a time for reunion. I wanted that assurance, I wanted the comfort it gave her, the comfort Gran had known too. I could only associate death with sorrow, with parting and pain, with loss of control and dignity. Suddenly a frail hand patted my arm, and I wondered whether I had voiced my thoughts out loud

"I'm not afraid, my dear. I am already at peace. But, before I go, I have a message for you. Rosa May paused. Her breath was laboured. I asked if she would like to rest for a moment. Maybe I could get her some tea?

"I will shut my eyes for a minute or two if that's alright." She was speaking very quietly now. "You're a good girl... sorry I do forget your name. I think I'm must be going again – don't you go though. Not yet. I've not finished yet. Polly's got something important to tell you, but for the life of me I can't remember what." With that, Rosa May closed her eyes and drifted off.

She looked so peaceful, I wondered for a moment if she had gone for good. I felt her pulse. It was remarkably strong. This old woman certainly had some stamina. I considered slipping away myself to allow her a proper sleep. I could easily come back tomorrow. But when I remembered how determined she had been to finish her story, I decided I should be here when she woke up. I owed her that at least,

I moved over to the window. Patches of blue sky showed through the gaps in the fast-moving clouds, enough to make a pair of pants for a sailor, as Gran would have said. And despite the lateness of the day, the air was no longer cold. A slight movement from the bed drew me back.

"I knew you'd be waiting when I came back." Rosa May's eyes were bright. I pulled my chair closer and bent near, so she didn't have to strain her voice. "Polly's been telling me about the letters, the ones from Phyllis. She said she wants you to read them if you haven't already. You're to stop worrying. Everything will be made clear in time." The old lady narrowed her eyes as if she was peering into the far distance. Maybe she was. When she began to cough, I held the water to her lips. She took the smallest of sips then pushed the glass away.

"Polly says you must ask Adollgar about his sermon, the one he preached for your mother. She says he'll remember it. I remember it too. It was powerful, one of his best, but I don't have the strength to do it justice. She also said Ethel sometimes gets things wrong, but I expect you've already realised that. Poor Ethel has never quite been all there if you know what I mean, but she means well."

As Rosa May's eyes closed, the door opened and Matron Madders hurried in, tut-tutting under her breath. She bustled over to the window and pulled it to, quite angrily, recoiling dramatically from the fresh air, as if it was blowing in from the Arctic.

"I think it's time for you to leave, Miss Evans." She addressed me without actually looking at me. "Mrs Davies's medication is overdue, and she is obviously exhausted." She was plumping pillows, fussing and snorting as she spoke.

Rosa May opened one eye. "Nonsense, woman! I've been having an enjoyable talk with Doctor Evans. I'll let you know if and when I'm exhausted, thank you very much." A frail hand reached out from the bedding and took mine. She drew me close and whispered, "Polly says she is that proud of you. She says, don't worry, all will be made clear. Trust her. Duw bendithia, cariad."

Chapter 32

Anxious to follow up on Rosa May's advice, I was knocking on Adollgar's door, bright and early the next morning. Aderyn answered, welcoming me with a broad smile. "Come in, come in, my dear. Adollgar is in the front room."

The reverend was sitting in his chair by the fire, the loyal Bryn curled at his feet. The old dog wagged its tail in recognition but did not stir. I placed a kiss on Adollgar's cheek.

Adollgar smiled up and offered me a chair. "And what can I do for you on this beautiful spring morning? Winter has been kind to us this year. Often, we are snowbound for the whole of February. And here we are bathed in sunshine, glorious isn't it?"

When I explained I was concerned about Rosa May's rapid decline, the minister nodded slowly and promised to pay his friend a visit later that day, adding, "Unfortunately, sickness doesn't always pay heed to fine weather."

"Rosa May was telling me about a sermon you gave just after my mother was born," I said. "She said it had a powerful effect on the town. I wondered if you could recall the gist of it."

The old man furrowed his brows, burying his eyes in bushy-white feathers. He was silent for a while before he said, "Well now, I'm pretty sure I know which one she meant. I remember it well. It was the Sunday after baby Megan was born. I preached on forgiveness. I told the story of how our Lord forgave the woman caught in adultery.

"My flock knew the story, but I wanted them to consider what would have happened if that woman had been with child? I told them that I had no doubt, none whatsoever – despite the opinion of certain 'God-fearing' people of this town, people who attend this place of worship each and every Sunday and only place their offerings on the plate when someone is watching – I had no doubt that the Lord Jesus would have taken that child into his bosom and blessed it as an innocent child of God. He would have baptised it and welcomed it into the body of the church. So, I simply asked my congregation 'Who am I to do otherwise?'

"We are all sinners, each and every one of us. We must each bear our personal cross for the rest of our earthly lives. Yet the Lord is beside us, ready to lift us should we fall. Let us ask the Lord for his forgiveness. Only he in his infinite wisdom and mercy can grant us peace. The penitent shall receive, and the unrepentant shall be turned away. No sin can be undone, but to repent of a sin is to have it washed clean. To have God wash your soul clean from the stain of sin is the very reason our saviour died. Thank him for his sacrifice, for his mercy, and endeavour not to sin again. There, but for the grace of God, go I. Amen."

Aderyn repeated "Amen" as she poured the tea. My mind flashed back to Gran's funeral, Adollgar stumbling and his wife reaching out to support him. She was still doing it. Her eyes smiled at me as if she knew what I was thinking, and she handed me a cup of tea.

"I remember that sermon so well," she said. "I was standing next to Polly. Felt her tremble, I did. My husband was a powerful preacher, powerful strong. I felt every word as if it was aimed right at me. Polly told me after that she felt he was talking straight at her, and I suspect Emlyn felt it was especially meant for him. Adollgar could make his words so personal. Awful. Fearful. Marvellous it was."

As the old woman stood behind her husband's chair, she laid a hand on his shoulder. "I have never been more proud of my man. The Good Lord must have been proud too, as he blessed his servant with many more years of service."

After sipping her tea, Aderyn placed her cup back in its saucer. Her face shone with a serenity that comes from loving and being loved. I think that was the first time I'd witnessed it so perfectly.

When she spoke again, it was expressly to me. "All the gossip, the malicious name-calling, the cruel finger-pointing, and the mean accusations ceased with that sermon. It was as if we had all been baptised anew. The town saw to it that Polly and baby Megan wanted for nothing. They even stopped calling young Phyllis names. It was as though she too had been washed clean. It was a miracle, a blessed miracle. A whole town united by God's word."

As if to prove the point, the preacher's powerful voice resonated around the little parlour in a loud, "Amen."

Chapter 33

I made the short journey back to Polly's house via the local off licence and emerged with a box labelled 'Vin Rouge'. (There was little choice in the wine department – unless you wanted Lambrusco or Mateus Rosé.)

I turned the key and let myself in. The house was horribly silent. Gran never locked the doors, had I less trust in my fellow man than she did? Or were people less trustworthy these days? Or were we all far more suspicious? Maybe we just owned more stuff worth nicking.

I felt a desperate urge to talk to Matt, but first I determined to tackle some more letters. If I rang him in my present sentimental mood, he'd tell me to drop it, as if I were a naughty puppy. But I was no pup. I was a big girl now. This was my quest, my life, my choice.

After a mind-numbing struggle with the wine box, I managed to extract a tumbler of red liquid and went through to run a bath. I had decided not to ring Matt until later. I needed to calm down. I also needed more evidence to convince him I had been right to carry on against his advice. I took my glass of 'Vin Rouge' and climbed into the bath.

I have always relished a hot soak after a hard day. The water's embrace is like a long, warm a cuddle, a 'cwtch' as Gran would say. I've never been one for scented candles accompanied by whales singing, but a glass of wine certainly helps me relax. I took a sip. Argh! It was disgusting.

My head sank back against the folded towel, and I let my fingers trace the roses on the tiles behind the bath. I could remember choosing those tiles. It was 1966, in a dusty little shop in Ebbw Vale. I wanted a jazzy, zig-zaggy, orange and black pattern, but Gran said it made her feel sick. She liked the boring pink rose-buds. How right she'd been. I let myself drift beneath the blossoms, my idle fingers now still beneath the comforting water.

When Morgan Williams had built the small bath-room onto the back of the house, we said goodbye to zinc baths by the fire. No more endless kettles of hot water. No more praying that no one came calling while you were naked and dripping. And no more trips to the stinky 'ty bach'!

That dreaded 'ty-bach'! (It means little house, but, in fact, it was a dark, slate-roofed, hellhole). Inside was a long wooden plank with three bum-sized holes. Flimsy partitions offered little privacy as every aspect of one's private business was unavoidably shared with any other occupants. Conversation was possible, but not readily welcomed, at least not by me.

Despite the copious buckets of soapy water with which it was regularly doused, the 'little house' remained gross. It made me gag just to think about it. I dreaded every visit I ever made. On the day our new bathroom was completed, we threw a party. It also happened to be the day England won the World Cup. But there was no question what we were celebrating. Well, we were Welsh after all was said and done.

I had watched Gran's house undergo various degrees of 'modernisation' over the years. Instead of candles to guide you 'up the little wooden stairs to gwely', electric lights operated at the flick of a switch. A boiler provided hot water and heated three radiators. Proper drains gave us a kitchen sink, a flushing loo and a plumbed-in bath. And last, but by no means least, a telephone appeared in the front room.

This contraption, this invention of the devil, gave Gran a heart attack every time it rang. Right up until the day she died, the sound of that bell made her jump out of her skin. She never got used to the electric stove either. She continued to light the range every day, summer and winter, to cook on the naked flame or in the tiny iron oven. Yet, despite her foibles, the later years of Gran's life must have been far easier. Mind you, Polly was a Welsh woman. She was far too stubborn to admit any such thing, look you!

As the bath cooled, my nostalgia faded. My mind began to focus on the events of the last few days. I began to analyse what Rosa May had said. Memory may play strange tricks, but her story resonated too powerfully to be a total fabrication. Something profound must have happened after Adollgar's sermon. The fact that Polly and her illegitimate baby were totally accepted by this narrow-minded little town was indeed a miracle of sorts.

As always, my thoughts had returned to the central question, who was the father of Polly's baby? Surely Polly must have confided in someone. It was an enormous secret to carry. I wondered what she told her daughter when she was old enough to ask questions. But then Polly had never mentioned anything to me either. And, as Ethel explained, children don't ask those sorts of questions. That curiosity comes later in life... as mine has now. I was beginning to conclude that Polly had indeed kept her resolve and gone to the grave with her secret.

I found myself agreeing with Rosa May that Emlyn was the most likely candidate. Actually, he was the only one. Who else would Polly have fought to protect so fiercely? Knowing how Polly valued her independence, she might well have forbidden Emlyn to speak up – especially as he was about to marry another woman. If Polly had refused to marry him herself, what was the point of him confessing? It would have ruined several lives and finished his career. No, Polly was too wise to let that happen.

Polly was strong. She was determined. It wasn't hard to believe, having vowed never to marry, her desperate urge to have a child of her own led her to resort to desperate measures —deception even? Nowadays, women often pick their most trusted friend to father their child. Maybe Polly was ahead of her time. Or maybe... and this thought did not sit easily with me... maybe she had tricked Emlyn into making her pregnant?

It was horribly plausible. Besides, what other explanation was there? I took another slug of wine and found it wasn't so bad taken in a large gulp. No, I thought, the whole thing is too out of character. But then, history is littered with un-plausible, unwanted, unlikely, unbelievable conceptions. Then I thought of Polly, her integrity, her dislike of hypocrisy, her devotion to honesty. No. It simply didn't fit. Something crucial was missing.

I climbed out of the bath, feeling none of the usual therapeutic benefits a good hot soak usually brought. Wrapped in Gran's old candlewick dressing gown, I sat by the electric fire in the sitting room and picked up the envelope the solicitor had given me that afternoon. When the phone rang, it was my turn to jump. Patting my beating heart, I reached for the receiver.

Chapter 34

"I'm calling early. I didn't want to drag you out of the bath or wake you up. Are you feeling better?" Matt sounded very chipper.

"I'm fine, I'm sorry I had a go at you. I slept late after you'd gone, then spent the afternoon at the solicitors."

"Ah, yes. How was it?"

"Okay. Good, in fact. It seems Gran owned this house. I'd assumed she rented it from the mining company, but it was hers. She's left it to me – along with some money. Mr Blackmore has sent me home with a pile of papers. I was about to open them when you rang."

"Right. Okay. Do you think you should wait so we can do it together? I don't want you getting all stressed out again."

"I won't get stressed. I'm fine. I'm sure I can deal with some house deeds and a few legal papers. I'm a big girl now, you know." I chuckled, not bothering to explain the irony.

"I was just offering to help." There was a slight hesitation. Then he said, "I'm going over to my mother's place later this evening. There's still some stuff in the basement that needs sorting before the agent can crack on. He's got a buyer chomping at the bit, so it's all systems go at this end. Any further thoughts about what you'll do with your gran's house?"

"Good God no! I only discovered it was hers to leave me a few hours ago. I thought the colliery still owned it. I need time to think about it – to get used to being an heiress." I laughed, and I heard a slight chortle from Matt. "Anyway, enough of all that. I'm sorry about the row. When are you coming back down? I miss you."

Matt began to make excuses: the distance, the pressure of work, the shortage of staff, all the usual, horribly plausible reasons. While he spoke, I refilled my glass. The vin rouge was definitely improving with age. The phone had fallen silent.

"I visited Rosa May today," I said, more to fill the void than to pass on information. "She's not well. I don't think she'll last much longer."

"I'm sorry. Still, she's had a good innings. Did she say any more about Emlyn and Polly? Are you any closer to solving the mystery?"

I thought for a moment then decided to tell a white lie. "No, she was too weak to talk – maybe tomorrow. I promised I'd pop back. You see, I have listened to you. I've been taking it easy, just like the doctor ordered. I don't want to leave until Rosa May is better. But I've got my assessment in a couple of months. I really should be gearing up for it. Can you survive without me for a few more days?"

We chatted about nothing for a while and eventually hung up. Should I have told him that Rosa May had also named me as her heir? And what of her message from Polly – that all would be revealed in time? No. He would certainly have treated that with derision. I needed to wait until I had something definite to tell him. I already knew enough about Matt to know he hated speculation. Maybe the next lot of letters would provide some precise facts. And if, in the meantime, I needed a shoulder or a sympathetic ear there was always Adollgar or Little Aunty Ethel. Besides, as I had already announced twice today, "I'm a big girl now."

Chapter 35

MATT: LONDON. 1979

I did not replace the receiver right away. I was trying to decide whether or not to leave it off the hook. I had a hunch Fliss was holding something back. I needed to tread carefully. She was still incredibly vulnerable. I felt sure she was making a mountain out of a molehill, seriously overdramatising the situation and obsessing in an unhealthy way, but I could hardly tell her that – at least not at this point.

Personally, I didn't give a shit if we had the same grandfather. To be honest, I quite liked the idea. But I knew that trying to stop a natural worrier from worrying could lead to madness. I knew Fliss well enough by now to know that she would do what she had to. Hopefully, something would surface that would cast a whole new light on the murky past and let us get on with our lives.

I settled back in my new chair and nursed a large tumbler of scotch. I was not on call; besides I had left the phone off the hook. The NHS would have to manage without me for one night. So would Fliss. I felt uneasy about having lied to Fliss, even if only a white lie because, to tell the truth, the house clearance firm had finished work on my mother's house two days ago.

Earlier this morning I'd popped over to give the premises a final once over before dropping the keys off at the estate agents.

After giving each room a cursory glance to ascertain they were quite empty, I spotted the cellar door. Damn! I'd forgotten to check down there.

There was a heap of rubble under my father's workbench. Cursing the men for not chucking it on the skip with the rest of the crap, I kicked it. My toe met a very solid object, and I cursed even louder. After removing several layers of dust, dried leaves and cobwebs, I discovered I had kicked a large leather bag. The hide was cracked and split, but on closer inspection, I managed to discern the initials E.M.J. MD. I ran my fingers over the letters, shot through by a surge of unexpected emotion. I was touching my grandfather's Gladstone bag.

When Grandpa died, he'd left me his antique stethoscope and a remarkably well-preserved skeleton, which I still counted among my few treasured possessions. The rest of his stuff came to me after my own father died. I had never thought to ask what happened to his bag. I simply assumed it had long since been thrown out. Yet here it was. How many times had it escaped being binned? It must have been moved 10 times or more. Each time it had survived. This time it had foiled the skip, patiently waiting for me to salvage it.

The bag itself weighed a ton, being made from solid hide with heavy metal attachments and catches. As I cradled it in my arms, I didn't care if it contained the crown jewels or a load of stones. The bag itself was the thing of greatest value. This battered, old bit of luggage was the embodiment of the man I had revered and loved beyond any other living thing in my entire life.

More than any other item, this bag represented my grandpa. He had kept it at his side every day of his adult life. Even after he'd retired, he used it as a travelling bag. Later it served as a portable filing cabinet. It was his talisman; it epitomised the man. It was him.

Having been de-cobwebbed and dusted the bag now sat in the middle of my room on the floor. I sat opposite on the only other piece of furniture – a sleek, new, very masculine, shiny leather armchair. From here, I stared at my new treasure. I planned to spend a blokes' night in, doing some serious drinking while partaking in a large overdose of nostalgia.

The bag was seriously scuffed. There was a deep dent on one side, and the four corners were dog-eared. I am no romantic, but this was an object of great beauty. Memories of the old gentleman filled the room. I could see him so clearly. Not some ghostly shadow, but Dr Emlyn Jenkins, strong, energetic, in his old, freshly pressed suit, tie knotted beneath a starched collar, boots spit-polished, fingernails manicured perfectly as he checked its contents. This was the ritual he carried out meticulously each morning before setting off on his rounds.

That bag contained life and death. I watched the way he set it down – carefully, almost gently, never letting it drop or be tossed onto a chair, cart or car-seat. It never left his sight. It was always locked and unlocked with precision. The small silver key hung from his fob along with his house keys and his pocket watch. The keys and timepiece were returned to his waistcoat pocket with a flourish and a pat, after use. As I sat, I could feel the past unfolding. My heart ached with feelings I had no words to describe. Totally overwhelmed by such unfamiliar emotion, I let the memories flow freely, like the whisky.

Grandpa had first shown me the contents of his bag when I began to show an interest in medicine. I remembered a strange tube-like instrument he called a stethoscope, umpteen bottles of tincture; files of morphine; large syringes; small syringes; rolls of bandages; wads of cotton wool; wooden spatulas, and an array of metal gadgets which could look into eyes, up noses and down throats. And that smell! It smelled of pure science.

I recall the frustration I had felt as a child, thinking how long it would take for me to be grown up enough, important enough, to have a bag of my own. I was impatient to acquire the knowledge that would enable me to use its contents as skilfully and professionally as my grandpa. I wanted to earn the right to have my initials Dr M.E. Jenkins MD emblazoned in gold, so the world would know I was a fully qualified medical practitioner.

By now I had left my chair and was down on all fours, stroking the bag as if it were a faithful old dog, come back after years of separation. It was dry and cracked, but a good rub down with lanolin would soon cure that. I tried to slide the catch to open the bag, but although the bar lifted, the case was locked. Of course it was! Emlyn always kept it locked. But the key would be on his watch-chain, which I had in the bedroom.

I confess I reeled slightly as I stood up to fetch the box of Grandpa's things from beneath my bed. Wrapped in yellowed tissue paper was his watch and chain. A large bunch of keys still hung on the fob. I unclipped the keys and sank into my chair, lifting the glass to my lips I took a long, slow swig of whisky.

One hand gripped my tumbler, the other held the keys. I began turning my hand from side to side, allowing the keys to flip from my palm to my knuckles and back again. The weight, the clink and clunk as they swung together was a sound that belonged in the surgery in Brynavon. This was exactly what Grandpa did whenever he wanted to think. He would toss his keys across his hand, making them chink and clink while he gathered his thoughts, exactly as I was doing now. I have never felt closer to him before or since.

I must have sat for some time idly playing with the keys and sipping scotch because when I stopped, my glass was empty. The keys rested in my palm, except for one small, square-topped, silver one, which I clasped between my thumb and forefinger, I offered it to the lock.

Chapter 36

FLISS: BRYNAVON

Among the papers I had obtained from the solicitor, were the deeds to Gran's house. As I had thought, 26 Somerset Street had been built by and remained the property of the Llewellyn Mining Company until the year 1917. At this point the property was purchased from the company by Captain Edward George Llewellyn, presiding at 29 Tite Street, Chelsea, London. Later that same year, the property was gifted by the captain to Miss Polly Aronwyn Evans, registered as living at the said address. On the demise of Miss Polly Aronwyn Evans, the house was bequeathed to Dr Phyllis Megan Evans, granddaughter of the deceased… me.

This piece of information, although fascinating, posed more questions than it answered. Why on earth had Edward Llewellyn bought the house and given it to my grandmother? I was beginning to feel I was on a wild goose chase.

I debated whether to return Matt's call. I didn't like the way we'd left things. It felt sneaky to be hiding things from him, especially when he had been so good putting up with my moods and obsessive behaviour for the last week. I poured another glass of wine, not caring if I liked the taste or not and decided I would phone

Matt later – before I went to bed. Knowing him to be a bit of a night owl, I felt there was little danger of calling too late. Polly's words, 'Never let the sun go down on your wrath' rang in my ears. Not that we had been wrathful – just a tad niggly. But I knew we would both sleep better having cleared the air.

Setting the deeds aside, I turned my attention to an envelope marked Births Deaths and Marriages. This contained various certificates, some very old and fragile. One was my mother's birth certificate, stating that Megan Polly Evans had been born on February 19th, 1917. The birth was registered at Crickhowell. The child's mother was clearly named as Polly Aronwyn Evans, but the word 'Unknown' appeared in the space reserved for the father's name. It appeared that Rosa May was right in thinking that Polly had taken my grandfather's identity to the grave with her.

I began to think of the difficulties a young woman would have faced by maintaining such a stand back in the early twentieth century. Most people thought single mothers were loose women and treated them accordingly. It was a comfort to know the town had rallied behind Polly, although I did wonder if my mother had been called a bastard by the kids at school. I remembered a school friend of mine being called names in the 1960s. Some things never change; others take a great deal of time.

When my roommate, Rosemary Wallis, got pregnant at university, she had gone to a 'back street abortionist'. It cost her 20 pounds, which was a fortune then, but she daren't tell her parents because of the stigma – her father was a lawyer and such abortions were illegal. The guilt proved too much for her and she had a breakdown, and that was the end of her education… academically speaking.

There was no doubt that Polly was a courageous woman – single-minded and fiercely independent. I admired her for that, but part of me was beginning to wonder if she wasn't also a little pig-headed.

I certainly have many friends who don't know who their fathers are. And probably lots more who have never known their grandparents. They manage to live perfectly normal lives. What would they make of my desperate, self-indulgent soul-searching? I know people who positively hate and despise their entire family. I'm one of the lucky ones, having been raised in a loving home by a woman who had given me everything a child could need. Why waste time looking for someone else? I decided to call off the search.

I was not yet ready, however, to phone Matt and tell him about my unexpected epiphany. To be honest, I was already doubting my ability to let go. Polly's unread letters were calling to me from their chocolate box. I could also hear Rosa May telling me, "Don't worry. Polly says, 'All will be revealed, soon.'"

Was Gran watching me? Willing me to open the letters? Armed with a mug of strong coffee, I decided to read them tonight, even if it took all night. Then I would definitely back off… maybe.

Meanwhile, back in London, unbeknown to me, Matt was unlocking the answers to many of my questions.

Chapter 37

MATT: LONDON

I was an excited eight-year-old as I turned the key and felt the lock spring open. It opened so sweetly as if it had been opened every day for the last 20 years. I released the bar and pulled the wide mouth open. Peering inside, I inhaled deeply. The leather interior, redolent with the nostalgic smell of liniment, whacked me in the face like a sock full of pebbles. That mixture of age, leather, mildew, medicine and wintergreen was sheer magic. I suddenly felt cheated, a unique moment had passed. I had blinked and missed the best shot. It could never be recaptured.

My disappointment was short-lived, however, when I saw what the bag contained, which was far more than its aroma. Realising just what I had discovered, I punched the air with my fist, and hollered, 'Yes!'

Eight leather-bound books nestled in the dark interior. These were Grandfather's diaries, eight volumes in all, each covering a five-year period. They spanned from 1910 to 1950. I had hit the jackpot.

I sat and stared at my find, an innate grin on my stupid face. To think, a day later and they would have been in the skip. If I'm honest, my hesitation was mostly due to the fact I was rather in awe of these private records. I poured myself another scotch, raised my glass to Grandpa and waited for my heart rate to return to normal before I lifted the books out and opened the first one – 1910—1915.

Lovingly, I stroked the script with my finger. It was Emlyn's unmistakable, sprawling writing. Like most of his profession, Emlyn used a fountain pen. In fact, I still have that pen – a black and green Conway Stewart, which still writes perfectly. The diary entries had been written in a rapid, spontaneous hand, with a minimum of loops, frills, dots or crossings out. I struggled to decipher the first few lines, but I soon grew familiar with the scrawl and found I could read it quickly and with ease.

Five hours later, I had devoured the first volume from cover to cover. To round things off neatly, I poured the last of the scotch and swallowed it down. My head was filled with a young doctor's boundless enthusiasm for medicine. I placed the phone back on its cradle and climbed into mine. I was asleep before my head hit the pillow. Minutes later, I was woken by Fliss, calling to tell me that Rosa May Davies was dead. It was four am.

Chapter 38

FLISS: BRYNAVON 1979

I remained in Wales long enough to arrange and attend Rosa May's funeral. There was little time to mourn or fret, I was so busy. Polly's house was on the market, I took her clothes to the charity shop and her furniture to a clearance company. Her personal stuff I boxed up ready to send Red Star to London.

By now I had read all the letters, and they too were in the box. I felt strangely calm – calmer than I had for a long time. The irrational urgency which had driven me since Gran's death had subsided. I had come to terms with the likelihood of never knowing the identity of my grandfather.

Matt's work prevented him from returning to Wales to attend Rosa May's funeral. We spoke every day, but our conversations were brief and to the point. He said nothing about the diaries, and I didn't mention that I had read all the letters. Neither did I tell him that Rosa May's death had left me feeling numb. A major connection to my gran had been severed. I felt I was losing her forever.

The last of Polly's letters did little to confirm or deny what I already knew. Now more than anything, I wanted to leave Wales. I wanted to put this all behind me,

I wanted to get back to London. I wanted to get back to Matt.

On the day after Rosa May's funeral, Uncle Jim asked me to go and see him. He suggested I went the next morning at 10 when Ethel would be at Brynavon House helping with their open coffee morning. I let myself into the kitchen and found Jim sitting at the table, tea already brewing in the pot beside a large plate of ginger-nut biscuits.

"Right, girl," Jim's voice came in gasps, gulped back by desperate attempts to get air into his congested lungs. I bent down and kissed his cheek. His face still looked as though a child had scribbled over it with a biro. Jim smiled, coughed a phlegmy, painful cough while thumping his chest with his fist. I knew he was in the final stages of pneumoconiosis, better known as 'miner's lung' or 'black lung disease'. Breathing had been a progressive problem for much of his life.

"Are you getting proper treatment for that, Uncle Jim?" I asked. He smiled wryly. "Oh yes. And I've ordered the undertaker to fit an inhaler in my coffin." He coughed again, hitting his chest as if willing it to behave itself. He produced a combination of gasps, chuckles and barks and eventually managed to say, "Mind I've told the man, I don't want no pure oxygen, ach a fi! That'd kill me for sure! No, I've asked for silica and tobacco smoke, I don't want to shock these poor old lungs before they have a chance to get used to all that Holy air blowing round those fluffy clouds, see?"

I laughed, being familiar gallows humour which was rife in the operating theatre. At times, laughter was the only thing to keep one sane.

We drank some tea, and Jim laid his blue-veined hand on mine. "Your gran was a good friend to Ethel and me. She's sadly missed is Polly Evans. Oh, life goes on, I know that as well as the next. But look you now, I've never had much education, I got little or no schooling, but I've seen a lot of life in my own deep furrow. I'm not clever like you. And I don't meet the folk as live in the wider world like you do. But then, they don't meet many like me, isn't it? So, I'd like to tell you my story – so as you can tell them what it was like for the likes of me.

"It's your great-grandfather's story and your gran's brothers' stories. Our lives hardly changed over the generations. But it seems that lately the world's got smaller. There isn't room for the likes of us anymore. There aren't many of us left as can cut the coal by hand. But I want our story to live on. It's the story of South Wales.

"Will you let me tell it you, girl? My name won't sit on any monument, see. That's not for the likes of me. But I've known so many brave, beautiful men whose names should be carved in history along with all the other heroes that fought for this beloved country."

*

And so, Jim began. And what a story he told.

Chapter 39

JIM LEWIS: BRYNAVON

"I was nine years old and a weedy little runt when I first went underground. I only come up to the crotch of most of the lads, even George Wilkins and he was no taller than a pony! Big, strong lads they was – fearless. I'd wanted to be one of them since I was old enough to stand up to take a piss. You just knew they were special. It was the way they carried themselves. Proud they were, too proud to show fear. And the pit was a fearful place, believe you me. I was scared – so scared I nearly pissed in my britches. But I was trying not to show it, not now I was a man, see?

"As we marched up the road, I remember thinking as this was the best day of my life. It was so early it was dark. The men had helmets with lamps on the front. Our faces were scrubbed clean, and I remember thinking, *Soon we'll be black as the very coal, we will.* I couldn't wait. It wasn't until we walked towards the cage that my legs began to shake. A hand dropped heavy on my shoulder. It squeezed the bones of me, and I knew that these huge men were all scared, just like me.

"We entered the cage, 10 at a time. The men towered over me, solid men – all shoulders and muscle. It was the smell of leather I remember, with my nose pressed against Alun William's belt in the crush. All I could see was that wide black belt. As the last three men piled in, I managed to turn my head so that I could breathe. A big, brass buckle dug into my cheek. But what I remember most, the thing I'll never forget, was the sudden silence.

"One minute they were chattering and joshing, pushing and shoving at each other, jostling for room. Then the chains started clutching at the ratchets, there was a grinding screech as the great wheel sang out. The floor started to drop with our steel-tipped boots rooted to it. Down we dropped, deeper and deeper beneath the mountain, the wheel grinding with each turn: the men silent as the grave. I thought it would never end. We just kept dropping down the shaft into a hole darker and deeper than hell.

"The men spread their feet, bracing themselves, their steel-capped boots ringing against the metal floor, as they shuffled to keep their balance. But they held their silence. All around us the mechanical thunder and clashing of steel on steel echoed in the dark. Suddenly there was a bump and a shudder, the cage clanged open, and the slapping, the joshing, the black humour began again – although I could see from their eyes they were listening for the noise of earth moving or the straining of the props.

"Alun Williams bent down so his eyes looked into mine. I gulped back a tear and returned his look as bravely as I could. 'Alright, boyo?' he asked, softly. 'That's the worst bit over with. Just remember, there's only one first time, only one. Just you remember that. It's over now. It'll be easier next time. Mind, there's not a man as doesn't say a prayer when that old cage starts to drop.' He slapped me on the back, and I wobbled but remained upright. I had passed the first test. I was going to be alright.

"Then Alun said, 'Soon you'll be an old hand like the rest of us, isn't it? Come on, boyo, you stick by me. I'll look to you today seeing as it's your first. You can be my pickup man, that'll get your muscles working. You'll soon have arms like mine!' I looked at the great tree trunks he called arms in awe. He slapped me on the back again, and we set off along the tunnel to the coal face.

"We walked for a mile or more, downhill with the roof getting lower with each step. After a while, even I had to duck it was that low. Water and sweat was dripping off me, yet I hadn't even started work. It was hotter than hell. Suddenly the tunnel forked sharp to the right, and I was knocked off my feet by a bitter wind. Alun Willams laughed. 'Takes us all by surprise does that old wind. God knows how it gets down here. You'll find the rain down here too. Rain and wind! Good to know we're still in Wales, isn't it, boyo?'

"I had to collect the smaller lumps of coal, the ones that hadn't landed on the wagons. I was given a bucket and told where to take my pickings. The men lay flat on their backs, swinging pickaxes too heavy for me to lift. It was an art, hewing coal at that angle. Above their heads, their picks worked a solid wall of shining coal. Those men were gods, and I was learning to be one of them.

"Each strike of the pick resounded like a giant bell, reverberating and echoing. The mine became a great underground belfry. I thought my ears would split. I prayed for the men to stop. When it was time to break, the ringing did stop, but the silence was even more terrifying, more deafening.

"Now there was nothing to hide the sound of the timbers creaking and groaning, see? Oh, they were stout enough beams, but they were all that was holding the world up. There was only them stopping hundreds, thousands of tons of muck, coal, sheep, roads, chapels, houses, streams, rocks and trees, from falling on us.

"As if he'd read my thoughts, Alun Williams pulled me close and gave me a swig of hot sweet tea from his flask. 'Don't think about it, boyo. This is your world now. Accept that, and you'll not go mad. You're a man, see. More than that, Jim, you're a miner. This is your life. It's a good life. Be proud of who you are. You're one of us. You're one of the lads look you, a boyo, just like us.'"

Uncle Jim's smile became a grimace, as his body shook, racked with a coughing and wheezing fit. Talking had taken every ounce of energy he could summon. Eventually his eyes closed, and his muscles relaxed, the blue scars on his skin became less prominent. Those criss-crossing scars covered his entire upper body. They were the price he had paid for each ton of coal he'd cut, that and ruined lungs, a life measured by each painful breath.

When the coughing eased, Jim's face relaxed into a smile. His eyes were full as he looked into mine. "So, that's my story. Promise you'll write down every word as I spoke it?"

I took his hand and kissed the top of his head. "I promise. I'm no writer, but I'll do my best."

"God bless you, girl. Oh, and mind you marry that young doctor. He's a good boyo, that one."

I walked out into the yard, Jim's smile following me from the window.

For a long time, I stood there on the dark, sooty dirt, surrounded by ghosts and memories. I knew now that my search for a grandfather was not about me. It wasn't about my identity. It belonged to Polly, to her sister Phyllis, to Ethel and Jim, to Rosa May Davies, Adollgar Griffiths, Emlyn Jenkins, Edward Llewellyn, Rhodri Evans, to this small Welsh town of Brynavon with its small-town dynamics. All had a share in it.

A seed had been sown that morning. I had decided to write a book, something that might help me make sense of things. At last, I had a purpose far worthier than simply identifying my grandfather. I had a story I wanted to share.

Chapter 40

LONDON SUMMER 1979
FLISS & MATT

By late summer, Matt's flat boasted two chairs and a coffee table. Not exactly what I would have chosen, but they were nice. Matt and I were okay too. In fact, we were more than okay. We were back to how we'd been in the beginning, I still had pangs of guilt about the letters (I still hadn't told him I had read them), but this particular evening was shaping up to what seemed a good time to come clean.

"Matt, you know Polly's letters? All that stuff Emlyn had kept?"

"You've read them."

"You know?"

"Well, I know I would have – and I'm nowhere near as impatient as you. Find anything interesting?"

"Mmm, yes and no," I said.

Matt put his book aside. Good. That meant he was prepared to discuss things. However, what came next came as quite a shock.

"I have a confession to make – quite a biggy actually." I held my breath.

Matt then proceeded to tell me about the diaries – how he had found them and why he had kept them secret. It was some confession.

"I knew I should have told you immediately I found them, but I didn't feel ready to share them. Not yet. Does that make sense? They made my grandfather very real to me – the man, Emlyn Jenkins MD, not the grandfather. I wanted to keep him to myself for a while. That's how you feel about Polly, isn't it? You're peeling away the layers, getting to know her private thoughts and secrets. It's very invasive but very addictive."

I moved closer and kissed him on the cheek. He understood. It would be easier now, knowing that he had so much to discover for himself. I still hadn't told him about my epiphany, and in some ways, this made me rethink my position. I so wanted to know if we were tied by blood. I wanted to belong to him and know that he belonged to me, but not as a cousin. Of course, I didn't tell him that. He would have laughed at such romantic rot.

Matt's enthusiasm over the diaries was contagious. "Grandpa was a good writer. Much of it is general practice bumph – a bit mundane, routine appointments and such – but every now and then he reveals something fascinating. For instance, I never knew he was such an authority on miners' lung. He'd had papers published in the *Lancet*. He never told me that. So you see, we all lie at times – even if only by omission." He grimaced.

I leaned forward and kissed him again, this time on the mouth, to let him know I'd forgiven him. Although I already knew him well enough to realise that in his eyes, his confession warranted immediate and total absolution.

"Did you ever play Chinese whispers?" I asked, getting up and wandering over to the window.

"I've never been one for party games." Matt pulled a face. Ignoring him, I continued my line of thought.

"You play it in a group. Someone whispers something to someone else, who whispers it to another and so on. By the time it has gone right round the group, the message has changed beyond all recognition. People can't help adding bits, changing a word or two – for fun, or to spice it up a bit. Maybe they want to make mischief, or maybe they really hadn't heard what was said.

"Anyway, Polly used to say a lie is like a Chinese whisper. Polly hated lies; I mean she really hated them. She believed that once a lie is told it takes on a life of its own and before you can say 'Liar', it's trapped in a web of its own making, unfathomably complex, what she used to call a bugger's muddle."

Matt had that wry look on his face that told me he didn't believe a word. "So, you think that's what happened? Polly told a little porky and it just grew? Listen, if she was half the woman everyone said she was, she'd have kicked it into touch before it took flight." We laughed – he because he'd ridiculed my theory, me at the thought of Polly playing rugby.

I stretched and yawned, I wasn't tired, but I didn't want Matt to think he had won. "That's as maybe," I said, "but, what if she had to lie to protect someone?" I was, thinking aloud, not sure where my thoughts were going, interested to know where they would lead me. "What if telling the truth would cause too much harm? What if she was forced to watch her little lie grow into something hideously beyond her control?"

Matt was sprawled in his chair, one leg hooked over the arm, his head supported by a large pillow (he hadn't got round to buying any cushions) utterly absorbed in one of Emlyn's diaries. I had been talking to myself.

I moved closer to the window and drew the blind aside. It was raining hard and looked as if it had been falling heavily for some time. The newly fitted double glazing was obviously effective, as I hadn't heard a thing. The light from the streetlamps rippled in round yellow puddles. Even the pavements were alive.

I knew Soho well, but Fitzrovia was new to me. It was less sleazy and more fun. It was just as cosmopolitan, packed with little delis and eating places. You could get food round the clock, from a Greek 'kebab in a sock' or a bag of chips in paper, to a slap-up gourmet dinner with fine wine and music and a bill to match. You could even crash plates to the sound of a bouzouki if you felt so inclined.

I could see why Matt had chosen to live here. Accommodation was still relatively cheap, and it was within spitting distance of the Middlesex Hospital, where he was now a senior register.

From my first-floor vantage point, I could see the whole street, including the busy corners where four roads met. This part of London never slept. Pedestrians hurried, dawdled, disappeared in and appeared out of pubs, restaurants and shops at all hours of the day and night. There was always something to see and I could see it all, unobserved, an unseen witness to all the goings-on, all the greeting, chattering and arguing – watching without hearing or speaking – Chinese whispers in reverse, a twenty-four-hour silent movie.

Directly beneath my window, a man and woman were deep in conversation standing in one of the rippling, yellow pools under a lamppost. They were wet through, but they were so engrossed they appeared oblivious to the weather. Their heads were almost touching. The man let his hand slide down the woman's spine until it rested in the small of her back. I thought he was about to pull her towards him and kiss her, but instead he pushed her, propelling her into the stream of traffic. I gasped as she pitched headfirst. There was a scream, a screech of brakes and a red Mini mounted the pavement, missing the lamppost by inches. Miraculously it also missed the woman. The whole incident was over in a second.

"Christ, what the hell was that?" Despite the double glazing, the sound of the brakes had alerted Matt. He rushed to the window, his book dropping to the floor. The man was still standing beneath the lamp, bandying words with the startled driver of the Mini. After a brief exchange, the Mini drove off. I looked along the street. There was no sign of the woman.

"What happened? Is anyone hurt?" The doctor in Matt was primed and ready to act.

"I think I just witnessed an attempted murder."

"You're joking!"

"Don't worry. It failed." I turned back to the room, feeling remarkably calm. It was as if a reel of movie had ended and the lights had come up.

Matt was salvaging his book. "I've only got a page or two left. Be a love and put the kettle on. I could murder a coffee. Then I think you should read this. It's fascinating."

As I moved from watchtower to kitchen, I could feel my knees trembling. Matt's choice of words rang in my head. Why do we say we could 'murder' something as innocuous as a coffee? Was it because we love it? Does murder always stem from extreme emotion, a hunger or an addiction? Had I just witnessed a jealous lovers' row, an act of revenge, or a convenient disposal? Would the man be more successful next time? I shuddered. Had I misread the whole thing? No! I saw him push her. It was a deliberate act.

I made two instant coffees and tossed the teaspoon into the sink, wondering if I should call the police. Feeling giddy, I gripped the edge of the basin and tipped my head back to take some deep breaths. A large cobweb hung from the corner cupboard. Suddenly I was back in Wales. I was about 18 or 19 years old, home for the summer vac. We were drinking mugs of coffee. No. I was drinking coffee; Gran had a cup of tea. Gran never drank coffee, and she hated mugs.

We were perched on the kitchen window ledge, enjoying the last warmth of a summer's evening. Gran touched my arm, and I followed her gaze up to the corner of the extension. She was looking up at the guttering and pointing.

"There." Following her finger, I saw what had caught her attention so intently: a spider, hanging by a single, silken thread. "Watch and learn, watch and learn," Gran whispered without taking her eyes off the tiny creature. I watched too. "She's spinning, see?" Gran said. "She doesn't know we're watching her. Watch closely now. You can learn a lot from a spider, clever little creatures they are, see?

"Look, there. She's fixed her thread up under the guttering. Now, off she goes, flying through the air to the opposite corner, see? Remember she hasn't got any wings. She's floating on the air – trusts it to carry her. There's trust. Her thread is the finest, strongest in the world, but her faith and trust is just as remarkable. Look you now, there she goes, riding on the air, spinning, spinning all the while."

We sat out on that ledge until our bottoms were numb and the air had grown chilly and damp. But the spider was still working. Over and over, she retraced her path, strengthening her line each time with another layer of silk. Over and over, until she knew her bridge would hold.

Next, she began to work across it, adding radii, like the spokes to her wheel. She worked faster now. In and out of the centre, weaving and spinning, checking and testing until she had secured each line to both the central hub and to her bridge line. Her wheel was complete. It was beautiful, ingenious and strong.

"There's clever," Gran said, not taking her eyes off the spider. "Mind, she's still got a long way to go. It was my da as started me off watching spiders. We used to sit out of a night, him puffing on his pipe, me knitting or chewing on a bit of taffy. It was him as taught me about spiders. He knew a lot about nature did my da. He knew a lot about everything, an awful lot for a man with no education, look you."

Gran and I sat on our shelf like a couple of owls, watching the beaded web glisten in the yellow light from the kitchen window. As the breeze caught it, or the spider moved, the whole thing shivered. It was so fragile, yet remarkably strong. By now the spider had woven concentric rings to form rungs between the spokes of her wheels. Like perfect little ladders, set to guide her prey to the central hub. All the time the master builder was checking her angles, testing for strength, she left nothing to chance.

Suddenly the spider stopped moving. I assumed she was resting. She had been working for a long time. But Gran explained that she was waiting while her glands were busy producing a new type of silk, one that was more elastic and toxic, to make her capture spiral a lethal trap.

Gran nudged me, and we watched the spider set lethal, sticky rungs across the radial ladders at the very heart of the labyrinth.

"Slowly does it now," Gran whispered to the spider as if she could hear her. "Don't put a foot wrong now, girl. That silk is as sticky as taffy. Watch how she keeps to the safe bits, Fliss. Slowly, carefully now, that's right. There's clever you are, little one."

I didn't know then that a spider is not immune to its own adhesive toxin. It instinctively knows that should one of its eight feet land in the wrong place, the result would be a slow, agonising death. No wonder she took such care to tread only on the spokes, avoiding the rungs, watchful not to get trapped by her own masterly genius.

"Oh, Look! There. See? She's got her first victim, a gnat. Oh well, we'd best go in now that the midges are out." Polly led the way through the kitchen door. I followed, vigorously rubbing my bottom and marvelling at my gran's knowledge of arachnids.

"Most liars don't have the brains of a gnat, let alone a spider. They think they're too clever to get caught in their own sticky web. But they always do – given time." Gran was talking to herself, but I was still listening.

The next morning Gran came in from the yard shaking her duster free from the last threads of tenacious silk. "There, all gone. Pity a lie can't be removed with the swipe of a duster. Now, listen hard and mark my words, lies only bring harm to the teller and pain to the listener. Believe me, we like to think we're as clever as a spider. We think we'll remember where to and where not to tread. But all liars get caught in the end – trapped by their own conceit and their own silly mistakes."

My mind went back to the young couple out there in the rain. Had I really witnessed an attempted murder? What deceit, what toxins had been woven to lead him to such drastic action? I was trying to make a connection between the two strands of thought when Matt called, "Have you gone to Columbia for that coffee?"

"No... only as far as Brynavon, but don't worry. I'm back now." I handed him a coffee and slid onto his lap, leaving the spiders, the liars and the murderers hang in the air. Right now, there were diaries to be read.

Chapter 41

DOCTOR EMLYN JENKINS'S DIARY

February 21st 1917

Last night I was called out to an emergency at one of the colliery houses on Somerset Street. I recognised the address. It was two doors down from the house of Polly Evans, a patient and a personal friend of mine. It was 11.23pm and snowing hard when I left my call and walked through the yard, past Polly's house. I was surprised and concerned to see a light burning in her kitchen and decided to check if everything was alright.

I tapped the backdoor before letting myself in. Polly was sitting in her rocking chair, looking unusually tired and pale. She had her shawl gathered tightly around her and was rocking gently to and fro. Then I saw she had a baby wrapped in the shawl. When I asked whose baby it was, she replied unflinchingly, "She's mine."

I had not seen Polly for a few days. The last time was when she had come with me to attend a complicated birth over in Tonypandy, and she had certainly not looked like a woman about to give birth. She was exactly as she always had been – calm, unflappable, in control. Now here she was, she sat in front of me, claiming to have just had a baby, without offering any further explanations. I assumed she was in a state of shock.

I reminded myself I was there as her doctor. There were protocols I had to adhere too. I told her I would treat her as any other patient, but that would incur my asking difficult, personal questions. I also advised her that I was obliged to record the incident in my surgery diary. She complied with a silent nod.

I told her to take her time, but I insisted she told me whose baby this was as I did not believe it to be hers. I needed to know how it came to be in her care. I also wanted to know why she been out on a night like this. Polly lifted her eyes, looked directly into mine and said. "She is mine. I'll say no more." I did not ask again. Instead we sat for a long while, sipping hot sweet tea, the baby sleeping soundly in Polly's arms, quietly content to be held and rocked.

I explained that I had to examine the child, and she handed it to me with a look that almost broke my heart. I knew that was why she had let me in – her common sense, her nursing instinct overriding her longing for secrecy. The baby, a little girl, was tiny, although it was a full-term birth. She weighed just over five pounds and appeared to be perfectly fit, if slightly undernourished. I deduced the child was no more than two days old.

It did not take a doctor, however, to see that this young woman was near breaking point. The last thing she needed was an interrogation or an argument, so I decided that, providing I was medically satisfied every-thing was well, I would leave things there until the morning. Polly nodded and I reminded her that if a woman had just given birth, I had a duty to examine both baby and mother. Polly swore to me that she was absolutely fine. For the first time in my professional life, I let my personal feelings rule my actions. She was a

227

good nurse and an excellent midwife, so I decided to accept her judgement.

I fully understand the risk I have taken. And I accept any consequence that may follow my decision.

*

That was the end of the diary entry for that night. However, a separate sheet of paper had been inserted on which Emlyn had written the following personal account. It was obviously written at a later date, although it was not actually dated.

Polly had shown no signs of her pregnancy, although she had been under considerable stress of late. She had only recently buried her father and been subjected to a great deal of hurtful gossip surrounding her sister's abrupt dismissal from Brynavon House, and her subsequent absconding with young Edward Llewellyn. Polly has made it quite clear that she does not want to discuss the matter with me, so I have deemed it best to leave well enough alone. Polly is a very private person, and she has made it quite plain that Phyllis is a closed book as far as she is concerned. Naturally, I respect her wishes.

However, my present concern is for Polly and her child. There is also the matter of her few days unexplained absence, which I now assume was arranged so that she could have her baby away from the wagging tongues and speculating gossips of Brynavon.

As I say, my concern now is for Polly and her child. I asked her directly to name the child's father and tell me whether he was able to offer her marriage, or at least provide for the upkeep of both mother and baby. Polly merely answered, in that way of hers that brooks no argument, "The identity of the child's father concerns nobody but her mother."

Suddenly I knew exactly what Polly had done. I asked her if she was sure she could cope, and whether she had thought through all the consequence should the truth become public, at which she touched my lips with her fingers, so softly, so sweetly, and whispered, 'I am sworn to secrecy, Emlyn. No one will hear anything from my lips. I swear to you, on this child's life, I shall never reveal my secret.'

I knew at that moment that she knew I was aware of exactly what she'd done. There was no need to tell Polly, she already knew my thoughts. I did, however, swear my secrecy too. It is strange, but I shall never forget the love, the peace and the joy that filled Polly's kitchen on that cold, winter night.

No more questions needed to pass between us after that. I watched Polly lay her baby in the dresser drawer, which was to serve as a makeshift cot, and knew I had made the right decision. Polly looked at me and smiled. I have never seen her so radiant, happy or fulfilled, and I swear I have never loved anyone as much as I loved Polly Evans at that moment.

I left, before the snow got too thick for my horse to plough home, having checked that Polly had milk and bottles to feed the baby. I shall always remember her serene smile, the smile that comes from the confidence of a clear conscience. Her fingers touched my lips again. "Hush now. Megan and I have everything we need, especially now that we have you on our side. You get off home to your lovely wife. We shall be fine. God in heaven, Emlyn Jenkins, this is not the first baby I've reared. Off home with you now, poor old Betsy will be frozen stiff standing so long in this blizzard. Out, now!" She kissed my cheek and I patted her arm. What else could I do? My God, just when I thought Polly Evans couldn't surprise me anymore, she up and does this.

I told her I'd call back in the morning, whatever the weather and let myself out into the night. I was smiling as my faithful old horse carried me safely home through the snow, content that I had done the right thing.

As the local doctor, I have considerable standing in this town. People will think twice before accusing me of falsifying a birth certificate. Polly's father, Rhodri Evans, was held in high esteem as a man of honour, a man of strong morals and of strict self-discipline. The townsfolk know Polly to be cast from the same mould. I believe the town will support the daughter out of respect for the father.

Adollgar and I make a formidable group. There will no doubt be idle chatter about the unexpected appearance of baby Megan. But our resolve will be more than a match for any ill-wishers and will squash any malicious gossip at source.

On a separate slip of paper, Emlyn had scribbled this pencilled note.

On Sunday 25th February 1917, the Reverend Adollgar Griffiths preached on forgiveness. You could hear a pin drop as he asked his flock to remember John 8:7, 'He that is without sin among you, let him cast the first stone.' After the service, Polly was inundated with well-wishers wanting to see the baby. She has since been showered with all manner of gifts, even teething rings and nappies. I wished her father had been there to see how much the people of Brynavon respected his memory. Even old Mrs Potter peered down at Megan and said, "She has the look of your mam about her, but those are Rhodri Evans' eyes. There's proud he'd be to see his baby granddaughter."

*

Later we found various personal notes and letters of Emlyn's tucked in among the diaries. One, written to Emlyn from Polly, told me more about my gran than anything else I had discovered to date.

*

My Dear Emlyn,

How can I begin to tell you how much your friendship means to me? To have you at my side now brings me such comfort. You always have stood by me, even when I know you are disapproving of my actions. I asked you to trust me in this difficult instance and you have. Thank you, Emlyn. You will never know how much that means to me.

I know there are feelings between us that have remained unspoken. Let's put all that in the past. You are happy with your Lucy, and I am happy for you both. I am about to embark on a new life as a mother and I promise I have never been happier. But I have never really explained why I refused your offers of marriage in those years before you married Lucy. An explanation is long overdue, and this seems the perfect time to offer it.

You know better than most that my one true dream was to become a trained nurse. As I child, I had seen a picture of Florence Nightingale – 'The Lady with the Lamp'— and imagined myself in a silken crinoline, gliding between rows of wounded soldiers, their hands reaching out to me hoping for a touch, a smile, or a kind word. I remember asking your father if he had ever met Nurse Nightingale. He laughed and told me no, but he had met Nurse Cadwaladr.

I had never heard of Betsi Cadwaladr, a simple Welsh woman who travelled all the way to the Crimea to help Miss Nightingale, only to be told she was too low born. He told me how she stayed out there, in spite of Miss Nightingale's rejection, working as near the front as possible, nursing the wounded and dying, risking and finally paying for it with her own life. She, like me, was from a little town just like Brynavon, Bala Llanycil. Here was a woman after my own heart, see? How I wanted to be like Betsi Cadwaladr.

I pestered my mam and da, and my brothers, to let me train as a nurse. I think I knew then it was an impossible dream. We had no money for dreams. Besides, as they never stopped telling me, I was needed at home, to take care of the family. Even if we'd had the money, it would have been a waste to spend it on educating a girl who'd get married sooner or later. Besides, the hospitals didn't like nurses to be married. It wasn't proper.

It is because of your belief in me that I got to work beside you as a nurse. I have learned so much by your side and hope you will continue to call on me for help when I am needed. Maybe Da was right and I was never meant to become a proper nurse. I have survived well enough.

Now I am building a new life for myself – one I shall dedicate to my daughter, Megan. My girl is going to complete her schooling to the highest level possible. I shall see that she is given all the chances I never had. She can be whatever she chooses, a nurse, even a doctor if that's what she wants. I swear to God she will have every opportunity going.

For all these blessings I have many friends to thank, but the first of them is you. I hope and pray, God willing, that you will play as precious a part in my daughter's life as you have and will continue to do in mine.

Your friend,
Polly.

Chapter 42

LONDON JUNE 1979

That summer, Matt and I moved in together, or rather I moved in with Matt. The flat in Fitzrovia was small and charmingly shabby. The area was lively and a joy to live in. My fanatical search for my past was put on hold while I concentrated on getting my neglected career back on track.

I had chosen my preferred specialism and had been provisionally accepted onto the team of Mrs Margaret Spencer, a leading light in paediatric orthopaedic surgery. Another 10 years and I might – with a great deal of slog, and a degree of good luck – make consultant, but that was a long way off. The good news was that all my doubts had vanished. I was solid in my choice of career. Life was good.

I didn't know it at the time but, as I was emerging from my crisis, Matt was plunging into one of his own. He too had been rethinking his career. Typically he didn't share any of this until he had reached his decision – that is crossed all the T's and dotted all the I's – guesswork and speculation being anathema to him. He was probably wise to keep me in the dark until he had arrived at a final solution. My fondness for 'whats', 'ifs', and 'buts', would have driven him insane.

Matt's itchy feet had not gone unnoticed, but the change in his demeanour was gradual. His phlegmatic easy-going nature became irascible, his temper shortened, and his face took on a grumpy expression at the best of times.

Matt had always taken a great interest in world affairs – constantly scouring the papers for information about the world's trouble spots. It never occurred to me that he was thinking of moving to Cambodia, Iran, or some sub-Saharan Africa war-torn state where his skills would be more needed. Although I had noticed he had been growing increasingly irritable and dissatisfied about his work.

I guessed that this irascibility stemmed from a sense of guilt. We did live a privileged life in a relatively prosperous country – although even in England life was increasingly insecure, with the IRA leaving bombs at random.

On the home front, I discovered that any confrontation merely served to exacerbate matters. Deep down, I knew that Matt was undergoing internal turmoil. Hopefully, he would discuss things with me once he had arrived at a decision. I decided to keep shtum until then. I had been biting my tongue for some time when he finally made his announcement.

We had just finished a late takeaway supper, eaten in silence, when he suddenly jumped up. "Right!" he said. "I have two statements to make and one question to ask. Which do you want first?"

I was still sitting on the sofa surrounded by the debris of Chinese cartons of half-eaten noodles and chop suey. I thought it might be nice to clear away first but decided in the interest of peace to opt for the statements.

"Firstly, I am taking a sabbatical – starting next month."

"Good idea. A break will do you good—" I'd not finished when he fired the second statement at me.

"Secondly, I have been offered a post with Médecins Sans Frontières. I leave for Vietnam when my sabbatical starts."

I pushed the debris aside and poured myself a large glass of wine. Matt was chattering on, more animated than I'd seen him in a long time. "MSF have chartered a boat, *L'Île de Lumière*. I'm going along as trauma surgeon, part of a team, three Brits, two French, one Cambodian." I was dumbstruck.

"Well, say something for Christ's sake," Matt exclaimed.

"Sorry – I don't know what to say."

"I'll be gone about three months, that's all. They work in relays, three months on three months off, when possible."

"Then what?"

"Back here for a while then hopefully to Sudan, or back to the boat people. It all depends where we are most needed – sub-Sahara or the South China Seas!"

So that was that. There was no point in arguing. Matt had obviously thought it through very carefully. He always did. He wanted to become a war doctor and I applauded his decision, although it terrified me. Yet, in many ways – in fact in most ways – I was extremely proud of him. I swallowed my misgivings and vowed to support him in every way I could.

I did ask what would happen about his post at the Middlesex, to which he replied, "They seem quite happy. They've agreed to let me go as and when it suits.

I'll be doing something useful and gaining specialist experience at the same time. It works out well for everyone."

Except me, I thought. To tell the truth, I felt neglected. "Right. That's the two statements. Didn't you say you had a question to ask?" Was he going to ask for my blessing, or was he about to drop another bombshell, I wondered, and might have mumbled something to that effect.

Matt looked hurt. I honestly don't think it had occurred to him that I might find this news difficult to accept, coming out of the blue as it had. Then he smiled, "Ah yes," he said. "The question. Will you marry me?"

Chapter 43

Marriage: I had no desire to get married. Even if I had wanted to become Mrs Jenkins, I was still unsure if such a union would be legal – given our possible blood ties. On the marriage stakes, I had always understood we were in agreement: we did not need a piece of paper or spoken vows to cement our relationship. It was a pleasant surprise and somewhat flattering to have been asked. However, Matt's obvious relief when I suggested we continued as we were was slightly hurtful, being delivered rather too promptly: his proposal was withdrawn with such immediate and total acquiescence. But no doubt that was just me being my usual stupidly, perverse self.

Matt's suggestion that it would be fun to celebrate our non-marriage with a slap-up meal removed any lingering sting. And we agreed to get dolled up and hit the town as soon as our busy schedules allowed.

*

When the day arrived, we got up late having planned to take in a matinee and grab an early dinner close to the Cambridge Theatre at Seven Dials. Of course, being Matt, he hadn't thought to book, and we arrived to find that they had no seats left. As *Chicago* was the only show we both fancied, we agreed to take a stroll around the West End and pop in for a slap-up lunch wherever our fancy took us. We meandered through Chinatown, along Shaftesbury Avenue and finally to West Street where we found ourselves outside the Ivy.

To my amazement we got a table. Deciding to be decadent, I ordered a martini cocktail followed by lobster thermidor. Matt chose the same and we sat back, allowing ourselves to be thoroughly spoiled. I was happier than I had been since Polly's death.

By now I'd had time to reflect on Matt's career move and decided it was no bad thing to spend intervals apart. I would fret until he came back in one piece, but then London was pretty risky in 1979. Besides, I really wanted Matt to follow his calling. Not many people can work under stress and extreme danger. Matt was ideally suited to the challenge. I had no doubt that it was the right thing for him. I would simply have to learn to be more self-sufficient.

After a truly indulgent lunch, we emerged from the Ivy into a bright, sunlit afternoon. We mooched along, holding hands, turning every now and then to kiss and bump hips. I felt like a teenager in love for the first time, and I could tell that Matt had also reconnected. We ambled round back streets I had never seen before and were approaching Charing Cross Road for the umpteenth time when I suddenly stopped and began to retrace my steps.

"Hang on," I called, grabbing Matt's sleeve. "Sorry, but I thought... yes. Look. There. See..."

I was looking into the window of a small shop displaying artists' materials. A poster stuck in the left-hand corner had caught my eye. It advertised an exhibition of 'seldom seen sketches and drawings from WW1'. The list of artists was impressive – Paul Nash, Edmund Blunden, James Montgomery and a certain Edward Llewellyn. The exhibition was on show in Charing Cross Road and had only two more days to run.

Matt scoured the window. "What am I looking at?" he asked, bemused.

I pointed to the poster and watched his eyes scan down. He whistled. "It's the right era, and your Edward Llewellyn was a painter. It's unlikely, but who knows. It could be your man."

I didn't hear him. I was already halfway down Charing Cross Road.

Chapter 44

The gallery was small. So was the exhibition. Collections of sketches, complete sketchbooks, some detailed drawings and a variety of quickly executed watercolours were displayed on all four walls in one small room.

The subject matter was stark, at times grim, but totally compelling, especially as the drawings had been executed in situ, in circumstances one couldn't begin to imagine. A sense of loss pervaded the work as if artists and subjects alike had reached a point where hope had been abandoned.

There were portraits of local civilians, washerwomen of Ypres, children of the Somme valley, soldiers relaxing in trenches, sharing a fag or writing letters home, offering glimpses of normality. Behind this burned a warning flare of certainty that this stillness was a mere interlude before the next burst of chaos and destruction. We were being shown fleeting moments in time – transient, fragile past.

Pictures of the dead – of soldiers, civilians, horses, bullocks, dogs and cats – were hard to look at, lives ended abruptly, minutes or seconds before the artist arrived. One minute they were there then – boom – they were gone. Only the scratches of nib or pencil on paper survived. The subjects lay beneath the mud and dormant poppy seeds of Flanders Fields.

I wondered if the artists had got to know the people they drew. Had they been talking to them, laughing with them, fighting alongside them, aware that tomorrow they too might be the subject of another's art?

I was, of course, imbuing these pictures with learned nostalgia, viewing them with the long lens of hindsight. It made me feel like a peeping Tom, unworthy to imagine the tragedy that infused these drawings. The artists knew reality for what it was. They didn't need statistics; they were the statistics. They smelled the carnage every day. It made them retch. It left them counting the odds that were stacked against them.

The gallery had grouped the work randomly, which offered a very comprehensive view of the whole. Many of the artists were unknown before the war. Some had been sent there to record, some drew from a compulsion to tell the truth. Thanks to their talent, we too could observe, we could look through their eyes. But we could never experience what they had. This was their gift to us – their art.

Many exhibits weren't signed. They were snapshots, aide-memoires for later paintings. They were not meant as works of art in themselves, but that was what they were. And they were powerful.

It didn't take long to recognise Edward Llewellyn's distinctive style. He worked mostly in pencil, using simple lines executed with the skill of a good draughts-man. He had an eye for detail, and a rare ability to convey form with a minimal mark or squiggle. He was good. Some might say his work was dated, but I loved it.

From the catalogue, I learned that Edward Llewellyn had been wounded twice and decorated twice. There was little about his civilian life, but I did learn that he had died in 1970. I also found the address of his agent. My curiosity was aroused. My search was about to resurge in earnest.

Chapter 45

Half an hour later, Matt and I were ringing the bell to a rather grand apartment overlooking Regent's Park. The door opened, and we were greeted by a middle-aged man in designer jeans and a pink polo-neck sweater.

"Come in, come in. I'm afraid the place is in a bit of a pickle. I'm moving out on Monday. So much stuff! It's amazing how much two people can accumulate over the years. Go through, straight ahead, the lounge is probably the least cluttered room. It's a splendid flat. Needs a bit of titivating, but then, don't we all, ducky!"

As we were ushered in, I tripped over my shoelace and bent down to retie it. Meanwhile, Matt followed the middle-aged man who was bombarding him with facts, as he led the way. "The views are sublime and ever-changing. Who needs a garden, with Regent's Park virtually in your living room? The rooms are all big, even the loos. And the bathroom..." He must have noticed Matt's quizzical expression as he stopped mid-sentence.

"You are not here to view, are you?"

Matt shook his head, and the man began to apologise profusely. "I'm so sorry. A couple are supposed to be popping round this afternoon and I just assumed. Silly me! You're from *Country Life,* aren't you?" Again, Matt shook his head. At that moment, the doorbell rang. It was the janitor, asking if any more tea chests were required. Having sorted out the logistics, our host returned.

"Sorry about that. What do they say? The three most stressful things in life are having a baby, moving house and getting divorced. Well, thank goodness this is the only one I shall have to endure! And it's quite enough, believe you me, ducky. Oh my goodness, how rude, I haven't introduced myself have I. I'm Terrance Holstein-Jones, art dealer. But everyone calls me HJ. Are you alright down there?"

I was still bent over my shoe. The lace had got into a knot, and I was struggling to fix it. HJ was shaking Matt's hand. I heard Matt say, "We were given this address by the Mayfield Gallery. I understand you used to represent the war artist, Edward Llewellyn. We're doing some research, and we were wondering how well you knew the artist as a man? I'm sorry, I'm Matt Jenkins, and my partner is the one who seems to be having a problem with her shoe." I mumbled something from my grovelling position while HJ addressed Matt's question in a most immediate and amazingly honest manner.

"Edward Llewellyn and I were lovers," he said. I pretended to continue concentrating on my shoe so that my look of amazement could pass unnoticed. "We met in 1930. We lived together until he died. That was nine years ago. Nine years, seven months and four days to be precise. So yes, you could say I knew him rather well."

Abandoning my lace, I stood up and extended my hand to HJ. He took it and to my utter amazement, he kissed it. Then as he looked up at my face, he let out a loud gasp.

"My God, look at you!"

I snatched my hand away while he continued to stare at me. After what felt like an age, he exclaimed, "It's uncanny... those cheekbones!" With that, he spun on the heels of his Saville Row slippers and hurried from the room, signalling impatiently for us to follow.

Baffled and amused, we scurried along behind as HJ led us through a large door into another empty room. I watched his slim, tightly clad bottom hurry through to yet another room. His backside wiggled ever so slightly as he walked, which made me want to giggle. I suspected that his well-groomed hair had been tinted, but the overall effect was subtly pleasing. I guessed he was in his mid-50s possibly 60, well-preserved and beautifully presented.

His manner was charming if somewhat eccentric, exhibiting the poise and confidence that comes with money and education. His accent was cultured, endearingly camp, and I felt I had known him forever. Matt's raised eyebrows indicated that it had never occurred to him that Edward Llewellyn might have been gay. Not that it was a problem. It simply added another dimension to the story.

The room HJ led us into was also practically empty. The far wall was almost entirely glass, comprising four casement windows, which spanned from polished floor to high, moulded ceiling. Behind them, spread out in all its summer glory, lay Regent's Park. Apart from an elegant, marble fireplace, twin chandeliers and three packing cases, there was only one other item in the room, a large package, propped beside the fireplace. It was expertly wrapped in corrugated cardboard and brown paper, obviously a painting or a mirror, and judging by the care with which it had been packed, it was of considerable weight and value.

"Right, young lady, close your eyes. No peeping until I say." HJ began pulling at the packaging as if his life depended on it. Realising this was too big a task for one man, Matt stepped forward to help. I waited obediently, eyes closed, ears taking in every groan and grunt as paper was torn and packaging discarded. Suddenly all fell silent. Then HJ's voice announced, "Voila! You may open them now."

Matthew released a long, low whistle, while I simply stared open-mouthed. I was looking into a mirror, although in truth it was a painting. I was staring straight back at myself and I was mounted on a fabulous white horse.

There was no mistaking the style: this large piece was unmistakably the work of Edward Llewellyn. The subject had been idealised and romanticised, adding a fairy tale twist to the narrative. And it certainly did tell a story. A lump rose in my throat as I continued to stare at the portrait. I knew at once that it was my great-aunt Phyllis. At last, I had a picture of her, my grandmother's pretty, headstrong, baby sister. And she was the spitting image of me.

Phyllis wore some sort of military uniform, totally unfamiliar to me. Her exquisitely fitted scarlet jacket was double-breasted, with brass buttons and elaborate white frogging. The skirt was long, heavy, blue-black serge, edged with bands of white braid. Her hands, though small and dainty, were clad in elegant white leather gauntlets. These tiny hands held her horse's reins in check with a confidence that told me this was an expert horsewoman. Having only ever pootled around on ponies as a child, I was in awe at the way she sat her mount. Her back was upright, her head erect as she sat side-saddle on her fiery white stallion, surrounded by a scene of battle and danger.

Instinctively, my hand reached out to touch the flying mane of the horse. I could feel the hot breath from his nostrils, smell the smoke from the scattered fires, hear the blast of bugles and the sound of distant cannon. The stallion's black eyes were stretched and wild, and those of the rider were shining amber, defiant, serious. Yet, behind the defiance lurked a spark of devilment, displaying a love of life which gave warmth to her awesome presence.

Great-aunt Phyllis looked directly at me, her eyes defying mine to look nowhere but back into hers. Only when a familiar voice called my name did I realised my face was wet with tears and that my eyes and nose were streaming profusely and, of course, I had no hanky.

HJ waved a very large, freshly laundered handkerchief under my nose. Once I'd had a good blow, the questions began to pour. Had he, HJ, actually met Phyllis? What had Edward told him about her? Did he know what had happened to her? My questions rolled out relentlessly so that HJ was obliged to hold his hands up in defence. The look he gave Matt was so comical, we all burst out laughing.

With his hands on his hips, HJ turned on me. "Listen, ducky, I can talk forever about my darling Teddy and dear little Phyllis, but I do need to be sitting on something a tad more comfy than a tea chest. How much time have you got?"

I exclaimed we were not going anywhere, but I felt obliged to offer a brief explanation as to why I was being so nosey. HJ waved it all aside as unnecessary, implying he was already more than satisfied with my reasons. Snatching his keys from the hallstand, he bellowed, "Right! Grab your things and suivez moi." He then proceeded to shoo us out of the flat.

Matt and I were frogmarched across the road towards a charming little restaurant called the Aubergine, which HJ referred to as, 'Chez nous de chez nous.' The place appeared to be full, but the maître d' welcomed us like long-lost friends and set up a round table in an alcove framed by French doors, open onto a small walled courtyard. The far wall was covered with roses of the deepest red I have ever seen. Heavy perfume hung in the air, which was warm and still, the perfect prelude to a perfect summer evening. Having ensconced himself in a large wicker chair, surrounded by cushions, HJ watched Henri pour three large Armagnacs. He swirled, inhaled and sipped his then he raised his glass, and we all drank to Teddy and Phyllis, and to what promised to be a very interesting evening.

Chapter 46

THE AUBERGINE

After savouring a large swig of cognac, HJ cleared his throat. He was preparing to make a speech.

"Hmm, hmm. Edward Giles Llewellyn – known to all as Teddy – was born in London in 1893. We met in 1930. I was a mad, gin-soaked twenty-year-old, and he was a serious, sober war veteran of 37. Remember this was 1930. We'd already learned that life was too short to take seriously. I realise now how extremely shallow, horribly spoilt and totally selfish I must have been. I saw the world divided into old or young, rich or poor, gay or miserable. (And gay meant something completely different in those days.) Well, duckies, I knew which side I wanted to be on. There was no middle way. It was grab what you can and to hell with tomorrow. Then, thank goodness, I met my darling Teddy."

HJ paused to sip the Armagnac, his eyes closed softly as if reliving something sublime. I tried to picture him as a young man, a glass of champagne in one hand, cigarette in the other, jazz piano in the background, but HJ had picked up his narrative, so my attention was returned to the present company.

"It was an after-show party. (I did a bit of acting in those days – just dabbling, nothing serious.) I don't recall the show, one unmemorable musical or another. As was his habit, Teddy was standing apart, observing rather than participating. I remember he was leaning on a rather swish, black, silver-handled cane. I remember that cane very clearly, it being the only stylish thing about him.

"I knew the poor old bastard had a stiff left leg. I'd watched him behind stage hauling himself up ladders or lugging hefty pots of paint around the set. He had to swing his gammy leg to get it to keep up. I learned later that he'd been wounded twice in the same leg. Rotten luck! Like many of us, he was filling time. I was acting. He was doing a spot of set design.

"A lot of that went on between the wars. One filled in. It wasn't easy to slot back into routine. Anyway, most routines had gone. Besides, things could never be the same after that lot. We did what we could, hoping the depression wouldn't suck us down with it. Mind you, Teddy was bloody good at stage design. Still, as I said, I thought he was a dried-up old crab. I thought he was all the things I never wanted to become – old, poor and miserable. Ha! The ignorance of youth!

"We fell in love within a week and spent four blissful decades together. Beneath his dreary shell, Teddy Llewelyn was witty, intelligent and extremely kind. He was also a brilliant artist. He taught me to feel passionate about the visual arts. Without him, I would never have entered the art world, let alone become known for 'having an eye' as they say. And I do have a very good eye, although I do say so myself. Talking of eyes, it was Teddy's eyes that finally did for me. They were grey, yet so dark as to appear black, with bright gold flecks dancing round the pupils like tiny satellites – penetrating and unfathomable. Looking into his eyes was like striking gold in a coalface. Quite, quite divine."

When HJ turned to me, his own eyes were misty, the pain tangible and raw. "I'm sorry, you want to hear about the girl in the picture, don't you? You'll probably have gathered I'm a bit of a softy with a touch of butterfly and a tendency to waffle. Teddy used to prod me if I went too far off-piste. I trust a little digression is permissible? But do feel free to poke me if I wander too far.

"The young lady in the painting is Miss Phyllis Evans, but you'd already guessed that. So now, where do I start? Forgive me if I tell you things you already know, but I stand more chance of keeping to the point if I chug along in chronological order.

"Don't forget, I wasn't born when Teddy and Phyllis met, so this is only hearsay. But Teddy wasn't one to exaggerate. He was always after the truth in his painting, and I'm sure he held the same integrity in his reporting. I shall use his words wherever possible. I have a good memory for speech. Probably something I picked up in my brief acting career."

*

Prevarication over, HJ proceeded to recount the strange story of the friendship between Edward and Phyllis. Throughout his oration, the waiter brought pretty glass bowls of nuts and crisps, tiny gherkins, mouth-sized morsels of delicious cheeses and round white cocktail onions. All the while, HJ entertained us with his story.

*

"When Teddy met Phyllis she was only just fourteen. Teddy was a twenty-two-year-old captain in the Welsh Fusiliers. He had been given leave, having been shot in the leg during the first few weeks of the war. He told me she cast some sort of spell over him, being 'an irresistibly bright, extremely pretty, rather gauche, abominably working-class nymph.' But he did say she was well-mannered and desperately eager to learn.

"You have to understand, Teddy wasn't so much a snob as a man of his time. It was all rather 'us and them' in those days. Anyway, it seems young Phyllis brought a breath of fresh air into a very stuffy house. Teddy could see why his mother enjoyed her company.

"Teddy had attended the sort of schools designed to turn out sophisticated young men. Men prepared to own things, to run things, to rule the world. Men like his older brother Paul. The Llewellyn boys were never close, in fact I got the feeling Teddy had never actually liked his brother. The ten-year gap between them didn't help. In a competitive world like theirs, poor Teddy was always going to feel inadequate. He was constantly being compared and constantly found wanting.

"Paul Llewellyn was cast from the same mould as his father, a man's man – sporting and brash, a drinker and a bon viveur. He was always, therefore, his father's favourite. By contrast, Teddy was studious and sensitive. Wanting to be an artist had not gone down well in such a patriarchal family. A love of riding and hunting was the only enjoyment the brothers shared.

"Phyllis was a good little rider. Her brothers had taught her to ride the local ponies, bareback and gypsy style, a skill that gave her confidence around the hunters in the stables at Brynavon House. She told Teddy she had watched Lady Brynavon ride out to the hunt and longed to learn to sit a horse 'like a proper lady'. Teddy found her a suitable mount and taught her to sit side-saddle. After that, the two of them would often go off riding around the estate.

"You know the Llewellyn family owned a mining company in South Wales? The actual mine, (coal not gold) was in Brynavon. The family home was just outside the town. The pit took the town's name and eventually when old man Llewellyn was made a Lord, he took the title of Lord Brynavon, a title which passed down to the eldest son, Paul. The estate was pretty large by all accounts, although Teddy seldom talked about it. I gather his early years were rather miserable, apart from his passion for horses, his art and, later on, his unlikely friendship with the little nymph.

"Once his leg healed, Teddy was shipped off back to the Front, poor darling! He hated everything about the war, but he always said it was the making of him as an artist."

*

At some unseen signal, the waiter brought fresh drinks and more snacks. The narration stopped for a while, and we chatted about the exhibition that had brought us to HJ's door. I took a loo break and ordered a glass of fizzy water. When I got back, HJ was refreshed and raring to begin the next lap.

*

"Spring 1916, Teddy had been shipped home with a second wound to the same leg. His left femur had been shattered. The army hospital had patched him up, but he was destined to suffer from a severely painful limp for the rest of his life. They gave him the Military Cross you know, for 'gallantry during active operations against the enemy'. His fighting days were over, and he returned home to rest and recuperate.

"He knew from letters to the front that his older brother had recently been appointed parliamentary private secretary to the Secretary of War, a certain Lloyd George. And as such, Paul was exempt from military service. The family were terribly proud of their eldest son. The post of PPS was considered a step on the ladder to becoming a cabinet minister. He was already an MP and had his sights set on becoming PM one day. I'm glad to say the bastard never made it."

At this point, HJ took an extremely long swig of cognac, which he proceeded to swill slowly and thoughtfully around his mouth as if removing a nasty taste.

"The family had always considered Teddy to be weak and unambitious. Having his leg shot up twice, even getting a gong, had done nothing to win him any brownie points with his father. Lord Brynavon was a hard, old bastard by all accounts. Thank God it was the older son who inherited the father's traits – and the effing title. Teddy was far too nice to be a member of that family, not that I met any of them. I'm much too common, ducky —among other things."

HJ laughed as he swilled his glass around. Then, emptying the last dregs straight down his throat, he sat for a few moments gazing into space. I wondered what he could see: if he wanted to stop all this reminiscing and go home, when all of a sudden he announced, "I'm starving. Where's Henri?"

Henri disappeared to return very promptly with a flambé dish and burner on which he proceeded to prepare crêpes Suzette – not in the least perturbed that we were diving straight into desserts without having starters or mains. I watched as he expertly beat the batter and fried the crêpes in butter. Deftly he folded them into perfect triangles and browned them in the now caramelised butter-sugar sauce. He then drowned them in a healthy slug of Grand Marnier and set light to them. We all cheered, as the flames shot up and the restaurant filled with a deliciously intoxicating smell.

I have never tasted anything so divinely decadent before or since. (The copious Armagnacs we had consumed before eating probably went a long way to enhancing my memory.) I have had crêpes many times since, often at the Aubergine, but they never quite live up to my memory of those first heavenly mouthfuls. From the familiar way the waiter served HJ, and the lack of words needed to explain exactly what was wanted, I assumed he ate these fabulous pancakes regularly, possibly daily. I think I was beginning to fall in love with this wacky, generous and rather lonely man.

HJ beckoned to Henri, who as if by magic was once again by his side, bottle in hand. The restaurant was indeed a real home from home with the scent of roses still heavy in the evening air.

"Aren't they glorious?" HJ said, watching me breathe in their fragrance. "Ena Harkness – you can't beat the old ones." HJ eased his chair closer to mine. "This was our favourite spot. It's at its best on an evening like this. The roses are most generous with their delights when they've been basking in the sun all day." He sniffed the air. "I still miss the old bugger, you know. Nine years feels like an interminable split second."

We sat in silence, sharing the roses. Eventually, I asked, "How did Teddy die?"

"The big C," HJ said, adding rather ruefully, "He was a chain smoker – well we all were, weren't we. Not anymore! Bloody hard to give it up though! Have you ever smoked?"

"No, I tried it once…"

"…and didn't like it!" We finished the sentence together and laughed.

Henri came over and started to close the French doors. Reaching over, I touched his arm. "Please don't," I pleaded, adding, "unless you have to. I mean it must be pretty late. You probably want us to leave soon?" I looked around and noticed with horror that we were the only remaining customers.

"No, no, I thought perhaps you were in a draught. There is absolutely no hurry." His reply was gracious and reassuring.

"Merci, mon ami." HJ's accent was impeccable. Henri inclined his head and proceeded to refill the proffered glass.

HJ continued smiling at Henri while explaining, "Henri is a dear old friend. He will always stay open for us… for me."

"So, Henri owns the Aubergine? I hadn't realised." HJ nodded. "Is he really French?" I asked quietly, half-joking.

"Bien sûr!" It was Henri who answered. He took my hand, raised it to his lips and kissed it. I felt my face redden. Twice in one day! I felt both honoured and stupid.

When offered another drink, I covered my glass with my hand. I looked across at Matt, wondering if he too was slowing down on the alcohol. He was leaning back in his chair, his eyes closed, a look of peaceful content-ment across his face. I knew I was extremely tipsy. I looked at HJ who was chatting away in fluent French to our host. He appeared completely sober. How had he managed that? I looked back at Matt and saw both images of him had their eyes closed.

I blinked hard, and the two Matts became one. This singular man held his glass with the short stem slotted between his third and fourth fingers, his palm cupping the balloon. Slowly and gently, with his eyes still closed, he began to let his hand make small circles, while his drink swirled around the edges of the large glass bowl. Once or twice his hand stayed and, without opening his eyes, he raised the glass to his nose and inhaled loudly. At this, his lips curled at the ends. I didn't actually see any liquid pass his smile but concluded he must be knocking it back when I wasn't looking as his glass was emptying at a rapid pace and he appeared to be as mellow as the brandy.

Chapter 47

HJ showed no signs of tiring. In fact, he was sitting forward in his chair, preparing to deliver the climax of his story. I blinked hard and found Henri beside me with a glass of iced water. Perfect. Meanwhile, HJ continued his tale.

*

"I should warn you this next bit is somewhat of a bodice ripper, but I assure you there is nothing romantic or melodramatic about it. It remains a sordid, shameful incident – one my darling Teddy hated to talk about. I repeat it was 1916. Teddy, Captain Edward Llewellyn, had arrived home unannounced to find the house empty. The servants informed him that Lady Brynavon was out visiting, His Lordship was in Cardiff, and the Honourable Mr Paul was in the vicinity but not in the house. They suggested he try the stables.

"Paul's hunter was in its stall. On seeing Teddy, Charger struck at the ground with his near side leg, anticipating an outing. He was saddled and bridled, clean and groomed, so he had obviously not been ridden. None of the grooms or stable lads would have left a horse tacked up alone in his stall, so Paul had to be somewhere close by.

"Teddy patted the brute on its muzzle and turned to leave, meaning to find someone to untack the horse or lead him out into the yard to be ridden. The horse snorted, wanting more attention. Teddy obliging him by blowing into the horse's nostrils when he heard the unmistakable sound of his brother's tuneless whistling. The horse recognised it too. Letting let his hand slide down Charger's neck to his quivering withers, he patted them gently to quiet the animal. He wanted to surprise his brother, so he stepped back into the shadow of the inner stable.

"From this new vantage point, Teddy could see his brother. Paul stood with his back to Teddy. From the steam which rose from the straw at Paul's feet, it was obvious he was taking a piss. Too occupied with the task in hand, Paul didn't see his brother approach. Teddy said he would always associate the pungent stench of human urine on straw with what he saw next. And until the day he died, that acrid smell would make him retch.

"Paul was stuffing his shirttails into his britches, which were unbuttoned and dangled from their braces around his bare buttocks. His jacket lay abandoned on a bale, along with some horse blankets and other discarded clothes.

"Delighted to have caught his pompous brother with his pants down, Teddy prepared to spring on him, when to his horror the bundle of clothes started to move – it was Phyllis.

"I remember Teddy saying he would never forget that child's face. It became etched on his soul, blank and colourless as a bleached sheet. The flesh around her eyes was puffy, while the eyes themselves stared lifelessly as though petrified. She turned, and he saw her left cheek was bright crimson, the result of having struck, or been struck by, something hard. Her hair, usually neatly tied back with a ribbon, fell loose, matted with dusty straw. Her dress had been ripped away from the shoulder, and her small, childish hand clutched at it in an attempt to cover her nudity.

"Phyllis raised her hand, first to her cheek, then to her mouth then back to her cheek. All the time, her pathetic little body shook violently, while her face remained too shocked, too bewildered, to express emotion, and those stony eyes retained their unnatural, fixed stare.

"The first time Teddy relayed this story to me he wept, even though some 15 years had passed by then. The tears poured from his eyes as he remembered her torn, bloodied fingernails, and struggled to find words to describe her damaged mouth. The memory never left him. Thinking of it made him gag as if it had been his fate to be forced down in the dung and the dusty straw, a man's weight pressing on him, ripping him apart with fear and pain and shame.

"Teddy always said little Phyllis's prettiest feature was her mouth. It was pink, plump and childlike. She held her lips slightly parted, which gave the appearance that she was perpetually, yet pleasantly, surprised. This delicate rosebud was swollen and bruised, crushed beyond recognition. Blood poured from teeth marks that had torn the soft fleshy inner lip. I shudder now at Teddy's rage when he described how she tried to hide it from him, as if she, the innocent victim, was ashamed of this... this act. Meanwhile, satisfied and mindless of the damage he had caused, the perpetrator had carelessly stepped aside to empty his bladder.

"Months later, Phyllis could not bring herself to look in a mirror. She also refused to speak. Later she told Teddy she had been terrified to hear what words might come from such a defiled and abused mouth.

"Paul continued to adjust his clothing, then to Teddy's disgust, he turned to her and smiled! It was too much. Before the older brother had finished buttoning his flies, the younger flew at him. He caught his chin with a powerful right hook which felled him. Seconds later, Paul, recovered from the surprise attack, was back on his feet. Being a good stone and a half heavier than Teddy, who was also hampered by a gammy leg, he retaliated and, in Teddy's own words, 'The bastard knocked the living daylights out of me.'

"By the time Teddy came to, it was dark. Paul was back in the house dining on mutton chops with his mother, as if he hadn't a care in the world. Teddy managed to crawl unseen past the dining room and crept on upstairs in search of Phyllis.

"Teddy said Phyllis looked like a broken doll. He asked if she was in pain, but she didn't answer. When he tried to lift her, she whimpered like a wounded puppy. Her face was already swollen and heavily discoloured, her mouth barely recognisable. Speech was impossible. Teddy offered to fetch her sister from the town, but at the mention of her sister's name, Phyllis grew hysterical. Knowing it wasn't wise for him to be in her room without a chaperone, he rang the servant's bell and sat stroking the child's hair, praying that it would be Betty who answered the call."

*

At this juncture, we all agreed we needed another drink. Nothing had prepared me for such a tale of rape and abuse. I was horrified. Matt also looked stunned. HJ, however, was determined to finish his story. He signalled for our glasses to be filled and, like the consummate narrator he was, picked up exactly where he had left off.

*

"Teddy was a kind, loyal creature. He had always known his older brother was cut from a very different cloth. Yet, he had gone out of his way, often leaving his rational reasoning behind, to find excuses or at least explanations for any past misdemeanours executed by his brother. Paul was far too old to be sowing wild oats, and by now, Teddy had learned to assess his brother as a man, not as an older sibling to whom he should look up.

"In short, Teddy had come to the conclusion that the honourable Paul Llewellyn was a pig. The man had done this because he could. No one ever challenged Paul, he was too powerful. He always got away with it. And he always had an answer for everything.

"Paul had often bragged, 'Of course, women always say no. It's part of the game. They like to play hard to get, to lead the chase – it's a form of hunting, and they all want to be bloody Diana. I ask you, what fun is hunting without frightened prey? Sex is primal. It's natural. And what's wrong with nature, eh? I tell you women love a man to be forceful. A real man knows when a woman wants him. You learn to read the signs.

I defy you to find one man who'd prefer to have a frigid little mouse.'

"Treating women as his personal property had become a habit for Paul. Of course, he could be charm personified – he was a gentleman after all. This wasn't the first time he forced a girl. It wasn't the first, and it wasn't the worst, but this time he'd gone too far. This time Teddy took it personally.

"Thankfully it was Betty, a woman of 40-plus, who answered the call. Betty had been with the family for years. She saw to the family's personal washing, changed their linen and made their beds. She was virtually un-shockable, practical, and especially fond of Teddy.

"The moment she saw Phyllis, she sent Teddy out of the room and began to check that the girl was physically alright. Satisfied that he had left Phyllis in capable hands, Teddy flew down the stairs, intent on beating the truth out of his brother.

"Mother and son were about to start on desserts. They were laughing, sharing little anecdotes, playing happy families. When Teddy burst in, Paul laughed. He denied having been near the stables that day, claiming he'd been in Whitehall first thing, a claim which he swore Lloyd George himself would confirm. 'So, you see, old boy, it follows that at the time of the alleged assault I was lunching on the London to Newport train. It was probably one of the stable lads. The little hussy probably asked for it, what?'

"The mother refused to believe a word Teddy said. Phyllis was dismissed on the spot over some trumped-up charge of petty theft, while darling Teddy was accused of jealously trying to discredit his brother. Mrs Llewellyn told Teddy she was ashamed of him and that unless he apologised to his brother, she would shame him in front of their father. Teddy refused and left the room, disgusted with his entire family.

"Paul followed him into the hall. Teddy said the look of disdain on his brother's face as he issued his final threat, was chilling. 'If you know what's good for you, you interfering young fool, you'll pack your bags and get back to the bloody war. With any luck, the Hun will finish you off properly next time.'

"Teddy called his brother a cowardly bastard at which Paul exploded, threatening to expose Teddy as a queer. Remember, in those days it was a criminal offence to be – to use the charming language of the time – a queer, a bugger, or a pansy. Ha! Now we have to refer to ourselves as gay! Another splendid word usurped by the unenlightened!

"Seriously though, the Honourable Paul Llewellyn MP was not someone you wanted as an enemy. He had friends in very high places. It would have been easy enough for him to get his brother cashiered, or worse. And by God, the bastard was mean enough to do it.

"From that day on, the brothers held each other in mutual contempt. They were never reconciled, although I know Teddy thought of his brother every day of his life. The bastard's still alive, you know – Lord Llewellyn of Brynavon. I curse him each and every day.

"When my darling Teddy first told me all this, I remember he couldn't stop shaking. Remember he was recounting something that had happened many years earlier. I felt as if I was hearing a confession. Teddy always was ready to take the blame, poor darling! The associated shame of his brother's crime never left him. Edward Llewellyn was a real gentleman."

Chapter 48

At this juncture, Henri brought a tray of much welcome coffee. Our raconteur, however, had not yet completed his tragic tale. Resettling himself, with considerable shuffling and rearranging of cushions, HJ proceeded to deliver the concluding chapter.

*

"Teddy left home immediately, preferring to disown his family before they disowned him. He no longer had the stomach to remain in such 'a nest of hypocrites' – his words, not mine. Besides, he felt obliged to help Phyllis. The poor girl was an innocent victim. She'd been abused, dishonoured, wrongly accused and abandoned, first by his family, then by her own. Did you know her own father, hearing the lies that were being spread about his youngest daughter, actually dropped dead! Who knows whether he believed them or not, anyway he never saw his girl again, never heard her version of events, never knew of the violent assault, never had a chance to stand up and defend her or her family's honour.

"Teddy, being the sort of man he was, felt responsible for his brother's actions. Talk about sins of the father skipping a generation. Anyway, he and Phyllis fled like the babes in the woods. They left all the scandal and shame behind and went to London. Apparently, she was in shreds. Teddy said she often talked of killing herself – of throwing herself in the river or under a train. He tried to let the whole incident die, hoping it would be forgotten the sooner by focusing on the future.

"He did write to the older sister, trying to explain exactly what had happened. I gathered from him that she agreed, for Phyllis's sanity, it would be best to help her begin a new life. Besides, apart from a loving sister, there was little left in Brynavon for the girl but gossip, hatred and a sullied reputation. Teddy was convinced that in time the sisters could be reunited, but it was better all round to distance themselves until the scandal had settled.

"As you will have gathered, Teddy was a very sensitive man. I hate to think what he must have gone through. Walking away from his family and from his inheritance took guts; it was a huge decision. Yet, he clearly never regretted it. In fact, he always averred he would do it again, given similar circumstances. And I believe him, bless him. You see, Teddy lived by a simple code of honour – one did the right thing, whatever the cost.

"He was convinced that a troubled conscience is the premier motive for most suicides. I don't know what evidence he had to back up his theory, but he certainly believed it. I don't think he could have lived with a guilty conscience. Poor, dear man, he was the gentlest creature you could wish to meet. He most certainly wasn't a coward. He was a brave, honourable man. He would have hated to bring shame on his family, which is partly why he kept shtum. Did he make the right choice? I don't know. But what alternative did he have?

"Teddy had a studio in Chelsea, an attic room in a pleasant enough little house. I like to picture him playing the starving artist. Actually, he was never on the breadline, but he'd walked away from a considerable fortune.

"Fortunately, he had a personal inheritance from his maternal grandfather, which had come to him when he was 21. The old boy was an eccentric, dabbled in the arts, that sort of thing. Teddy, being the black sheep, and the only one with a shred of aesthetic taste, was his favourite. And thank God for that. The rest of the family couldn't get their mitts on that money, so Teddy never actually faced hunger, let alone starvation. By the time his paintings began to sell – which was slowly at first, and for very little – he had enough to manage quite nicely, including making provision for Phyllis.

"When Teddy was declared fit for active service, he was shipped back to the front. Phyllis stayed on in the house. She wrote him long, chatty letters, I still have them. They're witty, ironic, often flippant. Her sense of humour was wicked. These letters betray nothing of the damaged girl she was. The fact that she was treading a tightrope between reason and madness didn't manifest itself until much later. I think we'd call it clinical depression now, or PDST. Then, it was a case of waiting and hoping the mind would repair itself.

"Anyway, her letters were the only contact Teddy had with England, and he always said they were the one thing that kept him alive. They gave him a purpose to live and the will to survive. His probably did the same for her.

"Phyllis was desperately homesick, especially for her sister. She hated the crowds and the busy, bohemian lifestyle of Chelsea. Then, purely by fluke, she discovered this warrior nursing troupe – hence the snazzy uniform in her portrait. And thank God she did. Teddy said he thinks she would have topped herself if she hadn't discovered that organisation. They were actually a topping group of women.

"I've still got all their letters. I have ALL Teddy's personal bits in his old campaign chest. It's positively stuffed with fascinating things – a veritable treasure chest." At that, Matt closed his eyes and sighed heavily, no doubt thinking, *Not more bloody letters!*

HJ was prattling on, but by now we all knew we had overstayed our welcome. "I know exactly where it is. I have a very efficient filing system, but I fear it must wait until tomorrow. It's packed up with all the other clobber. Pop round tomorrow. I'll have it ready for you.

"Oh dear, Henri is yawning, I fear we may have begun to smell! Poor darling, he looks shattered. Be good little ducks and walk me home. You'll pick up a taxi outside the flats easily enough. Bless you. I've had a wonderful afternoon. I love reminiscing."

With much flamboyant arm-waving, blowing of kisses and a stagger or three, we manoeuvred HJ to his door. Calls of farewell followed as Matt and I hailed a cab to take us home.

Chapter 49

LONDON 1979

The next morning, I called round as planned only to find a distinctly crestfallen HJ. The sale had fallen through, and he was faced with unpacking everything or putting it in storage while trying to sell a flat devoid of furniture. Despite all this upheaval, he had the letters ready for me as promised. He looked so dejected I invited him to join us for supper at nine, explaining we were both working 'til then. He accepted, and I realised I had nothing in the fridge. I would have to go to the deli for emergency supplies.

*

As soon as I got home, I pounced on the bundle of letters and carefully opened the first one.

Chelsea.

My Darling Teddy,

I trust you are wrapped up snug and warm in your monogrammed silk pyjamas. Would you like me to send your hot water bottle? I'd send you my sable, but I left it at Freddie's last night. (That's not a hint. I really do not want a fur!) Your trench sounds delightful, quite rustic, yet chic. I hear it is chilly in France just now, so I hope your butler is keeping the fire in throughout the night. It's just as well you have all that wine and cognac to fortify you. Do make sure you are getting enough exercise. Touch your toes every day and be sure to take a little stroll after lunch. I don't want you coming home looking like Billy Bunter!

By the way, I wrote to Mr Asquith, telling him it's a disgrace there are not enough young men left in England to go round. Parties are getting frightfully dull. I said we girls were planning to rebel if he didn't do something. Imagine how difficult that would make things for the poor darling. Why, fighting angry women would be worse than fighting the Hun! Anyway, he says he's going to get his boys home in time for Christmas. Won't that be nice? You can thank me when you get here.

Sorry. I'm being flippant. Sometimes I think I have gone quite mad, or I'm at least well on the way. Of course, I know how dreadful it is over there. You are so brave, all of you. It is just nicer to think of you surrounded in luxury, rather than trying to imagine the rats, the mud, the lice and the danger. Is that very selfish of me?

Take care of yourself and come home safely because I love you.

Your little sister,
Phyllis.

Letter number 2

Chelsea

My Darling Teddy,

You'll never believe what happened today. I can hardly hold my pen steady enough to write I am so excited. I was taking my usual short cut through Hyde Park – oh, Teddy, it is lovely at the moment. The leaves are all red and gold and the air is so cold you can see it when you breathe out. I like to walk along pretending I am smoking!

Anyway, I was about to leave by the north gate – I like to cut down Horse Guards, but I was late and in a bit of a rush – when suddenly we were all ushered to one side to let a column of riders pass. Two old gentlemen next to me were furious at being told to wait. They shouted all sorts of nasty things to the riders, calling them a disgrace to their sex! Oh, I forgot to mention... the riders were all women!

They rode beautifully, Teddy, straight-backed, legs still and a light hand on the reins, just like you taught me. They sat side-saddle, of course, and their horses – all magnificent dark bays – looked as if they had been polished with bees' wax. There must have been thirty or more, I didn't actually count. When they were well clear of the gates, they formed a double column and rose to the trot in perfect formation. I have never seen anything so breathtaking.

They wore uniforms of red, white and blue. You should have seen them, Teddy. They were magnificent, so proud and so confident. Oh, I wish you had been with me, my darling. I just couldn't stop staring at them.

Well, when the troop had passed, I followed them and watched them go through their exercises. I cut across the grass to keep up with them. When they finished, they dropped to a measured walk and fell back into single file. I continued to follow, still walking behind them, until they reached their garrison headquarters at Rochester Row. It was a long walk, but worth it.

Well, my dear, the long and the short of it is I have joined them – the FANY. FIRST AID NURSING YEOMANRY. I am going on a training course in two weeks' time, subject to a few practicalities, such as a medical and payment of a few subs. (I have to buy a uniform, hire a horse and a few other bits and bobs. Then there is my training in first aid, signalling and motor maintenance.)

Thank goodness you taught me to drive. I'm sure that was what clinched it. They were most impressed that someone of my age could drive a motor car. Of course, I lied slightly about my age, but it was only a tiny fib. I don't think it will matter, not when you think of all those poor soldiers dying from lack of immediate first aid?

Just think, I shall be in France or Belgium before the end of the year. If I come to France I can come and see you. I can't begin to imagine what this war's really like. Now I shall find out for myself. I know you don't tell me the half of what you men have to go through. I make light of it in my letters too, but only to make you laugh. Deep down, I am so scared. I pray for you all the time.

Don't you see, joining the FANY is my way of paying you back - you and my darling Polly. You have both sacrificed so much for me. Write and tell me you approve, my darling boy, please do. I shall write to Polly when I get to France. Imagine how excited she will be to get a letter from the frontline. I like to think that at long last she will have a reason to feel proud of her silly little sister.

God bless you, my dearest, Teddy.

May we meet again soon.

Your loving little sister,

Phyllis.

PS I might need some help with those payments.

Chapter 50

FITZROVIA 1979

HJ arrived bearing wine and flowers, the whole street must have heard him arrive, tumbling out of the taxi, insisting the driver get out to assist him and find the right doorbell to press. We met him on the doorstep and escorted him up to our humble abode. We had been discussing the very letters at the precise moment the taxi drew up. HJ immediately joined in with the conversation while I dished out a bubbling (shop-bought) lasagne.

When I confessed I'd not heard of the FANY, HJ exclaimed, "Never heard of the FANY! Oh, my poor darling girl!" He then proceeded to give a brief history of that extraordinary group of women, hitherto totally unknown to me.

"It started with some chap back in the Sudan campaign – think Charlton Heston and Lawrence Olivier, acres of sand and the mad Mardi, that sort of thing – well this young chap, this captain what's-his-name, was wounded in battle and discovered to his horror that the British army had a serious logistics problem with casualty arrangements. The method of transporting the wounded across miles of hostile terrain to a field hospital hadn't changed since Florence Nightingale's time. It was sheer chance whether the poor blighters bled to death on route or not. He'd been one of the lucky ones.

He'd survived, but many of his friends hadn't. As he lay in bed, counting his lucky stars, he came up with a plan.

"Back in England, he talked it through with his sister, a very resourceful young woman. They decided to try it out. She got a group of enthusiastic young women together, and work began in earnest. The women – all young, fit and able to ride, preferably with their own horse, i.e. mostly wealthy young debs – learned first aid, cavalry movements, signalling and camp work. His idea was that nurses on horseback could get to the front line very quickly, where they could administer basic first aid, staunch bleeding, dish out morphine capsules, that sort of thing, in situ, before ferrying the poor sods back to a field hospital.

"At first it was all a bit romantic – you saw the uniform in Phyllis's portrait – not exactly practical. Anyway, some forward-thinking women took up his idea, and by WWI the First Aid Nursing Yeomanry was up and running, already having proved itself in the Balkans and South Africa. That's the FANY in a nut-shell. And a bloody good corps they are.

"Of course, by the time Phyllis joined them they only wore dress uniform and rode side-saddle on parade. Divided khaki skirts and puttees had replaced the ornate tunics and long skirts. The new look was less attractive but far more practical. Even the horse was often superseded by the motorbike, lorry and van. Phyllis became a trained mechanic, you know, which was pretty rare for a woman in those days. But then the FANY were tough, brave and indefatigable. By the end of the war, several were highly decorated.

"I think they had to be tough cookies to survive. Phyllis told Teddy that the fact they were first aiders, not nurses, was drummed into them. But they tackled just about everything that was thrown at them. They never ducked a task, no matter how unpalatable. They even nursed cases of typhoid.

"In the beginning the Red Cross distrusted them. The British government disrespected them, and the British army tried to ignore them. The troops, of course, adored them from the word go – troops of all nations, the Belgians, the French and the Brits. Their motto 'Arduis Invicta' means 'In Difficulties Unconquered.' Colloquially translated as 'I Cope', it pretty well summed them up. They simply got on with the job. Eventually, they became accepted and trusted and even the powers that be acknowledged that they made a considerable contribution to the war effort."

At this point, I produced a bowl of oranges, which I served with a generous apology for the absence of pancakes and Grand Marnier.

"No need for apologies, my dear. That was a splendid meal – Italian simplicity, cooked with that special ingredient, love." HJ blew me a kiss then stared at me so hard I began to wonder if I had splashed something on my face. "I'm sorry." He laughed. "It's rude to stare, but the resemblance between you and your grandmother is quite remarkable. What a shame you never met her. She was a great storyteller and a wonderful mimic. You'd have adored her."

"My grandmother was Polly Evans, Phyllis's older sister. Phyllis was my great-aunt. You'd have loved Polly, she was amazing."

HJ wiped his mouth hurriedly and threw his napkin on the table. "Whoa! We seem to have got our wires crossed, ducky. I knew about Polly, of course. Teddy often spoke about her, although you are right, I never actually met her. I know you called her Gran, and she was indeed a grandmother to you, but I'm talking about your biological grandparent. That was the younger sister, Phyllis. And yes, I did meet her. In fact, I met her several times. And believe me, she was your mother's mother." HJ spoke with such certainty, I felt quite unnerved, offended even.

"I'm sorry, HJ, but you are so wrong." I realised I was talking rather loudly by now, but I was anxious to make my point. "Polly Evans was my biological grand-mother, and I have the birth certificates to prove it. That means that her sister, Phyllis, was my great-aunt. I also have a telegram informing Polly that her sister, Phyllis, was killed in Amiens, France, on August 8th, 1918. If I remember correctly, you were born in 1910, so I really don't think you could have met Phyllis... unless, of course, you were at a séance.

"I never met Polly's sister – she'd been dead for 36 years by the time I was born. I didn't even know she existed until my grandmother died. I certainly had no idea that I looked anything like her until I saw Edward's painting. And that's the God's honest truth. I'll show you the telegrams and certificates if you don't believe me." Mentally I rested my case. I also looked to Matt for support.

Matt shrugged. HJ remained unflustered, then he patted my hand and addressed me softly, but with that same unwavering conviction. "I'm so sorry, my dear Fliss. I assumed you already knew all this and I'm afraid there is still an awful lot more you don't know. Some of it is going to come as quite a shock."

At that point, Matt intervened. "Sorry, guys, it's going to have to wait. We have a crisis. We've drunk all HJ's booze. I know, I know, I was supposed to get some, and I forgot. Sorry. I suggest we adjourn to the Fitzroy Tavern, it's two minutes away, okay?" Before we could object, we were being bundled down the stairs and frogmarched to the large, friendly boozer on the corner of Windmill and Charlotte Street.

I made for a corner table, while HJ ordered three large Armagnacs at the bar. He instructed the landlord, Frank, to keep them coming until we left or fell down drunk. "Whichever occurs first, my good man." Joining me, HJ then ensconced himself in a large Windsor chair, waited until we were all settled and continued. "Now, my darling girl, I suggest I clarify all that business about who was who, before we tackle the mix-up regarding Phyllis's demise. Agreed?"

I was rather preoccupied with a battle between butterflies and lasagne which was raging in my poor stomach, but I smiled optimistically – a little apprehension was a small price to pay for the relief that hearing the truth would bring. Hopefully, at last, HJ would put an end to all the conflicting suppositions and varying versions of 'truth' I had already been fed.

Chapter 51

TEDDY'S STORY

With consummate aplomb, HJ picked up the story exactly where he had left off.

*

"Shortly after Teddy received Phyllis's letter about her joining the FANY, the army discharged him. He had taken a bad fall, and his gammy leg could no longer support him. His riding days, his fighting days, were over.

"He got home to find his ward just returned from a week at training camp. Phyllis was a changed woman. She was eating again, her cheeks were rosy, her face wreathed with smiles. What's more she was animated. He described her as 'a woman on a mission'. The whole experience of living under canvas, learning new skills and meeting like-minded women had inspired her.

"However, just a few days later, Phyllis took to her bed. She complained of an upset tummy, nothing too serious, but debilitating. They laughingly put it down to the result of camp cooking and expected it to go as quickly as it had come. It didn't. It got worse. When Teddy insisted she see a doctor, she called him an old woman for 'making a fuss about nothing'.

"A few days later, Phyllis began to suffer acute pains in her abdomen and back. This time a doctor was consulted, and having examined her thoroughly, he announced that she was seven months pregnant.

"Phyllis was just 16, a total innocent. She had no knowledge of the facts of life. Her mind, therefore, made no connection between Paul's brutal attack in the stables of Brynavon House and her condition. In fact, the very idea that she was expecting a baby was beyond her comprehension. Teddy tried over and over again to explain, but the only way she seemed capable of accepting what was happening was to assume it was punishment for something sinful she had done.

"It was soon obvious Phyllis believed the 'thing' inside her was evil. 'Only a very evil thing could come from such an evil act,' she cried out, screaming and tearing at her belly to try to force the thing out. Teddy could not get her to understand that she had done nothing wrong, that this was just a cruel twist of fate.

"Phyllis believed she was possessed, convinced that this 'thing' was sent to kill her. She swore that if they did not take it away, she would kill herself and the 'thing' with her.

"In desperation, Teddy contacted Polly. He swore to stand by Phyllis and his brother's child. He even offered to marry Phyllis and take the child on as his own.

"Polly, in her calm, practical way announced she would come to London to be with her sister and help with the birth, which the doctor predicted was only a matter of weeks away. 'If, when delivered of a healthy, normal baby, my sister still cannot accept the prospect of motherhood, that will be the time to make other plans. Until any such time, the best thing for Phyllis, and her unborn child, is to ensure they are safe and loved.'

"Poor Phyllis, still embroiled in her own private hell, knew nothing of all this. Apparently, the next few weeks were hellish for everyone. Phyllis could not be left alone for a second, nor was she allowed to leave her room. She reverted to eating only when forced. Her days and nights were spent crying and pleading that the 'thing' be taken away from her belly before it killed her."

*

At this point, HJ adjusted his position and reached for his glass. "Good God!" exclaimed Matt. "Imagine that happening today?" There were several nods and verbal grunts of agreement, and I looked up to see a small crowd had gathered round our table, while in front of HJ a row of Armagnacs, no doubt supplied by the narrator's fans, sat awaiting his disposal. He downed a couple, cleared his throat, took a deep breath and resumed his tale.

*

"On February 19th Polly delivered Phyllis's baby – a girl, weighing four and a half pounds. The mother, who was both mentally and physically exhausted, refused to see the baby. She never held it, never asked after it, never acknowledged its existence, or indeed had any-thing to do with it.

"Whether Phyllis had any understanding of what had happened to her, who can say. As far as she was concerned, the ordeal was over. She believed her sister had heard her cries and come to save her. The 'thing', whatever it was, had gone, and she felt purged.

"All the poor deluded girl wanted to do was resume her life with the FANY. Her tired, fragile mind had to find a way to survive the future. She spun a new world around herself, one in which she was still an innocent, happy sixteen-yearold, and safe in a cocoon where the past could not touch her. She never mentioned the rape, the birth or the child again as long as she lived.

"Only Teddy and Polly knew how close to insanity Phyllis still was. They dared not raise the subject for fear of triggering a relapse. Phyllis was in total denial – although that state had not been invented back then. Polly felt it best that her sister should not be made to confront the truth, unless or until, God willing, she recovered her wits enough to address and accept the facts herself. Meanwhile, it was agreed that Polly should take the child and raise it as her own. Before totally committing to this, Polly insisted that no one else was to know the child's true identity, except for Edward Llewellyn and herself.

"Teddy and Polly made a solemn pact to take their secret to the grave. And, as far as I know, both kept their word.

"And so, in a state of blissful ignorance, Phyllis threw herself back into the FANY. Feeling relieved and somewhat vindicated, Teddy watched as Phyllis completed her training and eventually set off for France. His actions had been unorthodox, totally unofficial, possibly even illegal, but they appeared to have saved the girl's sanity. To all intents and purposes, the two conspirators had found a satisfactory – if not ideal – solution."

A general sigh of relief was heard, but knowing it to be premature, HJ raised his hand. His voice had a solemn note, as he continued. "On August 8th, 1918 Polly received a telegram. The very one you read aloud earlier this evening, my dear Fliss, informing her that her sister had been killed at the battle of Amiens." There was a loud gasp from the audience, which HJ acknowledged with a dramatic pause.

I was nodding, aware that everything was suddenly, horribly real. "Imagine poor Polly's reaction," HJ continued, "to have gone through all that, only to have her sister cut down so cruelly? Polly relayed the distressing news to Teddy by letter, for fear of local gossips reading telegrams or listening in to the telephone. Her baby sister, the last of her family, was dead at just 17 years old.

"I'll remind you that this was long before I had met my darling Teddy. But he talked about it so very many times that I often feel I was there with him during his ordeal. The astounding thing was that it took 27 years to discover that the War Office, or whoever the buggers in charge of casualties were in those war-torn days, had made a monumental cock-up. Phyllis hadn't been killed at Amiens. No! She had been severely wounded, suffered shellshock and had been put into a mental hospital – in Blighty."

Another collective gasp escaped, this time enhanced by whistles and expletives.

"Oh yes!" HJ exclaimed. "I remember exactly when she died because Teddy and I arranged her funeral. It was May 25th 1950. A Thursday, to be precise."

"So, she lived another five years – to 1950." I was counting rapidly on my fingers. "Jesus! That poor woman was stuck in a mental hospital for 30 years!" I think I may have squealed at that point.

Matt mumbled something blasphemous and looked up at the ceiling, tipping his chair back, so it balanced precariously on its back legs. One of the other punters whistled a long, descending scale. I was firing questions, rhetorical and unanswerable, my voice getting louder as the words tripped over each other in their hurry to get out.

"You're telling me that Polly's sister was institutionalised for 30 years?" I exclaimed. "Why didn't someone let Polly know? Someone should have told her. The War Office must have contacted her, once they realised what a monumental blunder they had made? Someone must have known about her? I can't believe no one did anything for 30 bloody years. It doesn't make sense."

"As often happens, fate intervened. Let me explain." HJ raised his voice, trying to be heard above my incoherent rambling and Matt's vociferous insistence that I 'shut the hell up'.

Suddenly, we were silenced by a loud voice, demanding that HJ, "Get on with it, mate. My last train goes in half an hour, so cut to the bloody chase."

The audience applauded. "Yes, cut to the bloody chase," they shouted. They began whistling, jostling, vying for HJ to answer their personal questions.

"What happened to the kid?" A heavily made-up woman cried, streaking her cheek with mascara as she dabbed moist eyes with a soggy tissue.

Another demanded, "Didn't the bloody government admit they'd made a cock-up?" Only to be shouted down by another calling, "Nah! Of course, they bleeding didn't – they'd've had to cough up if they admitted it was their fault!" There was loud jeering and laughter at this, when suddenly a bell rang, and the entire bar erupted.

Someone exclaimed, "What a fucking balls-up!"

Frank's loud shout of, "Time, ladies and gents, please," cut through the din. Questions hung in the smoke as the landlord ushered us out into the rain. Amid a general struggling and jostling for raincoats and umbrellas, I was wrestling with the idea of spending more than half one's life lost, not knowing who one was, or where home was.

Out in the dark and wet, I looked around for Matt. He was striding up the road at a hell of a lick. I had to run to catch up with him, I kept yelling at him to wait, and eventually, he stopped and turned.

"That was a fucking pantomime," he shouted, rain dripping off the end of his nose. "Is this what you wanted? Eh? Are you happy now you know the truth? Your grandfather was a rapist bastard. And your 'gran' wasn't who she claimed she was, in fact she was a consummate liar. Has it helped you? Have you found yourself now you know your real grandmother was a traumatised kid, born before anyone understood the long-term effects of trauma? What do you hope to achieve from all this… from all this… this… madness?"

Someone had let all the air out of me. "Where's all that anger coming from, Matt?"

"Where from? From having to sit back and watch you dig yourself deeper and deeper into this self-indulgent bog, that's where. It was obvious from the start it wouldn't end well. You do realise don't you, you'll have to live with the consequences? Can you do that? Honestly? Don't you wish you'd left well enough alone? Do you know how many human beings are lost, killed, maimed or disappeared every day? Every day the numbers increase. The victims have no choice. They just have to get on with it. But I know whose life they'd rather have. Think about it, Fliss. You're healthy, strong, educated and free. Drop this now."

I squirmed, not knowing what to say. Matt wouldn't have listened anyway as he still had a lot more to get off his chest.

"You need to grow up, Fliss. Life's a shitty business for most people. It's a cruel world. Wars happen. Casualties happen. Collateral fucking damage happens. Things don't get rounded off, neatly tied up in ribbons, resolved to everyone's complete satisfaction. You have to let the past go. You can't change it. You, we, have to concentrate on the here and now. If not, we'll all go fucking crazy."

Matt spat out the last two words, spun round and marched off into the rain. I wanted to run after him, to call him back, to apologise, to kiss him, to tell him he was right, but I couldn't because deep down, I knew he was wrong.

If I have learned one thing from my work, it is that every death, every injury is a one-off. It's personal. It's life-changing for someone. Tragedy is only ever felt personally. Numbers don't magnify the pain, they simply replicate it over and over, in equal doses of the same. Universality means little to a bereaved mother. That's the whole point, isn't it? Isn't that why we are moved to care for others? We understand their grief because we too can feel it.

Looking back, I think it was there, standing in the London rain, that I realised how much I loved Matt.

I am not as shallow as Matt thinks. Not now. Tracing my past has given me an insight into the lives of others, a glimpse of the times in which they lived, and an understanding of the ways they struggled to find a meaning to it all. Life does have meaning. It's finding it that's so hard.

A hand touched my shoulder, making me spin around. HJ stood beside me, shielding me with his umbrella.

"Alright, duckie?" he asked, giving my shoulder a squeeze.

"No. But I will be." I pulled a face, hoping to mask my misery with a pathetic attempt at clowning.

HJ smiled ruefully. "Matt's a good man, but he's angry. He wants to heal the whole world on his own. Believe me, my darling, you never be able to stop him from trying." HJ kissed my cheek and turned to hail a passing cab. "Call me. There's more you need to know, but not now. You go and look after that man of yours. The rest will wait."

The taxi pulled away, trailing twin ribbons of red which blurred with my tears. I wiped my eyes and traced Matt's path to the front door. Inside, the flat was empty, and the phone was ringing off the hook.

Chapter 52

BRYNAVON 1979

Next day I was back in Brynavon sitting beside Uncle Jim's hospital bed. Despite oxygen, his breath came in desperate gasps. Poor Little Aunty Ethel, the future must have looked bleak as she watched her beloved Jim fight for his life.

Jim died later that day. I was there to help Ethel fill in the forms. When asked who was next of kin, I replied, "His wife, Mrs Ethel Lewis."

Ethel became very agitated and tapped my arm frantically. "No, no, no..." she twittered, shaking her head so violently that several hairpins fell free from her hairnet.

"Jim is... was... my brother. I'm two years older than him, but he has always looked after me." I was flabbergasted.

All my life, I had assumed they were a married couple. They had shared the same house and the same bed since I had known them, and probably since the day Jim was born. I remember not feeling shocked, but I was very surprised. Did it matter how they were related? Even if their relationship had been incestuous? No. It was none of my business. They had loved each other. That was enough.

Poor Ethel looked as though she had been torn in half. One half was now gone forever. I was only too acquainted with the trauma caused by amputation. This was no different. Ethel's pinched face, the fear and hopelessness in her eyes told me she no longer had the strength or the will to carry on alone.

Jim was buried on the Wednesday. I agreed to stay on until Ethel felt a little stronger. Things between Matt and myself were left hanging. It was far from ideal, but what else was I to do? I decided to spend no longer than necessary in Wales. Meanwhile, I assumed Matt was preparing to leave for Vietnam. Lives were about to change dramatically, but my days were too busy to waste time dwelling on such things.

My nights were different. Alone in the dark, my mind would not turn off. Cold waves drenched me, leaving me shivering and nauseous. What if I never saw Matt again? Never! We hadn't even said goodbye. Nothing had been resolved.

The next morning, I woke with a raging temperature. I ached all over. It even hurt to move my eyes. I had flu. I lay in Gran's bed for three days, unable even to manage the stairs to get to the loo. I didn't care as I spent most of the time in that limbo where reality and dreams merge. There was a chamber pot under the bed which was miraculously emptied, cleaned and covered with a linen cloth. At regular intervals, a cup of tea was placed on the bedside table, alongside a jug of clean water and a little plate of biscuits and grapes. Mostly I slept. Images came and went in a bizarre haze. I didn't know, and little cared if I was alive or dead.

On the fourth day, I was human again. I drank the tea by my bed and nibbled one of the biscuits. I got myself downstairs and had a bath. I was just finishing a bowl of cornflakes when the back door opened, and Little Aunty Ethel trotted in whistling a tuneless ditty. She stopped whistling when she saw me.

"Oh, there's lovely. All well now is it? Funny thing that old flu. It comes down like a ton of coal then flies away like a little sparrow." That dear, frightened, confused, old woman had put her own problems aside and nursed me. It may well have been the saving of her.

A couple of days later I was back to normal. Ethel had been a tower of strength. Maybe looking after me was what she'd needed – that meaning of life thing. Anyway, there was nothing left for me to do here, so I booked a ticket to Paddington.

*

I'd still heard nothing from Matt. I didn't know if he was in the UK, if he had cleared out of the flat, or if he had left me for good. With no idea what was waiting for me inside, I turned the key and bulldozed my way through a pile of letters, circulars and general junk-mail that littered the narrow hallway. My heart sank as I realised its significance. Matt was no longer here. He would have sorted them into piles.

I shuffled them with my foot. Among them was a card from dear HJ inviting us to join him for dinner. The dinner date had come and gone. Dear HJ. He must have wondered what had happened to us. Everything had happened in such a rush; I hadn't thought to let him know I was going to Wales.

Upstairs I found a letter on my pillow. Matt's familiar script rambled over the pages, free and undisciplined, in stark contrast to the succinct logic of the words. He wrote clearly and concisely, always straight to the point, at times harsh and unpalatable, but never cruel. He wrote exactly as he spoke, which made his absence even more acute. I wanted to cry.

Matt explained that the day after I'd left for Wales, he was directed to travel to Saigon. He warned that correspondence from Vietnam could be very slow, but I was not to worry. MSF took great care of their staff. He would write when possible and send me an address. He hoped to see me at Christmas. Three months – an eternity.

A sense of schoolboy excitement lurked behind every word. This was exactly what he had been waiting for. This was the work he knew he was destined to do. At last, he was doing something purposeful. This was his way of making sense of a crazy world, a world that seemed determined to tear itself apart.

Typically, he made no reference to our row. He was in the moment. The past was over, the future not yet begun. This was how he lived, which was why my machinations, my introspective nit-picking, fell way beyond his sphere of comprehension. It was why I loved him. It was also the cement that would hold us together for so long. Isn't hindsight a wonderful thing!

The next day I phoned HJ.

"Hello, stranger. I thought you'd abandoned me." The warm, refined voice flowed over me like honey. We arranged to meet the following evening. When Matt was invited too, I said nothing.

Chapter 53

THE AUBERGINE 1979

Henri greeted me like a long-lost sister before escorting me to the window table where HJ sat nursing a large cognac. He rose to embrace me, making me feel loved, wanted and better than I had felt for several weeks.

We dispensed with any preliminary, chit-chat. HJ took a large swig of Armagnac, cleared his throat and in his usual fluid style, picked up the thread exactly where he had last left off. It was as though he had merely taken a breath since the last instalment.

*

"We fast forward to 1945. Another war ends, and Teddy finds himself visiting an old pal (who's in a unit for victims of shellshock). The two mates are taking a turn in the grounds when suddenly Teddy stops dead in his tracks. He stares. He can't believe his eyes. Is it? It can't be. Yes, my God, it is. There was no mistaking her.

"The hair was thinner, the auburn lustre faded, but the face, though horribly scarred, is as lovely, as familiar, as ever. It was the way she held herself that had caught his attention – that aristocratic carriage, the tilt of the head, high and slightly to the side; the rounded gestures of hand and arm; a natural grace controlling each movement. Teddy said that, despite the shapeless uniform of an asylum inmate, there was no mistaking Phyllis.

"After 27 years in the wilderness, Phyllis was waking up. However, this was no fairy tale. Her physical injuries had been severe, the mental damage, devastating. Phyllis was, and always would be, profoundly deaf in both ears, both eardrums having been perforated. She could remember nothing about the rape, nothing about the baby, nothing about the war. In her own mind, she was still 16. Maybe that was just as well. Who can say?

"After that first meeting, Teddy visited her regularly. Eventually, she showed brief flickers of recall – small isolated episodes, which crept back like dreams – vague and ephemeral. Amazingly, the one thing she eventually recalled with absolute clarity was the moment of her 'death'.

"She described the whole event in great detail. It was quite unnerving to listen to, although she was very matter-of-fact about it. Teddy wrote it all down, wanting to record her own words in case her memory failed again, and she lost this crucial moment of her life... or death... forever."

Chapter 54

PHYLLIS

"After a hideous sea crossing and a terribly bumpy drive across country in the back of a lorry full of manure, I arrived at the base hospital, about 25 miles behind the front line. The CO told me I was to be teamed with an older woman. 'Her name is Thompsett. The family are titled but don't hold that against her. She's one of the best, a regular poppet.'

"I was scheduled to meet Thompsett in the morning. But just as I was about to leave to find my quarters, a very jolly, rather plump woman bounced into the room. She grabbed my hand and began shaking it rather too vigorously. It was Thompsett.

"Thompsett (we only used surnames in the camp) was lovely, keen and kind. Like on that first night, she'd stayed up so I would not spend my first night without a pal. Really nice people had been given affectionate nicknames; her's was Tomps.

"Tomps was my senior by four years (plus the two more I'd lied about). She'd already got three years' experience of France and the war. I was in awe of her; she knew so much and had such sound common sense. It reminded me of... of someone, but I don't remember who... Never mind. However, despite being brilliant at most things, Tomps was no mechanic, while I loved engines and driving. That's why they had put us together.

"I spent several weeks at base camp, working in the hospital, familiarising myself with the work, or 'bedding in', as Tomps called it. Then the CO sent six of us to clear out an abandoned butcher's shop in a nearby village, to serve as much needed bed space. It reeked of rotting meat, and the only place to sleep was on the sawdust floor, amid the offal and dried blood. We scrubbed it out until it shone, although it still stunk to high heaven.

"Eventually, I was considered 'bedded in', and Tomps and I were assigned to the front, which was about 25 miles south of base. We were actually going to use our training in the field. I was excited and terrified in equal measure. This was why I had come to France, but I was scared I wasn't up to it. Tomps said there was only one way to find out and she was right. So, off we set, me as designated driver and Tomps definitely boss.

"Our vehicle was an old truck that had been converted into an ambulance of sorts. It was a Renault. Tomps immediately christened her Foxy, she said Renault sounded like Reynard, which was French for fox. Little did we know how apt the name was.

"The base hospital was 20 miles north of Amiens. We drove at night, under cover of darkness. Headlights were strictly forbidden, so visibility was nil. Did I tell you it had been raining for weeks? No? Well, it had. French rain is just like Welsh rain. When it comes, it comes proper hard. As a result, the first stretch of road was a quagmire. Foxy skidded and slithered, behaving more like a Keystone Cops' car than an ambulance.

"No one had thought to warn me that darling Foxy had an aversion to cornering or that she disliked being driven at anything less than 10 miles an hour, and positively hated going under five. She showed her disapproval by stopping abruptly and stalling, pitching us headlong into the windshield. Although Tomps was the navigator and by far the senior officer, she was the passenger, so it was her job to climb out whenever Foxy stalled, and with only a Lucifer to light her way, crank-start the engine.

"On the first leg of the journey, Foxy managed twice to slide into the ditch that ran along the nearside of the road, and once into the one on the far side. These ditches were full of mud and were surprisingly deep in places. Hauling the slippery Fox out was extremely difficult, not helped by the fact that I had forgotten to pack the torch. All three of us were caked from head to foot and tyre to roof, in slimy French mud.

"Foxy came nose to nose with several trees which loomed from the dark if we got too near the edge. Potholes pitted this stretch of road, and I had no light to help me avoid them. We pitched and rolled so much we both felt seasick and kept the first two fingers of our right hands crossed, for fear of getting a puncture. It was a miracle Foxy didn't beach herself. By the time we joined the main road, all three of us were nigh on exhausted, and we hadn't even started the real work.

"Eventually we turned onto the main road to Amiens. This was long and straight (most roads in France are long and boringly straight), which was just as well considering Foxy's aversion to cornering. This was the 'open road' the CO had talked about. She hadn't mentioned the snaking, narrow, mud-filled ridge we had just conquered."

*

"Day was breaking by the time we reached the 'open road' only to find it was anything but open. It was a crawling crush of horses, wagons, motorbikes, trucks, staff cars, soldiers (hundreds of them, on foot, all heading north). Nothing was moving at more than two miles an hour. Foxy hated it. She stopped and started, spluttered and coughed, each time incurring a barrage of abuse for halting the already halted traffic.

"At this point, Tomps pulled rank. Now when Foxy stalled, I had to get out and crank the shaft, incurring jeers and wolf whistles from the slow marching men.

"We had heard the rumble of distant guns at base camp. With each mile they got louder – a stark reminder that we were heading towards danger. Now the volume increased with every slowly gained yard until the pounding was deafening. Wounded and dying men on stretchers, crutches or on foot, inched their painful way against the traffic. I wanted to stop Foxy, to start work, to do something, but Tomps was adamant. Our orders were to reach the front.

"Some of the men were bleeding profusely. Some were blind or minus limbs. All shared the same dazed look, the same question on their lips, 'Why?' But behind the question was a sad resignation to a fate they had no control over.

"Eventually, Tomps told me to find a safe spot to leave Foxy. She planned to run on ahead to find our colleagues and ask them where they need us most. It was difficult to think in such chaos. It was all around us. The noise so loud it was physical; you could feel it. Every thud, each sudden boom, made my whole body shake. The pounding was relentless. The air choked me, thick with smoke and screams. Orders were being bandied from all sides, swallowed up by the general din of war. Men and vehicles clashed and swerved, trying to leave or reach destinations which no longer existed.

"I found somewhere to leave Foxy, ominously close to a sign which read *'Beware of Mines'*. Tomps shrugged saying, 'They're the least of our worries, old bean.' I had never realised there were so many ways to die. So, I shrugged too and raced to catch up with my friend.

"In her haste, Tomps had left her first-aid bag in the ambulance. I saw her turn and shout at me, but it was impossible to hear her above the din. She began pointing frantically to my bag and back to Foxy, showing her empty hands. Realising what she wanted, I hurled my kit to her, then wove my way back to the ambulance.

"Seconds later, clutching Tomps' bag, I was racing back, less than 10 yards from my friend when the world exploded with a blinding flash. Lifted off my feet, I travelled through a wall of light. Suddenly I was in a bubble where there was no sound and no movement. In a split second, the light turned to darkness. I was cocooned in my bubble, floating in outer space. It was beautiful."

Chapter 55

THE AUBERGINE

HJ sighed. I noticed his eyes brighten and knew he was thinking of his lover. He must have loved Teddy very much. His eyes met mine, and he smiled.

"Darling Teddy! He never failed to appear surprised when he remembered how peaceful Phyllis was when describing her death. There was no trace of fear, no horror, no remembered pain.

"It was easy to see how the identity of the two women had got switched. Thompsett had taken the full blast. A moment of forgetfulness, the chaos of the moment had cost her life... and saved her partner's. Phyllis was taken to a local French hospital – not the field hospital where they could have identified her. She remained in a coma for several weeks. Her only possession was Tomps's first-aid bag, it was, therefore, assumed that she was Margery Thompsett. As a result, Phyllis Evans was pronounced dead.

"The appropriate telegrams and letters were sent and Phyllis – now officially Miss Margery Thompsett – was shipped back to Blighty. As fate would have it, Margery had no family. If she had, then the mix-up might have been resolved much, much sooner. Phyllis had no idea who she was: it made little difference to her whether she was Thompsett or Evans, her memory was gone. When the authorities told her she was Margery Thompsett, she believed them. And so it remained for the next 27 years."

*

HJ and I sat in silence. Such cruel irony was almost too much to digest. Eventually, he rallied, and fortified with cognac, continued the saga.

*

"Naturally, once the authorities had been informed, they realised there had been a right old cock-up. Teddy managed to get Phyllis moved to a private nursing home in Hampshire. By now, there was no doubt in anyone's mind that she was indeed Phyllis Evans. She was alive and safe, although Teddy had been warned that her recovery, if there was one, would be by a gradual, spasmodic progress. Nothing was guaranteed."

At this point, I interrupted. "Didn't you mention meeting Phyllis? I assume Teddy told Polly he had found her. My God! What a wonderful surprise, or rather what a shock! How did she react? How did Phyllis react, discovering she had a sister? What a meeting that would have been. Why on earth did Polly keep it all secret? I wonder if she told Megan. I wonder why she never told me. Do you know?"

"Whoa! Steady on, old girl – one step at a time. I promise to tell you everything I know. First, I insist we eat a little. I'm starving."

I conceded but ate very little. I already had more than enough to digest. Eventually, HJ placed his spoon in his dessert bowl and pushed the plate away. "Now, I shall attempt to explain all," he said, and dabbing his mouth with his napkin, he was off.

*

"Of course, Teddy told Polly. It was the first thing he did. I can't begin to imagine how she must have felt. It was the doctors who advised against her visiting her sister, for fear of causing a setback. As a result, Polly never visited the nursing home, but she was eventually reunited with Phyllis. I, however, did accompany Teddy on one of his visits. So, in answer to your question, yes, I did meet your grandmother.

"Phyllis really was quite beautiful. I had of course seen her portrait, and I assure you that young girl was still present in her demeanour and aura. There was noticeable scarring, and age had also taken its toll, but the bone structure was still there. She would still turn a head or two. Of course, the poor thing had no idea who I was – she barely knew who she was. For some peculiar reason, she insisted on calling me 'Doctor Jenkins', which Teddy found extremely amusing.

"Other than that one occasion, Teddy kept his visits private. This was probably wise, as Phyllis was very fragile, and he was terrified of losing her again."

"That's sad!" I exclaimed. "But you say Polly and Phyllis were reunited. How did that happen?"

HJ came back like a flash, "Oh yes, they certainly did meet. Every first Sunday of the month, Teddy would collect Phyllis and escort her to Newport station. Here the sisters would take afternoon tea together, just the two of them, in the Station Hotel tearoom. On these occasions, Teddy left them alone.

"Sadly, Phyllis never recognised Polly. She had no idea they were sisters. They did become very close, though. It was like two strangers meeting and discovering an existing affinity. Communication was difficult at first, because of Phyllis's deafness, but she got very excited about these little outings. Teddy said, she was always talking about her friend Polly, but she never regained any memories of her childhood, or having had a sister, or the tragic circumstances that had led to her sorry situation."

I wanted to cry; it was all so sad. Eventually, I managed to say, "How awful for Polly. She never really got her sister back – just half, just the physical half."

"Oh no. Her spirit remained intact," HJ interjected. "Phyllis's personality was remarkably unchanged. Yes, she was still locked into her childhood. She was still innocent and vulnerable. Polly had to be very careful. That was why she never mentioned Phyllis's child, who was a young woman by now. Had Phyllis shown the slightest flicker of memory, it might have been different. So, you're right, it must have been very hard.

"As far as I know no one but Teddy, Polly and myself knew about these reunions. Phyllis, of course, never realised that was what they were, so she too never really knew."

*

It took some time for me to take all this information to heart. The fact that Polly continued with these meetings, always smiling, always treating her sister with love and

303

respect, reflects the Polly Evans I knew and loved. But I had to resign myself to never knowing anything with absolute certainty. Unfortunately, without Polly to enlighten me, I would never know how she really felt about these strange events. I realised that should I ever get round to writing this down, I would have to speak for Polly – I could only hope she would approve.

Chapter 56

LONDON 1980

At long last, the story of the two sisters had an ending. Yet the jigsaw was not quite complete, there were still one or two gaps. Some pieces didn't fit comfortably. Had I put them in the wrong place, or jumped to the wrong conclusions? Something was missing, an emotional element was lacking. For instance, why did Polly pretend Megan was hers?

Motherhood is a tremendous responsibility for a single woman. Did Polly have time to think things through, or was she swept along by the speed of events? Had she been trapped by the narrow confines of the times in which she lived? Or was she an exceptionally modern woman, willing to face harsh criticism in order to fulfil her dream of motherhood?

If only Polly was alive. If only I had known what questions to ask. How hard had life been for her? Did she resent having to sacrifice her own childhood for her siblings? In later life, were there times when she resented raising two little girls, neither of which was her own? Did she blame her sister or my mother for standing between her and her dreams of becoming a nurse? And what about my arrival?

Were there times when Gran had resented me for entering her life just when she should have been putting her feet up? Here I was, landing out of the blue, making her start all over again – changing nappies, writing name tags, reading kids' books, always having to put another person's needs first. When was she going to have a life that was entirely her own? A life to enjoy as herself?

Oh, Gran! What would you say if you were here now? How would you explain your actions? Would you feel the need to defend or justify them? Did you ever live to regret them? Would you have acted differently if you had known how things would turn out? Of course, there was no point in speculating about these things. I knew I had to resign myself to never knowing the whole truth.

*

Time passed. Christmas came and went. Matt did not come home, and the new year arrived. Nothing changed, yet everything changed. I missed Matt so badly. I had not heard from him for three months, and I was sick with worry.

In February, a much-travelled postcard arrived. It was originally posted in Addis Ababa. Matt was well. He loved me. He would be home for Christmas. The next day another arrived, one with a hurriedly drawn smiley face, a scribbled cross for a kiss and the words HAPPY XMAS. It was the best Christmas card ever.

There was also a note from the post office informing me they had made three attempts to deliver a parcel, which I would now have to collect from the main branch.

Late that night, Matt came home.

Chapter 57

LONDON 1980

We breakfasted on hot croissants and strong coffee from the deli in Charlotte Street. Benjamin, the Jewish deli-keeper, burst into fits of laughter at the sight of me – Matt's anorak thrown over my pyjamas, my slipper-clad feet blue in the February frost, grinning from ear to ear like a Cheshire cat.

The next hour was spent luxuriating in bed, licking melting butter from the corners of our mouths, relishing its creaminess highlighted by the bitter taste of Arabica as we kissed and shared the same breath.

Luck would have it that I had an early shift and had to leave within the hour. I faced a heavy day ahead, but that was fine, Matt was home. Poor Matt, however, was exhausted. He had said very little about his time in Cambodia and even less about Sudan. I deemed it wise to wait until he was ready to talk and share. He never responded well to probing. Besides, I had him back for three whole months – there was no rush. Long days and longer delicious nights lay before us, like the endless expanse of a child's summer holiday. I stretched and yawned lazily, before snuggling against the heat of Matt's strong back.

"Ouch! Your feet are freezing. They're like bloody great icebergs. God! I've missed you, Dr Evans." Matt turned over, wallowing in a bed with a mattress and clean sheets, rolling like a hippopotamus in a bed of mud.

"I missed you too, Dr Jenkins, but cold feet are the price you have to pay if you want your slave to bring you breakfast in bed."

"Thank you, slave."

"You're welcome, Dr Jenkins."

"Don't mention it, but if you want to remain my slave, I'd better give you a name. I think I'll call you Jenkins."

"That's your name, sir. My name is Evan—" Sitting bolt upright, I stammered, "Was that a proposal?"

"Yes. It is the third and final chance for you to make an honest man of me. A simple yes or no will do."

"Yes. Yes, yes, yes. I mean, yes please, Dr Jenkins, sir."

Matt's head flopped back against the pillows. His eyes were closed. He was already asleep and looked as if he would sleep for the next three months.

I stared at my rumpled-haired man. His brown hair was bleached like straw, long and tousled. A single strand flopped over his closed left eye. White lines fanned from the outside corners of both eyes, and I thought of him squinting into the African sun. His chin was hidden by a shaggy blond beard, while the rest of his face was tanned like leather.

His term overseas had obviously affected him physically. But what, I wondered, had it done to his mind? "Please don't let it have changed you too much," I whispered. He replied with a loud snore. Some things never change.

No doubt he had witnessed awful atrocities. There had been constant reports in all the papers. I'd seen pictures on the telly that had made me turn away. Would he share any of this with me? Should I probe him? Would he think I didn't care if I didn't ask questions?

Lying with my head propped on my elbow, I stared down at him. He was scruffy, underfed, worn out, and beautiful. Had he really just asked me to marry him? Had I really just said yes? What had happened to our vows of never marrying, of staying independent, of being happier cohabiting? What a horribly cold word – cohabiting. Still, it doesn't apply any more. Soon I shall be Dr Phyllis Jenkins. Wow!

That morning I was late for my shift. Several colleagues remarked on the twinkle in my eye, the spring in my step. I was light-headed during the ward rounds and performed my stint in the consultant's outpatients' clinic in a semi-dazed coma. My feet barely touched the ground until, a few weeks later, we stepped from Westminster registry office into a small patch of wintery sun as man and wife. A beaming HJ stood at our side, acting the perfect 'bridesmaid'.

Chapter 58

With all the excitement of the wedding, I had quite forgotten the undelivered parcel languishing in the post office at Russell Square. It was Matt (my husband!) who finally collected it and brought it home.

Something about the packaging evoked a strong nostalgia for a lost past. Maybe it was the brown paper or the string, tied and secured with a dollop of red wax. It had been posted in Cardiff. I had absolutely no idea who it was from. Excitedly I began to tug at the knots. I was a child again, full of the anticipation that comes with birthdays and Christmas.

The parcel contained several cassette tapes and this covering letter.

Dear Dr Evans,

Please accept my sincere condolences for the loss of your grandmother. I regret I was unable to attend her funeral, as I was out of the country at the time. Polly Evans was a very great lady who will be sadly missed by a great many people. As a child, I lived next-door-but-one to your grandmother. I know there are many wonderful stories about Mrs Evans and her good works, but one in particular is very personal to me.

It concerns an incident in 1924 when a little boy accidentally sat in a tub of boiling water. Polly Evans's quick thinking, her incredible foresight and wealth of practical knowledge, saved his life, and his manhood. Using freshly made dough as a nappy, she let the yeast draw the heat off the child's scalded skin. By the time he arrived at hospital, there was barely a mark on him. The doctors said it was nothing short of a miracle.

The boy went on to make a full recovery and referred to Mrs Evans as 'his guardian angel' from then on. He kept in touch with her long after he'd left school and became a junior reporter with a local newspaper. In fact, he went on to become editor of the Cardiff Times. *He has never forgotten Polly Evans.*

I know this as fact because I was that little boy. My name is Tommy Morgan, and I shall be forever in debt to your grandmother. I shall never forget her singing to me, stroking my head while nursing me. With each stroke of her fingers, I felt the pain lifting, while her sweet, soft voice made me forget how frightened I was. She really was an angel.

Now I am in my sixties and have recently been clearing and sorting through my archives. I am a great hoarder, but, having retired, I decided it was time to have a thorough clear out. While sifting through my collection of reel-to-reel tapes, I came across one I'd recorded back in the 60s. I was researching for a series of articles on 'Women of Wales between the Wars'. Your grandmother was among the many women I interviewed. A book of the same title was published in 1964, to coincide with the fiftieth anniversary of the outbreak of WW1. It didn't sell very well, but I am still rather proud of it.

I made reel-to-reel recordings of all my interviews, and they make fascinating listening. Sadly, the book is no longer in print, but I have enclosed a copy for you as a memento of your grandmother, who is mentioned and quoted in the text.

I have taken the liberty of re-recording the appropriate reels onto a tape cassette for ease of access. There is also a separate cassette dating from the 1970s, which was actually recorded by your grandmother, under my instructions. I forget how it came to be in my possession. I confess I have listened to it, but on rehearing it, I believe it was meant for you alone to hear.

I have said it before and I cannot repeat it often enough, Polly Evans was a truly remarkable woman. I know she was extremely proud of you. I hope you do not mind me contacting you like this, but I should hate these tapes to get lost, or remain unheard. I hope you can find a use for them – maybe a book about Polly's life? Anyway, I am glad that they are at last coming home to you, where they belong.

With my kindest regards,
Thomas Morgan

My hands were shaking so much I couldn't slot the first cassette in. Matt stood watching with a smug grin on his face, then he took over, muttering, "Come here, butterfingers, I'll do that. Call yourself a surgeon!" I sank down on the rug and watched him throw one of his raised-eyebrow looks at me. His finger was poised dramatically above the play button. I nodded, and a few seconds later, we heard Thomas's deep Welsh voice.

"This recording of Polly Evans was made Tuesday 14th April 1964, as one of several interviews I conducted to use in my book. *WOMEN OF WALES: BETWEEN THE WARS.*" There was a short pause, then I could hear Polly's voice. It was strong, confident, and so wonderfully familiar. I had to pinch myself to check I wasn't dreaming, but I really was listening to my gran's voice; the voice I loved so much.

*

"Hello. I am Polly Evans. I was born in Brynavon, in South Wales. I was the first of ten children and I was born in 1893. Owen, Thomas, Rees and Alun died when Brynavon pit collapsed in 1913. The twins, Dafydd and Fred, and young Morgan were killed on the same day, at Mametz Woods on the Somme in 1916. My only sister, Phyllis, died in 1950, although I had been told she had died in France in 1918 and did not see her for twenty seven years. My mam died in 1904, giving birth to my baby brother, Dewi. who drowned in the Low Pond on his fourth birthday.

"Mam suffered from poor health, which meant I had to grow up very young. Like lots of us girls before the Great War, my education was short and brief. I sometimes think I was a woman by the time I was seven. I looked after my brothers and my sister and ran the family home. I did all the washing, ironing, cooking, shopping, cleaning. Water came from a pump. Cooking was done on the range, and we slept top to tail in two huge beds, one in my parents' room, with a cot for the youngest, the other in the second bedroom, with a ceiling too low for my brothers to stand up.

"I never felt times were hard, although thinking back on them they were. We knew no different, so we were content. I would do it all again, quite willingly, if it was needed.

"But I did have dreams. I dreamt of a future where I would be free to choose what I did for my living. By the time I was 12, I knew I never wanted to marry. I knew what it meant to be a mother and a 'home-maker'. I'd lived in a house full of men whose needs always came first. I didn't want to spend all my life with a man telling me what I could or couldn't do. I wanted something more for the grown-up Polly Evans. I wanted to be my own woman.

"I really wanted her to be a nurse, like Betsy Cadwaladr. But God had other plans for me. I never did marry and have no regrets. I have always made my own decisions and kept my independence.

"Life in the valleys was tough for us working people. Food was hard to come by, as money was scarce, see. Women had the task of eking out what little money there was, which often meant going without to provide for the large families they had in those days. Today it seems daft to have had so many babies, so many mouths to feed. But women had little say in the matter back then.

"Men saw children as a sign of manhood. Large families were a source of pride. But I ask you, where's the pride in having more kids than you can feed? Silly beggars! Most women would stop at one or two, given half the chance, but like I said, it wasn't up to them. It was the men as decided the big things, like whether to go down the pub, or whether to come out on strike, or what choir should sing at the Eisteddfod. And there's proud they were when they won.

"Woman couldn't afford to be proud. It was them as had to put food on the table, whether the men brought a wage home or no. What good is pride when you're begging for an extra week's grace to pay the rent? Or running cap in hand to borrow a cup of flour or a screw of tea from a neighbour?

"The trouble with men is they don't know how to swallow their pride. It sticks in their throats and chokes them. Women can't afford such luxuries. It isn't that we don't have any pride. Oh, we've got plenty pride, but we don't crow about it, see. Men can't understand that. They don't understand that it is pride that makes a woman get up at crack of dawn and scrub the living daylights out of her front doorstep. Men don't see a scrubbed doorstep as a badge of honour. But that's what it is to a woman. God knows no one's going to give them a bloody medal for anything else. A scrubbed doorstep tells the world you take a pride in your house – even if there's no rug on the floor or bread in the cupboard. And it's an achievable goal, see. Besides, what else do we have to take pride in? Not a lot.

"Mind you, when it comes to responsibility and blame, us women carry more than our fair share. Men take all the praise and all the glory. Women get the blame and shame. Take children. When I was a girl, the legal age of consent was 13, although I never knew that or what it meant. There was no such thing as birth control then. A single woman had to keep her legs crossed. God help her if she got raped or tampered with by her father or brothers. It was always the woman to blame when a baby came along. Married or single, it was their fault and their responsibility. They always shouldered the blame, as I know only too well. When I was young, an unwanted baby was called a 'fatherless' baby. Now there's clever!

"Married women had no choice. They had to give their husbands what they wanted and accept what they didn't want as a consequence. It was up to them to bear it, feed it, clothe it, raise it, cherish it, and bury it, or die giving birth to the next. My mam was poorly all her life, but she still had 10 babies. The last one killed her, and I don't think that was her choice.

"If little Dai's backside hung out of his trousers, or he cheeked the teacher, played hooky from school, or played knock your neighbour out of bed, it was the mother's fault. If he scored a goal or sank a pint or got himself a girl at the age of 15, he made his father proud.

"When I look at the world today, after two world wars, the great depression, general and local strikes, I think us women have reason to feel proud too. We have fought for and achieved suffrage for women. I might even live to see a woman elected as prime minister. Women can get to the top of most professions nowadays. We have birth control, and it is in women's hands for the first time ever. We can plan the size of our families, when to start our families and when to add to them. One day we will have women ordained as priests and vicars, even bishops. Women might even be walking on the moon. There is nothing the women of today cannot do.

"Mind you, there are still some things the men won't let go of, but times are changing. By the time my granddaughter is my age, who knows what she will have achieved. The young Welsh women of today are educated. They are healthy, determined, ambitious and independent. Good luck to them, I say. Today, Wales is a fairer, better place for women. And I, Polly Evans, am proud to have played my small part in that progress."

There was a click, then silence.

I slid the second tape into the machine. My heart was racing, thudding and pounding in my ears. What had Thomas said about this last tape? 'It was meant for your ears only.' I looked at Matt, swallowed hard and pressed the start button. After a second or two there was a click, a pause, another click, then Polly was beside me, chatting directly to me, her lovely Welsh voice wrapping me in a warm cwtch.

*

"Right let's see now, I've connected the microphone thingy and pressed the red button, now what else did young Tom say? Oh yes, don't hold the mike too close. Oh dew! Is this too close? How am I supposed to know what's close? How long is a piece of string? There. I can't touch it with my nose, but nearly. How's that? Can you hear me? Oh, it's no good. Hang on a minute."

There was a rustling sound followed by a few tuts and three loud, hollow thuds, presumably Gran tapping the mike. A few more tuts, a sigh, a click, then silence. I reached forward, but Matt stayed my hand, urging patience. The machine was still running. There was another click, a cough, then:

"Right, that's it! Can you hear me, Fliss? I'm sorry if you can't. I'm doing my best, see, but all this is a bit what's it? 'Technical' I think you call it. Fancy me being technical! Last time young Tommy did it for me. He made it look so simple. He said as even a two-year-old could do it, so here goes. Not too close, am I?"

"No, Gran, that's perfect," I answered.

"Hello there, my lovely. It's me, your gran, talking from beyond the grave. Not that I've gone yet. No. I'm still very much alive and kicking. But it's funny to think that I will be gone when you listen to this. (Funny peculiar that is, not funny ha ha!) Seriously though, I can't imagine not being here anymore. I know I'll be missing you.

"You came as a wonderful, unexpected gift to comfort me in my later years. I am so proud of you and what you have achieved. Never give up, cariad. You can make it right to the top if that's where you want to be. Go for it. I will always be here, wherever here is. And I'll still be dishing out advice, whether you want it or not.

"I'm not afraid of dying. Well, you know how I feel about death. It can't be that hard. We all have to do it sooner or later. I am quite ready to meet my maker, and it will be lovely to see Da, Mam, my brothers and my sister, and my darling Megan again. But I'm happy to wait until the Good Lord sees fit to send for me. And I do hope it's later rather than sooner, isn't it? Anyhow, thanks to modern technology, it seems I can talk to you even after I'm gone. Now, there's clever!

"I'm sorry I left you with so many unanswered questions. Emlyn always said I would live to regret not telling you everything before I went. But I can't say as I do, not really. You see I wanted to go with you still loving me, still thinking of me as your gran. I always thought of Megan as my daughter, see, which really does make you my granddaughter. Was that so wrong of me? Was I wanting too much? Was I being selfish? I'd already lost my sister or as good as. Then my Megan was taken so soon. I couldn't bear to lose you too.

"But now there's no one left as can be hurt by me telling you the truth, so I shall tell you everything. Hopefully, by now, all the others will have forgiven me. That just leaves you, cariad. Now I am asking you to forgive me too. I hated having to lie to you, but the last thing I ever wanted was for you to get hurt.

"By now, you will have discovered that I had a younger sister called Phyllis. Phyllis was so beautiful, so full of life. She meant the world to me. I named you after her. Sadly, she was not meant to have a long life. She died – twice, although I lost her three times. Bear with me. I'll come to all that later. You probably already know some of it, but you can't know everything. No one knows that but me and my maker.

"Phyllis never grew up. She was always a child, an innocent. At 13 she went to work at the big house working for Mrs Llewellyn. The woman had taken a fancy to her. I blame myself for giving in and letting her go, her being so young. But she was that keen, and it was a chance for her to better herself, I could see that. It was the only time Da and I fell out. In the end, he won, and I let her go. I wish to God I'd stood my ground. If only I could have seen what would happen, but no one could have foreseen that.

"There's no nice way of putting this. Phyllis was raped by Sir Llewellyn's oldest son. It was a brutal attack, after which she was dismissed and accused of all sorts. She was dismissed, slandered, disowned by her own da, and driven to the brink of insanity. The youngest son, Edward, was a good man. He managed to take Phyllis to London, where she could recover away from the lashing tongues in Brynavon. Seven months later I heard she was expecting. As if the poor child hadn't gone through enough, it was a cruel twist of the knife.

"I fetched the baby and brought her home with me. That baby was your mother, Megan. The baby's father, your grandfather, was, and is, the Right Honourable Paul Llewellyn MP, not a very apt title seeing as he was far from being right and far from being honourable. As I am recording this, he is still alive. He's in the House of Lords now, with the title of Lord Brynavon. I can hardly bring myself to speak his name.

"Brynavon was a coward. He denied everything and came up smelling of roses. I can't allow myself to tell you what I think of that... I know this must come as a shock. Luckily, you take after the rest of your family. You are nothing like that horrid man.

"The Llewellyns were a rich, powerful family. There was little I could do. In the end, the actions I took, and the lies I told, were, God help me, to protect Phyllis and cover her shame – and believe you me, she was greatly shamed. As I've always said, it was always the woman who was blamed in those days.

"I hated having to lie. I tried to fight the Llewellyns, but they were too big and too powerful for me. I couldn't see another way other than the one I took. I did what I did for my sister and her unborn baby, and I'd do it all again. (Although happen by the time you listen to this, I'll have been shown a better way of dealing with it – if the Good Lord sees fit.)

"There is, however, one thing that still really worries me. It haunts me at times. It is haunting me now. I have never said this to anyone before, so this is hard for me. But, well, here goes. I don't know what I would have done if my sister had recovered her wits, grown strong and wanted her child back. I'd like to say I'd have been over the moon... and in many ways I would have been but – and look you now, this is the hard bit – deep down I don't think as I could ever have shared little Megan once she had become mine, let alone have given her back.

"I'd fallen in love with her, see. Honest to God, I would have died for her. Yet when I say I'm glad I never had to make that choice, it's as if I'm saying I didn't want my sister to get well. Do you understand that, Fliss? I hope you do. Tell me now, and I shall know. The Good Lord will let me know because he knows how much I need your forgiveness. I believe He has forgiven me."

Here there was a long pause.

"Well you see, by the time we discovered Phyllis was expecting her baby, she was already seven months gone. She was so much better in herself, almost back to her old self. She liked living in London as Edward's ward. Now there was one of the Llewellyns you could call good. It's hard to believe the two of them were brothers. Edward, bless him, offered to marry her and claim the child was his.

"But it wasn't that simple. Deep down inside, Phyllis was still very ill, see? Sick in the mind she was. When she heard she was expecting, she couldn't come to terms with it. She became worse than ever. Demented she was, kicking and screaming, saying she was possessed by the devil and that she wanted to die. Poor Edward was at his wits' end.

"Phyllis was my sister, my responsibility. The London doctor wanted to have her committed to an asylum, but

Edward and I couldn't bear the thought, it was so harsh. That was when I had the idea of pretending the baby was mine. It seemed such an obvious solution. All I had to was drop a few hints that I was in the family way and let the gossips do the rest. By the time the baby arrived, the scandal would be over, and I could look after the little one as if she was my own.

"In the meantime, all we had to do was keep Phyllis safe until the baby was born. I said I would come up to London nearer the time and help with the birth. Then, if necessary, I'd bring the baby back with me until Phyllis felt she could cope with being a mother.

"I had to find a way to explain the sudden appearance of a baby. That's why I pretended that I had got into trouble and that the young man involved was willing to make an honest woman of me. I went to see the Reverend Griffiths, to pave the way so to speak. I didn't actually lie, but I tried to mislead him. In other words, God forgive me, I didn't tell him the truth.

"Anyway, Adollgar knew me too well. He was having none of it, was he… not unless I told him who the father was. So, I sort of hinted it was Dafydd Jones. Dafydd was a nice enough boy, but not very bright. He'd been making sheep's eyes at me since we were at school, so I knew he'd do anything I asked – including marrying me.

"Honest to God, I was getting desperate. I think the reverend thought I'd gone mad. He knew Dafydd was a most unlikely culprit, so he refused to read the bans. I think he thought Emlyn was the father… although he never dared ask me outright.

"Everyone knew that Emlyn was my closest friend. I knew he too would do anything for me. I also knew he was in love with me, but although I loved him dearly, I wasn't in love with him. How could I take advantage of him? I had turned him down twice already, isn't it? Eventually, he'd given up on me and started courting Lucy Morton.

"I could see he was happy for the first time in years. I couldn't mess his life up now. Besides, it would have been wrong to marry him and expect him to bring up another man's child. He would have done it though: he's such an honourable man. But to be honest, I would have hated being a doctor's wife. And I couldn't have been his nurse and his wife, he wouldn't have allowed that. So, it wasn't difficult to decide what to do.

"I've never wanted to get married, see. I was always meant to be my own woman. I'd watched the lives of so many friends change as soon as they got married. Husbands can be very demanding – in more ways than one. Even a man like Emlyn would expect his wife to give up her independence to support his work. She would only ever be 'the doctor's wife'.

"That's why I chose Dafydd Jones. Being a bit simple, he would have been putty in my hands, see? Oh, don't get me wrong, I'd have been loyal to him, a good wife, but not a real one. Mind you, he was so excited by the whole idea, being simple, he didn't need persuading. Then he went and got run down by a horse. So that put an end to that.

"It seemed that Megan and I were meant to be alone. I'd just have to get used to any finger-pointing and name-calling. Sometimes I think that old horse did me a favour. But for him, I'd have been Mrs Dafydd Jones. Anyway, thanks to Emlyn, Rosa May and Adollgar, the town supported me. They were actually very kind to me. Everyone called me Mrs Evans, and that was that.

"I never told you about my sister Phyllis because I thought it for the best. It was all in the past, see? I have always thought of Megan as my child. So naturally, when you came along, you were my beautiful granddaughter. And, in my heart, that's what you always will be.

"So why am I raking over cold ashes? Well, they're not completely cold, are they? I always knew the day would come when you would ask who your grandfather was. You were always a great one for asking questions. I'm sorry. It was wrong of me not to tell you the truth, Fliss, especially as I was always warning you of the perils of lying.

"Well, it turns out I was right, look you? I got caught in my own sticky web, isn't it? I began to believe my own lies. I had begun to believe Megan was my child. It was the only way I could live with what I'd done. Maybe that's what all liars do in the end. They lie to themselves. They make themselves believe in their own lies.

"But I wasn't a very good liar. I always knew the truth would come and bite me on the backside one day. What I did was wrong. I'm sorry if I have hurt you."

There were a few indecipherable words, very muffled and disjointed. Then a loud sniff. Then...

"I'm going to stop for a minute. I need to get a hanky. Hang on, don't go away, Fliss, I'll be right back."

Click.
Pause.
Click.

"Right, that's better. Sorry, just a sniffle. I hope I'm not starting a cold. No, see, I'm alright now.

"I know Rosa May probably told you some of this – all she knew and a bit more. She always was one to let on she knew everybody's business better than they did. Mind, she was a good sort and a good friend to me. Still, there was more to this story than she ever knew. More than anyone ever knew, even Emlyn. As I said before, I had to keep it secret to protect my little family."

"I have never told anyone this next bit. It's very personal and I don't think it's of much interest to anyone but you. Anyway, I want to tell you, Fliss. I'd like to record it from an historical point of view. Oh, there's posh! Me talking history! Fancy. It's really just an account of the very first time I went up to London – the reaction of a simple Welsh woman to the big metropolis! I'll start at the beginning.

"A got a telegram late afternoon on February 18th, 1917. I thought I was ready for it, but it set my heart fluttering something awful. I'm not one to panic, but I can tell you when I read those words, I came very near to getting in a tizz. I had to make the journey to London all on my own. I kept telling myself there was nothing to it. I could do it easy like. But I was still physically sick as I packed my bag.

"I hadn't told anyone about the baby. Not even Emlyn. It was better that way, with no one knowing. This way no one could point a finger at my sister, see? Any more stress would have tipped her right over the edge, and I dared not risk that. But it meant I had no one to share my fears with. Oh dew, cariad, I have never been so scared.

"Edward said he would meet me in Paddington Station at three o'clock under the three-faced clock. I had never been further than Ebbw Vale before. Today I was going up to London all on my own. It was more terrifying than going down the mine that time when the pit collapsed. Then I'd had no time to think about it, whereas this had been planned. I'd had a long time to worry about it.

"I took the little train from Brynavon to Newport, where I changed onto the London train – so far so good. The train was full, but no one talked to me, although we were packed together like sardines. The train raced along, but it still took hours to get there. I was feeling quite ill by the time it reached London. When I tried to stand, my legs felt like jelly – partly from the motion of the train, mostly from fear. What if Captain Llewellyn wasn't there? Or we couldn't find each other?

"I waited for everyone else to get off before I moved to the door. Honest to God, Fliss, I nearly died. The only thing between me and a gap as deep as Brynavon pit was a strip of wood no wider than my boot, and I only take a size three. Normally I'd have jumped, but my best blue-serge skirt was hobbled, see. I closed my eyes and stood there dithering like an idiot when suddenly I was lifted up and swung around. Only when my toes touched solid ground did I dare open my eyes. A Welsh Fusilier had hold of me, a soldier, look you!

"The ghosts of my brothers were everywhere. It was only eight months since my three brave boys had marched off in their smart new uniforms, pressed and steamed by me, the badge of the Welsh Fusiliers proudly sewn on their caps. Now, here I was, in London, in the arms of a stranger, my face as red as the dragon on his sleeve. He looked straight in my eyes as I pushed him away. I'll never forget those eyes. Baby blue, they were, beautiful. He grinned, saluted and marched off, leaving me ashamed to have acted so ungraciously.

"I shouted to him, praying he'd hear me above the din. "Thank you, soldier. Duw bendithia," I yelled. He turned and winked. I laughed and blew him a kiss. My boys were the same age as him when they'd marched off. How I hoped they'd kissed a girl or two – and been kissed back before... I found myself praying that this young lad would make it back safe and sound if only to be kissed again.

"I thought of my other brothers, buried under that mountain of earth and coal. The older two left sweethearts behind to grieve for them. At least they'd known love, but the others had been too busy being lads, shooting slings and catapults, riding Farmer Ward's ponies and defying Da by swimming in the dark water of the Low Pond. They were all old enough to go down the mine. They were old enough to die. But it seems they would never grow old enough to fall in love.

"I was standing where they'd stood. I wondered if they had felt as scared as me. Had their hearts pumped hard at the thought of adventures waiting for them in France? What they found were bullets and bayonets, lying in wait in the woods of Mametz. I prayed. *Please let them have been together. Let them have died together. Not alone. Not forever lost in a foreign wood.* That was the first battle of the Somme.

"These thoughts and more filled my head as I stood in that vast station. I was no longer praying – I was cursing now, tamping against a God who'd let a man die before he'd lived. It was wicked that so many left as boys only to come home lost. To be remembered only as a name on a stone in a cemetery or etched on a brass plaque by a redundant mine. I didn't need any engravings to remind me. I had my anger. My thoughts were as black as Welsh coal. I didn't care if that damned me to hell. I had no desire to meet a God that I despised, a God who allowed such dreadful things to happen. And for what? What purpose did they possibly serve? Nothing could justify such waste.

"Dear Fliss, by the time you listen to this I hope I have some answers. If I do, I shall try to let you know. Maybe I'll find some helpful angels – or naughty devils? There's spooky, isn't it?

"Listen to me blathering on about angels and devils when I should be answering your questions. I'm sorry, my lovely, I'll try to keep on track. Oh, there's clever – seeing as I'm talking about Paddington. On track, trains and things, see?

"Well, there I was watching my young soldier disappear into the smoke, my angry thoughts making my poor head spin, when I realised time was marching on and I still had to find the three-faced clock and Captain Edward.

"I had been told Paddington Station was big and busy, but I never have imagined this. It was bigger than the mountain above Brynavon. I have never felt so little – not even when gazing up at the stars with Da. I was lost in the middle of a mountain of glass, iron, stone, noise, steam and smoke. It literally snatched my breath away. Yet for all its wonder, it didn't touch my soul. Not like the real hills, not like the streams and valleys of Wales.

"There were dragon-like locomotives belching fire, coughing, smoking and roaring so loud, I pulled my hat over my ears. Wheels clunked, pistons puffed, doors slammed, guards shouted. Whistles shrilled. It was so thrilling I forgot to be terrified. I could actually feel the energy, Fliss. This was man-made energy. A mist of curling smoke and steam hung over everything, like the mist on the mountain above Brynavon but this too was man-made. I was surrounded by the future, and it put the fear of God in me. I could breathe it in, but it still didn't touch my soul.

"As I wove and ducked between the lines of service-men in search of the three-faced clock, I saw a long banner promising "REFRESHMENTS FOR SOLDIERS AND SAILORS". Women – in starched shirts with wide leg-of-mutton sleeves and wide-brimmed hats – kept a long queue of men fed and watered with a constant flow of tea and buns. These women didn't stand for any non-sense. It was heartening to know the women of London were doing their bit, even if all they had to offer was tea. Dew! As if a cup of tea was the answer to everything. What those men needed was a booth offer-ing kisses.

"Dew! That bloody war! Everything I loved got taken and blown up. Why is it men are so keen on war? Has it got something to do with their damned pride? It isn't in them to back down, see? Us women would never have let things get that far, look you? We'd have put an end to it long before it ever got to out-and-out war. Oh, there might have been a bit of a scrap, some pulling of hair, a bit of name-calling, but women would never have let it get to the point where they were blowing each other to kingdom come.

"No. Left to us women we'd have all been sat by the fireside by that first Christmas, taking a nice cup of tea, all friendly and cosy, having sorted our differences with no more than a slightly bloody nose, but with very little face lost. But that's the trouble with men, isn't it, see? They just can't swallow their pride.

"How did I get to talking about to pride? I'm supposed to be telling you about the day Megan was born. Oh dear, now I've forgotten where I was."

Click.

Pause.

"Is this thing this thingy still working? Tom said as I'd hear it click and it would stop going round if the tape runs out. Then I've to turn it over and use the other side or put a new tape in the whatsit."

Pause.

"Hang on a moment, Fliss, I'm going to try 'pausing'. Hang on."

Click. Another click.

"There now. I think it's working. Mind, all this talking's made my mouth go all dry. Hang on, I'm going to pause again – seeing as how I know how to – and have a cup of tea. Back in a minute – all being well, that is."

Click.

Click.

"That's better. There. I hope I didn't keep you waiting too long. I expect you've had a cuppa too. There's lovely. I hope they have tea in heaven, if not I'm coming right back, look you! Right. I've pressed the start button and the thingy's going round, lovey, so here goes."

Gran took a deep breath. It was as if she was in the room with me. I could almost feel her breath on my cheek.

"Now, where was I? Oh, I know, I was telling you about me going to London the day your mam was born, isn't it? So, I'm in Paddington, lost. I was wondering what to do when I heard someone calling my name. I turn, and there's Edward Llewellyn, or Captain Lewellyn as he was then. Handsome as a film star he looked, stood there in his uniform – long shiny boots and a Sam Brown polished to perfection. It was only when I looked up, did I see I was stood standing right under the three-faced clock. You could read the time from three different directions, look you! There's clever! How I'd missed it, God only knows, and he wasn't telling. I expect I hadn't seen it for looking.

"Captain Edward took me by the arm and led me to a waiting cab. London was so full. I don't know how anyone actually lives there. I could hardly breathe. The air down the pit was cleaner than in the street here. It was a long way to Chelsea. I couldn't believe we were still in London. It seemed to go on forever. Eventually, we arrived at a nice terraced house, much bigger than my house. It had a front with a gate and a porch over the door. I hurried straight upstairs to see Phyllis.

"I'll spare you the details, but after a long, difficult labour she gave birth to a little girl. I called her Megan. Well someone had to give her a name. Phyllis wouldn't look at her, let alone hold her. She seemed terrified of the poor little thing. The baby was perfect, although too small if I'm honest. Still, it was just as well, as it had been bad enough for Phyllis as it was.

"Who'd have thought that little thing would grow up to be your mam! As I said, she was small but quite perfect. Poor little mite, her mam wouldn't go near her. She looked nothing like her mam either. Maybe she looked like me? I'd never seen a photo of me as a baby, so I couldn't say. When you were born, you looked exactly like my sister. There's pretty you were. Megan wasn't a pretty baby, but she was a lovely little thing. And she was alive and well.

"My poor sister was in a bad way, though. The birth had been very hard, despite the baby's size. Phyllis had been damaged inside by the rape, see? Poor dear, she just lay there weeping and begging me to get rid of the baby, 'that thing' as she called it. 'Don't let it near me, it wants to kill me,' she sobbed over and over again. It was pitiful.

"Edward and I agreed it was better for me to take the baby and leave immediately – out of sight, out of mind, so to speak. Phyllis was convinced the baby was the devil incarnate. She kept shouting that only evil could come from such a sinful act. We were afraid of what she might do to herself and the infant, so I left.

"I took a taxi back to Paddington. I could still hear my sister's screams as the cab drove off. God knows what the neighbours thought. Back in Brynavon they'd have been round the house like a shot. I don't think Londoners share the curiosity of us Welsh – at least not the ones in Chelsea. Too posh see.

"I found a corner seat. The whistle gave a mournful cry, and I clutched little Megan close to my chest. Then the train pulled away, and it was too late to change my mind.

"Dew! It was a long old journey home. As the train sped through the dark, I kept my eyes on the baby. She was so tiny, so helpless. I felt I had the weight of the world in my arms, although she weighed next to nothing. The burden I was carrying was guilt.

"Believe me, Fliss, keeping all this a secret has been the hardest thing I've ever had to do. As the train rattled on, the full weight of what I'd done began to dawn on me. From now on my life would be very different, but there was no going back.

"Brynavon station had never looked so small as it did when the train pulled up on the single track. I climbed down, relieved to be back on Welsh soil. It was dark, the sky was starless. A bitter wind blew off the mountain, whipping flurries of snow around me. I pulled my shawl over my head, pulling the baby as close as possible for fear of her catching cold. I could not see my own feet for snow.

"The first thing I did was light the fire. I'd only been home half an hour when there was a rap on the door and Emlyn let himself in. I don't know what made him call round at such a Godforsaken hour on such a dreadful night, but I had never been happier to see him.

"Poor Emlyn! That was the only time I ever saw him lose his temper. He demanded to know whose baby it was. I kept insisting it was mine, adding each time that it was none of his business anyway. It wasn't anybody's business but mine. He didn't like that.

"Oh, how I hated not being able to tell him, him being such a good friend and all, but I've always said, 'A secret that's been shared is no longer secret.' Mind, when he asked to see the child's birth certificate, I realised I hadn't given a thought to registering the birth. I don't suppose Edward had either.

"After the anger died down, Emlyn said he would take care of everything, even if it went against his better judgement. That sweet man was always my most loyal of friends. He risked his career, his reputation, everything he held dear, to protect my secret and provide a birth certificate for little Megan. I shall never forget that. May the Good Lord reward him. Maybe we shall be sitting together, sharing a heavenly cuppa, watching you listening to this. Dew! There's lovely!

"From that day on, I brought Megan up as my own. Adollgar christened her, and it was thanks to his powerful persuasion that the town accepted her without too much gossiping. No one ever suspected it was Phyllis's child. It was Polly Evans's baby daughter, which was exactly how I wanted it.

"You must want to know what happened to your real grandmother, my sister, Phyllis. Well now, my lovely, that's another story – one that very few people know.

"Tragic, it was, her being so young and so beautiful. Her life should have been full of joy, but then only God knows why such things happen... and like I always say, he never tells.

"Phyllis stayed in London, in Edward's care. Gradually her health returned. Even her mind grew stronger and calmer. She never once mentioned having given birth. She never asked about any baby. I think nowadays we'd say she was in denial. I don't know, but whatever it was it allowed her to get on with her life, what was left of it.

"In time, she signed up with an organisation called the FANY, an amazing group of very brave women. When she'd finished her training, she was sent over to France to nurse the wounded. I was that proud of her, and although I never said so, I was more than a bit jealous. Probably Edward was the only one to have seen that courageous side of Phyllis. She was both brave and caring. But her dreams didn't have long to live. In 1918 a telegram came telling me she had been killed at a place called Amiens, in France.

"She was just 17 – blown up by a landmine. There was no funeral as such, well there was no body see. I met Edward in Newport, and together we laid flowers on the local war memorial, it wasn't much, but I felt better for doing it.

"Edward and I agreed it was best to keep our distance. Besides, why would Polly Evans be in touch with a member of the Llewellyn family? It was sad though. Edward had done so much for my sister and for me, I should have liked to keep in touch, properly.

"Then in 1945, I got a letter from Edward, posted in London, sealed with sealing wax. He said he'd been visiting an army pal who'd been wounded in the second war. They were taking a walk in the hospital grounds when he saw her. He'd found Phyllis!

"My poor, sweet Phyllis! She'd been shut up in a mental hospital since 1918, registered as Miss M. Thompsett. She had no memory, no idea who she was or where she came from. We all believed her to be dead, so no one had been looking for her or coming to claim her. There's terrible, to think of my own sister lost and alone, with no one to love her for all those empty years

"I hardly dared believe Edward's letter. He was so caring, so generous. I think he loved my sister as if she was his own. He had her transferred to a beautiful home in Surrey, where I think she was happy in her own peculiar way. I can hear you asking if I met her again. Of course, I did, thanks again to Edward's generosity.

"Every first Sunday of the month, Edward would collect Phyllis from the nursing home and take her by train to Newport. We'd spend an hour together in the tearoom at the station. Edward made himself scarce so that we could talk. I'd sit beside her, and we'd hold hands, just the way we had when Phyllis was little.

"It hurt that she never recognised me as her sister. I don't know who she thought I was. But I knew who she was, and I like to think she grew to love me as a friend. Anyway, we met every month until she got ill. The doctors said the journey was too much for her. She died in 1950. But we had five precious years, thanks to dear Edward.

"I never told Megan about Phyllis being her mam. She knew she had an aunty who had died in the first war, but that was all. How could I tell my grown-up daughter she wasn't really mine, that her aunty was her real mother? Then to have to try and explain that her aunty hadn't died after all, and that I had tea with her in Newport every month.

"So, I didn't tell her. Was that so wrong of me? I was that proud of my girl. I couldn't bear the thought of losing her too. So, I added another lie – or rather, I kept another secret. Am I just making excuses? Anyway, as always, the lie took on a life of its own.

"Lying is hard at first, then it gets easier, or so you think. Little by little, a word here, a hint there, it starts to grow, until it's so heavy it drags you down. The only thing that will get rid of it is the truth. But why did you lie in the first place? To hide something you thought was too awful to tell, isn't it? Telling the truth becomes too dangerous. One little fib and everything has changed. Before you know it, you're trapped.

"I knew it was wrong of me to lie, very wrong. I know that now and knew it then, but I was a lonely, selfish woman. I am sorry, Fliss. Forgive me? Let me go to my maker knowing I am forgiven. I loved your mother, and I love you too. I was that proud of her and now, what with you becoming a doctor and all… I think my heart might burst with pride."

There was a deafening boom, which made me jump out of my skin. Polly must have blown her nose right next to the mike. I laughed, then I felt the tears start as she cleared her throat. She too was obviously crying now. I wanted to tell her there was nothing to forgive and that I loved her too and always would. But she hadn't quite finished…

"Right! Sorry. I got a bit emotional then. I'm alright now though, so I'll just say cheerio for now, my darling girl. It's not goodbye. It will never be goodbye. We'll meet again, God willing. Then we'll cwtch up close with a nice cuppa tea and everything will be beautiful, just like always. I love you, Fliss. Be happy, be strong and remember me kindly. I am beside you now and always will be. Nos da, cariad. Duw bendithia."

There was a long pause, a silence then a click. Gran had come home.

Epilogue: Brynavon. 2019

Matt and I did retire to Brynavon. We now live in a small cottage with two adorable border collies and a glorious view across the valley to the mountain of our childhood. I am sat at my desk enjoying that view as I write.

I promised to commit Polly's story to paper and, at last, I have done so. Unearthing the past has been an adventure, a joy and a privilege. Hopefully reading her story has been as enjoyable for you, as the writing of it has been for me.

Thank you for allowing me to share it with you.

Fliss Jenkins.

The End

About the Author

Jennifer Button lives in Kent with her husband Alan and two dachshunds, Daisy and Lily. This is her fifth novel and, although a work of fiction, much of the inspiration for this book comes from happy childhood memories spent in south Wales with her lovely grandmother, Polly.

Lightning Source UK Ltd.
Milton Keynes UK
UKHW010739060223
416537UK00003B/1023

9 781839 753299